BODYGUARD

HOLLYWOOD A-LIST

BODYGUARD

HOLLYWOOD A-LIST

NEW YORK TIMES BESTSELLING AUTHOR

CD REISS

Montlake
Romance

Published by Montlake Romance, Seattle

www.apub.com

Amazon, the Amazon logo, and Montlake Romance are trademarks of Amazon.com, Inc., or its affiliates.

ISBN-13: 9781542049009
ISBN-10: 1542049008

Cover design by Shasti O'Leary Soudant

Printed in the United States of America

To my son.
I prayed to have you, and you're everything I prayed for.
But faster.

CHAPTER 1

EMILY

When we became friends, she was just Darlene McKenna. She wasn't even in third grade when she started singing in her church on Sundays. I sang a little, danced a little, but gymnastics was the love of my little heart.

We met during gymnastics camp in Chicago. I was awesome. We were in the same group, and I was already on the team. My parents had put a bar across the garage door so I could practice my casts. Which I did. A lot.

My parents worked. They were lawyers, and I was a ten-year-old kid who talked like a buzz saw and couldn't keep still. So they sent me to lessons and camps to keep me happy. All they ever wanted was to keep me happy. The gym I went to was a second home in a massive warehouse space just south of the city. Banners with team members' names over the colleges they attended. They'd trained Olympians and champions. There were so many banners they were running out of space. I grew up thinking the odds of winning all the chips were in my favor.

Camps were fun enough, but gymnastics wasn't fun. I wasn't into the leap-into-the-ball-pit-bounce-house fun. That was for *babies* and I was *team*.

"What's your name?" Darlene asked me the day we met. She was bigger than I was by a lot. Taller, thicker, bursting with confidence. Her skin was honey and her hair was kinky and dark. She was pure power, in one direction. Up.

"I'm Emily and I'm team. We're going to the state championships in May."

I pointed my toes when I walked and when I sat on the mat. I pointed them when I stood there fidgeting between stations. My coach, Tammy, tried to be funny, calling the constant practice at toe pointing "good habitizing." I got the joke, but gymnastics wasn't funny.

"Let's be friends!" She jumped up and down, clapping as if this was the biggest idea since the iPod. "I'm Darlene!"

I didn't have a lot of friends. I left school seconds before the bell rang and had no time for playdates or parties.

"Sure. I'm Emily."

Space had opened up on the red floor, and I wanted to get on it. There wasn't a coach around, but I was better than all these girls. I didn't need no stinking coaches.

"Where you going?" Darlene bounced after me to where kids were leaping in a line and young coaches spoke the language of encouragement. Her leotard was hot pink and just a little too tight, as if she'd had a growth spurt.

"The red exercise floor. Wanna come?"

"There's no coach by it."

I shrugged her off. It was just a springy floor. I'd been coming to that gym seven years already. Forever.

I lined up in the corner. Feet together. Arms up, right knee bent, toes pointed, visualizing the run, then the cartwheel.

"How many you gonna do?" asked Darlene.

"Two. Cartwheel then flip."

"Do three." Hands on hips. A two-word challenge. I wasn't made of stone. I was made of 100 percent US grade-A kid. I'd never done three, but it was just one more.

I took two big steps, turned, landed on my hands, flipped, spun, did a perfect cartwheel. I bounced on my toes, did the flip, and somehow found a tiny bit of torque. Enough for an ugly half-assed third thing that didn't have a name.

I landed on my bottom, ashamed of my failure. Then angry. Then resentful. I got up to try again.

Darlene held judgment. I might have been mad at her for that for half a second. If I was, it was gone by the time I got into the corner again.

"Hey," Darlene said, "did you know I sing in my church? The AME church on Pico. I'm the youngest they ever had."

"That's really cool." I did my run, finally nailing the landing. Darlene clapped and stuck two fingers in her mouth to whistle. That made me smile. It was nice to have a fan.

"Do you know about acoustics?" she asked when I came back to her.

"Yeah." I knew everything. Of course.

"That whistle I just did, man. The acoustics in here are insane."

The whistle had been really loud. It had drawn attention to us, and Coach Tammy blew her little metal whistle.

"Girls! What are you doing over there?"

I waved, letting her know we were fine.

Darlene leaned in and whispered, "I bet we could sing 'Ain't I Your Baby?' so loud the roof would come down."

I giggled.

She looked around the huge space. "I bet if you went by the vaults and I went by the uneven bars and we both sang, it would be crazy."

Something about the way she said it made it seem like the best idea ever. She had an infectious sense of fun. Besides, it was just camp. It wasn't team practice.

"I can hold the note in 'yours' longer than you can." She held up a finger and stuck her butt out. That sealed the deal. She had no idea who she was dealing with.

3

"Is that a dare?"

"Yeah. Sure."

The space took up half a city block. Even as an adult, it looked huge. As a kid, it was planetary. I just had to go to the opposite corner and sing a long note. Easy. And better than doing baby stuff with the other campers.

I held my hand up, and she slapped it.

We were on.

"Go!" she said, and I ran. She found her corner first and started the first verse. I joined in with lyrics we weren't old enough to understand. Darlene belted it out from the bottom of her lungs, and when I joined her, we sounded so good under the thirty-foot ceilings, I barely heard the sound of my voice without hers.

And that note, in "yours"? The one we were competing to hold? It was magic.

Gymnastics was my life, but if I could pin down a moment when I started to love singing just as much, it was that moment I harmonized with Darlene. I felt us becoming friends. It was inside the note.

The applause was deafening.

We both hopped to the red floor and bowed.

It was the last time we'd take a bow together. Which was fine. She was Darlene McKenna, and I was just Emily.

CHAPTER 2

EMILY

I was late. I figure the whole thing could have been avoided if I'd been on time. But the auto lock on my front gate had jammed, and the back gate wasn't set up for leaving. It was set up for coming in, so the keypad was on the outside. I had to go back into the house, which took a few steps, then I had to find the key to the back gate, and then the phone rang. Darlene wanted me to bring the video of the Sexy Badass Tour, which I didn't have loaded on my laptop. So I loaded it. Then forgot the key.

This kind of stuff adds up.

I couldn't be late. A dancer could be late and get a slap on the wrist because the practice could continue a dancer short, more or less. But when the choreographer was late, everything stopped. Darlene's time was wasted, and her time was expensive. Liam, her manager, drilled that home to the entire team at least once a week.

I managed to avoid an accident going Downtown and parked on the street. The lot was full, and because I was late, they'd put someone else in my spot.

Deep breath.

Darlene and I had met in gymnastics camp during spring break, then again in summer break, before I invited her over to my house. She became my best friend. She got taller, and her physical power compacted into a tight, womanly frame. Her voice matured, and she used it like a weapon to cut through anyone who stood between her and fame.

I landed on one leg coming off a triple pike vault and blew out my knee. It wasn't even at the state championships or anything. It was a practice the weekend before. I let my team down. I couldn't even look at them when they visited me in the hospital.

I wasn't good at holding grudges unless they were against myself.

I'd continued singing lessons, though, and took up dance, which I loved and which my knees could handle. Darlene and I had the same instructor in our teens, and we did recitals as a team. If there was an audition for a commercial, we cut school to go. We were perfect together.

We plodded through college, but all we wanted to do was sing and dance. When Darlene had the brilliant idea to move to Los Angeles to "make it," I agreed. Work in Chicago was tough to get. Not enough commercials. Not enough stage. Not enough of anything.

That went well for a while. Darlene was always going to be a star, but something happened to me on the way, and she saved me by making me her choreographer.

Who was late.

I took half a deep breath and got out of the car. I didn't have time to de-stress in the front seat. I had time to yank my bag out of the leg space in front of the passenger seat, open the door, and get out all in the same move.

I almost closed the door before I realized the engine was still running. *Deep breath, Emily.*

I took the rest of the breath with one hand on the car door, closing my eyes and pretending the deep breath I had the time for was a full five-minute relaxation exercise.

Keys. Tote bag. Clean clothes. Laptop. Close door. Chirp doors locked. Look around. Check the early morning shadow for someone coming from behind. The laptop wouldn't fit in my purse, and it took an entire arm to carry. I'd have to cross the length of the building to enter on the parking lot side. I had a key card for the back door, but it was in the bottom of the clothing bag. When I got to the rear of the building, I stopped by the metal door to dig around for the key card.

I had this.

All I had to do was move my purse to the left side, shift the laptop, search around the clothing bag . . . but no. Wasn't there.

Switching everything back, I let the purse slide down to my wrist, rebalanced everything, leaned the laptop on my knee while digging around my bag, taking stuff half-out. Wallet. Charger. Vitamins. Checkbook. Notebook. Sunglasses. Pistol. Tissues.

A breathtaking force hit me from behind, and as I was on the way down, with the black asphalt getting closer and closer, my hand locked around the key card, and I wondered if the laptop was going to break when it fell.

Half a breath took five minutes, and by the time I hit the ground, my lungs were empty. The air made an *oof* sound when it left me. Hard pressure fell on my wrists and lower back. A person. A man.

I had a stalker. His name was Vince, and I'd loved him once.

But with my face to the pavement, love wasn't in the equation anymore. It had been replaced by anger, fear, and action.

Was it Vince? Had he followed me?

I smelled charcoal and gunpowder.

"Stay still." His voice wasn't Vince's. I was in a shitty position, but it wasn't him.

The voice was so commanding I obeyed it without thinking.

No normal woman would have relaxed in that situation, but I did. I couldn't see anything but the glare of the sun between two buildings. My face was pressed against the dirt. I felt the guy move above me. I didn't know if he was getting ready to drag me or hit me, but I wasn't going to have a second chance to get away.

He didn't drag or hit me. He snapped the key card out of my hand, giving me time to mentally prepare.

He got off me, and I jumped to my feet and went for him. I'd taken enough self-defense classes to get close with a kick, but I became distracted.

He was the most gorgeous man I'd ever seen, and I'd seen a lot of gorgeous men. Nice scruff. Blinding blue eyes. Gray linen suit. Precisely untidy dark hair. And a perfectly formed hand that grabbed my ankle just as I was kicking him. He turned it in a swift move, and with his other arm, he kept me from falling on my face by grabbing me by the waist and holding me to him—my back to his front. His body was hard and thick as it curved against me. His arm was strong but not painful, and his hand held me tight at the rib cage without hurting. Three inches higher, and the flood of arousal that weakened my knees might take over.

What was I thinking?

"Let me go," I barked.

"Calm down first."

I jammed my heel into the arch of his foot and jammed my elbows back. I felt the air go out of his lungs, but he didn't let go. Every time I inhaled, his arm got tighter around me. Something about it wasn't threatening but secure.

"That's not calming down," he said into my ear. God, his voice.

Fine. If he wanted me to calm down, I'd calm down. He could have done much worse in the past few seconds, and it wasn't like I had a choice.

"I'm not leaving this parking lot with you." My voice was steadier than it should have been.

"Count backward from five, and I'll let you go."

Let me go? What kind of deal was this?

Not a deal a rapist would make. That was all I knew.

"Five. Four."

"Don't make a move for the gun."

Is that what this was about? Darlene always said it would get me killed before it would save me.

"Three. Two." I went slowly. I had no motivation to, except to collect my thoughts.

"You'll never make it."

"One."

He let me go, took a step forward, and picked up the black pistol I kept in my bag. As soon as he had its weight in his hand, his face changed.

"You're joking," he said. "Are you trying to get yourself killed?"

"Yeah." I crossed my arms. "By you. Whoever you are."

"Why would you carry a fake gun?"

"Because I couldn't get a license to carry."

He laughed. On top of everything, he had a wonderful laugh. His face lit up, and his chest expanded the fabric of his shirt. His jacket opened to show a dark shape and a bulge under it. Unlike me, he had a license to carry.

"You a cop?" I asked, picking up my bag by one handle. "Because if you're going to give me a ticket for having a fake, can you just give it to me so I can get to work?"

"I'm not a cop. Not anymore." He dropped the fake gun in the bag and picked up the clothing tote. "You all right?" he asked as he brushed off my laptop. It looked undamaged. I tucked it under my arm and held my hand out for my things.

"I'm fine. What the heck was that about?"

I grabbed my things from him. I was so torn between wanting to get away from a man who had physically attacked me and wanting that same man to put his arm around my body again.

"You're supposed to come in through the staff parking lot on the other side. Not sneak in on this side with a firearm." He handed me my key card. "And this picture doesn't do you justice."

I didn't snap the card away. I held it between my thumb and my index finger, imagining I felt his heat through the plastic. I was supposed to thank him for the compliment, but after having his arm around me and his breath in my ear, I was sure we'd moved past small courtesies.

"You're really forward for a security guy."

He let go of his side of the card, and I took it.

"I'm not exactly security."

"What exactly are you?"

Besides impossibly handsome.

"I'm Darlene McKenna's new bodyguard."

That was great. Just great. He'd be around all the time now, and I had to work and keep my head together while he watched me dance. This was not going to work out well.

"Well," I said, holding up the card, "you know who I am. This is my face. Remember it. I'm running late. So. Nice to meet you."

"Carter. Carter Kincaid." His deep voice made the name all the sexier. "Nice to meet you too."

My right hand was full of crap, so we couldn't shake. He offered me a fist, and I bumped it. The gesture seemed natural on him, but I felt like an awkward goofball.

"Okay, uh, better get to work." I slid my key card into the slot, and when the door clicked, he opened it for me.

A gentleman too.

I didn't think I could stand close to this guy another minute.

CHAPTER 3

EMILY

I made it my business to be on time from then on. One, because it was my job. Two, a few minutes before call was a great time to get coffee at the craft services table and make conversation.

The third reason, limited parking, yielded a firm statement from Darlene that no one was to park in the choreographer's spot. Even if she was late. Even if she was sick. If an ambulance pulled in to take Darlene herself to the hospital for a life-threatening stroke, it could park in the street.

Darlene took care of me, but she was still a star.

She stopped short in the middle of a move. "I cannot do that, Emily." The music cut out. The dancers flopped from inertia.

"Yes, you can. Look." I did the move, landed, and turned to her. "That."

"Stop showing off."

"We can make it easier."

The Downtown space she'd rented was called Citizens Warehouse. It had windows everywhere and glossy wood floors. Big show. Ton of people. Dozens. I didn't know what half of them did, but they were all busy, all the time.

"Who here thinks Darlene McKenna can do these steps?" I called out, raising my hand high. Simon, her dance partner, came all the way in front of her so she could see his hand up. Behind her, ten professional dancers raised their hands, while the four-time Grammy winner who could stack platinum records higher than her Malibu mansion stood there with her arms crossed.

Her publicist raised his hand. Her three tech guys. Liam the manager. The DJ. The costumer and the six foot two of pure muscle poured into a perfectly tailored suit, aka the dude from the parking lot two weeks before: Carter Kincaid.

Sexiest name ever.

Darlene briefed me on him. Fans had discovered the studio space and parked an RV across the street to watch her coming and going. Not dangerous in itself and not illegal, but creepy. And there were letters recounting all the interesting things that could be done to Darlene's body. One compared himself to Genevieve Tremaine's killer, who was famous for murdering the actress, her estranged husband, then killing himself.

Fun times.

Darlene stopped looking at the scary letters and just brought on the best security money could buy.

Carlos, her head of security, had hired Carter on a contingency, assuring her that he was highly sought-after and she was lucky to get him.

He scanned the space constantly. It made me nervous whenever his blue eyes crossed my part of the room. I caught myself tucking hair behind my ear, shaking, sweaty-palmed, knees knocking, can't-do-the-fucking-steps. It wasn't his job to speak to me, but he said hello sometimes, and we exchanged complaints about the food over the craft services table in the morning. Then I got rubber-legged and stupid. All he had to do was look at me, which he was doing right the hell now. I could see him in the mirror. Was he still looking at me? Why did he do that?

"Don't matter what they think," Darlene said, distracting me before my palms got sweaty again. She knew damn well she could do it.

"If you want Chantelle to outperform you . . . ," I said, invoking the name of her competition. The dancers hooted and clapped before I even finished. "One-two-down-and-up-and-*over*." I did the move, which was difficult. It's true. But fuck that. She was who she was, and she knew as well as I did that if the dance moves didn't accentuate the pace and power of the music . . . Well, Darlene McKenna didn't do almost-got-it-right. That was the bottom line. Period. End of chapter. The end. No cliffhanger.

When I looked over at Carter, he was looking at me. There was a little hiccup in my body.

Darlene lowered her eyelids enough to let me know the challenge was accepted and one-two-down-and-up-and-*over*ed herself without a word, landing with legs crossed and arms up the way she was supposed to, tipping only a little.

"You got this!" I clapped twice, and the music lifted. "One-two-down-and-up-and-*over*—"

A booming voice from craft services interrupted.

"Lunch!"

Everyone stopped midstep.

"We're working on 'More Than a Sister' after break!" I shouted. I snuck a look at Carter. When he saw me, he turned away as if he'd been caught looking.

CHAPTER 4

EMILY

Organic, artisanal, handmade meals were catered on steam tables with a staff to spoon out salads, vegetables, high-protein lean meats, and whole-grain desserts. I was fine with that to a point.

"More," I said to the hipster behind the chafing dish. A warehouse floor full of dancers could eat a farm-to-table establishment out of house and home.

"Give her that big piece." Darlene pointed her fork at a giant piece of chicken. "Everything we do she does ten times." She leaned into me. "I left a surprise dessert for you."

"I think we need to change the opening on 'Make Him Yours.'" I took the extra chicken and pushed it to the side to make room.

"Make it harder." Darlene's assistant handed her a salad with the tomatoes taken out.

"Is that a dare?"

She winked at me. She complained and begged for more at the same time. Hard work was her MO, and diva was her brand. She honored both sides, and I understood them. I wondered if I would have been the same way if I'd been the one to race in front of the pack instead of drop to the back of it.

"Yeah, it's a dare." She walked away to manage something for the afternoon. She'd be working on vocals until after dark, and I'd continue with the performers.

"One day, just one day." The voice behind me was deep and resonant. I turned fully and recognized Carter before I could turn back away.

"One day?"

"One day they could have cheeseburgers. Just one day."

He smiled at me and popped a cucumber slice in his mouth. Our eyes met for a second before his went back around the room. Scanning. I wondered if he ever looked at anything for more than a second.

I came to the pie. I loved pie. That must be the surprise Darlene had for me.

"If we fed these guys cheeseburgers, they'd be useless the whole afternoon." I took a slice of cherry, then let my knees go weak and my eyes go half-closed to show him how we'd be on a fat-heavy lunch. "Blar blar blar." I moved like I was drowning in mud, letting my tongue loll.

What was I doing? This wasn't funny. And I was going to drop my pie.

Except he caught it, tilting the plate back as he steadied the edge.

I turned hot pink.

"We certainly don't want that." I couldn't look at his face, so I dropped my gaze to his hand curling around the edge of his plate. It was so masculine, with veins on the back and long fingers. I had to look away from that too, only to find him watching me. I felt trapped in him, and it wasn't at all bad.

"Do you smile?" I asked, moving down the line.

"How would it be if I asked you that question?"

"Shitty. So don't ask it."

He smiled, answering my question.

"Emily," the caterer said before I took my pie back from Carter. "These were in the dessert cart. I'm assuming they're for you." He held up two brownies in tinfoil.

Even more than pie, I had a soft spot for brownies. Sometimes Darlene had the caterer make them for the whole team on Fridays. It was Thursday, and there were only two, but whatever.

They were rectangular, near black, dotted with walnuts and delicious-shaped.

Two desserts. A girl needs a little joy sometimes.

"Thank you."

"Do you share?" Carter reached for a slice of apple pie. "I prefer brownies."

"Nope." I popped my *p* and went to the patio overlooking the freeways of Downtown. All the seats were taken except a small round table with two chairs. Carter surprised me by following me and pulling out a chair for me as if he wanted to sit with me.

After I sat, he placed himself across from me. This was a better surprise than a couple of desserts.

"You're really busy around here." His eyes kept going to the door. Normally, I'd find that insulting. In his case, I found it reassuring.

"We have a tour in a month. Doesn't get much busier than that."

We'd spoken a few times in the past two weeks but never with intention. We'd never sat together at lunch.

"I never asked you why you carried around a fake gun."

He said "carried" in the past tense as if he knew I'd stopped carrying it after he attacked me in the parking lot.

"I'm afraid of the real ones."

"You could carry nothing."

"Protection." Even I didn't believe me. It was the most ridiculous reason I'd ever concocted, and I didn't insult him by waiting to see if he bought it. "Deterrent."

"What are you going to deter? Or is it *who*?" He raised one eyebrow. The arch was so perfect I was disappointed when it dropped.

"I have an ex-boyfriend who can't take a hint or understand the big words in an order of protection."

"Ah." He poked his food, looking at it for the first time since he'd sat down.

"Which ran out three weeks ago. So I've been a little nervous."

"You didn't have a three-year restraining order?" He snapped up the Tapatío and slathered his food with it.

It was a simple question if you were a victim or a lawyer. The levels of protection orders became clear to me only after Vince had hit me, then stalked me. Before that, I wouldn't have known one from the other.

"Criminal protective. Judge wrote in a year." I pointed my fork at the red-hot sauce on his chicken. "That's going to be really spicy."

"It's fine." He put it in his mouth and didn't even cry or scream. "Twelve months is unusually soft."

"The judge was unusually hostile to women. Said Vince only hit me once so he'd probably forget about me in a week. No need to inconvenience *him* further." I flicked a piece of salad across the plate. "And he insinuated I was going back to him anyway. Judge Croner, and I'll never forget his name, didn't want to 'remove incentive for Ms. Barrett to work on the relationship as opposed to lean on the courts when things get rough.' Which was another way of saying I was crazy enough to deserve it."

"I know Croner. I think his wife hasn't fucked him in a decade."

When I was done laughing, I put my elbows on the table and leaned forward. "You know judges by name, and you know how orders of protection work. You a lawyer in your spare time?"

"Former LAPD."

"Detective?"

"Uniform and badge."

"Bicycle?"

"Cruiser."

"Singing or dancing?"

"Neither. What about you?"

"Both."

CD Reiss

"You sing? I didn't know."

I didn't talk about it, ever. But he'd told me about himself without my reciprocating, and for reasons that had more to do with feelings than facts, I wanted him to know me.

"Darlene and I came to LA together to 'make it,' which obviously she did, and she deserves everything she has and more. But we were on an even keel. Same auditions, same agent. Same contacts. We even did some duets with a band in little clubs and stuff. But then . . ."

Could I find a way to tell this without looking like a complete doormat?

Probably not.

"Then I met this guy. We can call him Mr. Order of Protection. You'll remember him from two minutes ago. I must have been really weak or insecure. I don't know. It's embarrassing to tell it. But he got really jealous when I was onstage. Even if I didn't dress sexy at all. He hated people looking at me. So. I kind of stopped performing. Little by little. I stopped doing the little shows and skipped auditions. I got a data entry job that wasn't threatening. Darlene didn't even realize what was happening until my momentum was shot. Then, blah blah blah. Darlene had me choreograph her first show, which went great, and I thought Mr. Order of Protection wouldn't have a problem with it because it was a backstage job, et cetera, et cetera. Simon had to touch me to demonstrate a lift. He saw it. He went nuts. Yada yada."

We ate in silence for a while. I was grateful he didn't ask for details, shame me, or even say the usual platitudes. It was nice to just sit and eat after telling him.

"I'd like to hear you sing," he said.

"I probably sound like a frog after so long." I opened the foil around my brownies. "Do you want some?"

"I'll stick to the pie today."

I bent a corner off the brownie and ate it. It was exactly the kind I liked. Trader Joe's in the yellow box. Perfectly moist, dense, dark.

18

I wrinkled my nose. Took another bite.

"What?" Carter asked. "You got a face like there's a bug in it."

I chewed. Swallowed.

"I think they got arty with it."

"Two minutes!" a voice called from the dance space. If the rest of the dancers had two minutes, I had one.

"Arty? Looks brown to me."

He was so good-looking. The parts of his face clicked together like a puzzle. I could see the sections in a way I hadn't before. The high cheekbones. The square jaw. The full lips. Click, click, clickety-click.

"They got fancy with the taste. They put something else in it."

"Like? Describe it with words." He'd scoffed at the salad with his cheeseburger comment, but he speared the last flat leaf and ate it.

"Thirsty."

"You have water right there."

I ate the rest of the rectangle and folded the tinfoil over the other.

"No, they *taste* like thirsty." He had no idea what I was talking about, and to be honest, neither did I. "But good. Really good." I handed him the foil packet. "Not as good as a cheeseburger, but in case you're hungry later."

He took the foil, and I ran back to the studio.

I could hear Darlene working with her voice coach in an adjacent room as I went through the next set of moves with the dancers, chanting the counts I'd designed to help them remember the steps. I felt fine at the first break, but about two hours later, as we were doing the last of the moves for the day, Darlene got far away. I lost my connection with distance and time. My body pulled out like taffy. My stomach felt sucked in on itself and the thirsty taste took over my mouth, but I kept working, hoping I wasn't coming down with a stomach bug.

Monty was a very good dancer. He threw himself into every step until he got it right, and in this case he threw his torso too far left and his shoulders too hard around, and he fell over.

19

It was the funniest thing I'd ever seen, and I laughed. I never laughed at a mistake. That was rude and unprofessional. But I couldn't help myself. I laughed and laughed until I fell down, then I laughed more. Laughing was for the sake of the laughter. Hands and heels on the floor, I wasn't even the one laughing anymore. It was separate from me, and I was so separate from the room I had no idea what everyone else was doing. My chest hurt, and that was funny. I couldn't breathe, and that was funny. Carter was leaning over me, and the hilarity of his concern was shattering.

CHAPTER 5

CARTER

You need to lighten up.

Gotta admit, when I saw that note under the brownie, I thought it was directed at me. But it wasn't my dessert. It was Emily's. She was a serious girl. Cute but serious, and for good reason. I wanted to wipe all those reasons away and give her a reason to laugh.

But I'd never tell her to lighten up. It's not a friendly suggestion. It's an aggressive demand. I put the tinfoil packet on a speaker and flipped over the paper. Nothing. Just brownie crumbs and oil spots.

Were brownies *oily*?

I sniffed it. Cloying. Sour. Garlic. Eggs. Skunk.

I took a tiny bite of the brownie and had my suspicions confirmed. I folded the brownie away and grabbed a bottle of water to wash out the taste. I wished the story of her ex-boyfriend washed away as easily. Stalkers had a special place in my heart. The place where I kept violence and foul language.

Emily cackled from the studio area. I hadn't heard her laugh like that in the past two weeks. I went to the sound.

She was the center of attention in the middle of the floor, laughing so hard her face was magenta. That tiny slip of a thing in her black dance clothes laughing so hard her face was red? The tears streaming down her cheeks? Now that was cute.

"What the hell are you doing, Em?" Darlene pushed past her dance team to stand in front of Emily with her arms crossed. I kneeled over Emily and held my hand up to Darlene, because she needed to shut the fuck up right now.

"Emily?"

She was gasping for breath, up on her elbows and ass, chest heaving, eyes bloodshot and slick with laughter. I wanted to lick those tears right off her. I'd seen her out of breath, and I'd seen down her shirt plenty, but I'd never seen her or anyone laugh like that. It was the sexiest thing I'd ever laid eyes on.

"Yeah?" She licked her lips.

"Thirsty?" I held my hand out for her. She took it.

"Uh-huh."

"Hungry?"

"Yeah. And I feel weird."

Darlene put her hand on Emily's arm when she was close enough and looked into her eyes.

"Girl! What the fuck? You're stoned?"

"It's not her," I said. "It's . . . She ate a brownie. Do you know where they came from?"

I handed Darlene the note, but Emily swiped for it, missed, and slapped it out of my hand on the second pass. It fluttered down, and I caught it before it hit the floor.

Both women held their hands out for it. One swayed; one was steady. One woman paid my salary; the other was the owner of the note itself.

I gave it to the woman who paid my bills.

"That motherfucker," she said, holding it up for Emily.

"Vince," she whispered, nearly falling. I held her up, and she gripped my biceps like a vise. She looked at her hand on my suit, then made eye contact with me.

"It's okay," I said. "You're not hurting me."

She was about to start laughing when Darlene cut in.

"No, I said just no. This is not gonna work." Darlene was a force of nature. Everything she brought to the stage and studio could be leveled against one person. I was bigger, stronger, and more able, but she was damn intimidating. She paced two steps one way, then two the other, a ball of sharp intensity.

"I'm sorry," Emily said, cowed even while high.

"Vince Ginetti and his twisted shit are not okay." She pointed at Emily as if she'd done something wrong. "I knew he was too quiet. Guy like that doesn't stop wanting to hurt you just because you don't hear from him. No, no. He's been waiting. Biding his time. I told you he'd be back."

"I'll talk to him," Emily said.

I didn't know Emily that well, and I knew even less about her relationship with this Vince guy, but she wasn't talking to him.

"No," Darlene shouted. "No, you will not. He's a stalker. He's a classic, unoriginal ex-boyfriend stalker. He's the guy you see on TV in some still picture with an Uzi. And everyone watching hears how he killed his ex-girlfriend's cat before he chopped her into pieces, and they all wonder why no one did anything."

"He really killed your cat?" I asked.

"Maybe," Emily said.

"Yes. Yes he did. For the millionth time, yes he did."

"I left the poinsettia out. It's poison."

Darlene wasn't done. "I am not going to sit around and wait for you to turn into Genevieve Tremaine."

My skin crawled at the mention of the dead actress. The gruesome scene of death and everything after it. Every stalker story started and

23

ended with a comparison to that double murder. I went blank for a minute while Darlene continued.

"You will not go near him," she was saying as I made a decision. "Because if he hits you again, I'm going to kill him, and I'm not doing jailhouse shows."

"I'll talk to him," I offered. That special stalker place in my heart was getting blacker and blacker.

"No!" Emily stiffened.

"Yes. I'm assigned to the UNICEF thing tonight. I can go after."

"Never," Emily insisted. "How about before or after never?"

"I'm paying him to protect me." Darlene waved over her assistant. "Which means you too."

Emily looked at me with big, pleading brown eyes. They were really expressive. More expressive than I realized. She didn't want me to go see her ex-boyfriend the stalker. Did she still love him? I wanted to break every bone in his body.

"I know where he lives." Darlene took a clipboard from her assistant. "Unless his one ball sack actually dropped and he got his own place, which I doubt." She scribbled something on her assistant's pad and ripped the page off. "He lives in Loserdale with his fucking mother."

The last insult stung even though it wasn't directed at me. I took the slip of paper and pocketed it without looking at the address or Emily's big brown eyes.

CHAPTER 6

EMILY

I wasn't protecting Vince. I was protecting myself. I didn't want to get spun into Vince's world again. His little dramas. His begging and pleading. His poking and prodding. I just wanted to pretend I'd gotten a brownie meant for one of the assistants or grip guys. The electricians stank of skunkweed and propane lighters. It was probably meant for one of them.

Darlene didn't buy it either.

That night, she went out to some fancy event after a day of breaking her ass. Her stylist came with an extra gown for me, but I begged off. I didn't want to deal with flashing lights or people being *so nice* because *the* Darlene McKenna was in their presence.

I just wanted to go home and eat a dozen eggs. I let Carlos, her not-as-hot security guy, drop me at the door. He wouldn't leave until he heard me lock it. Apparently he was picking me up tomorrow because I couldn't get from the driveway of my house to the parking lot at work without getting jumped by a brownie.

I couldn't argue. Maybe he was right.

I was the one who had dated a pot dealer. Caretaker. When you bought weed in bulk from medical dispensaries and delivered it to clients, you weren't a dealer in the great state of California. You were a caretaker.

He didn't smoke it. I thought he was a very clever guy, making money on product he didn't use. Alcohol was his drug of choice, and everyone drank. It was nothing. It was a laugh. We drank a little together when we went out, getting happy-tipsy, then coming home, fucking and crashing, and after I got bored of mai tais and Long Island iced teas, he drank without me.

Which made him feel stupid and out of control.

Which made him *act* stupid and out of control.

Which made me not want to deal with him.

Which made him feel inferior.

Which made him mad.

Which made me want to placate him.

Lots of other girls have it worse. It takes more than a single black eye for a lot of them. I was lucky. Darlene got me out. Our friends descended on the apartment I shared with Vince, packed me a bag, broke some shit for fun, and poured maple syrup in his gas tank. Darlene was seen taking me to get an order of protection. TMZ got wind of it and surmised she was playing keep-away with her current guy. So the guy, Jinx Smootchum (real name: Joe Stevenson), who should have just called, then had an excuse to post a selfie kissing China Santiago in some club.

Darlene said she didn't care. He was an asshole anyway. And he was. Because you don't just go off kissing China Santiago because you read some shit on TMZ, and for the love of God, you don't post the kiss on Instagram.

Not only did that end the relationship, it sent Darlene into a rage. She was an artist with her voice, but if her energy is misdirected, she could make art out of spite.

Instagram will never be the same.

Let's just say she lost her account and the 16.7 million followers she entertained with her square-framed shenanigans.

So I was not interested in getting Vince involved in my life again, even if he'd just tried to interject himself. He'd played a nasty trick with the pot brownie. Carlos had dropped me home half an hour before, checked behind the couch and shower curtain, had a moment of intimacy with the security system, and left. I was on my second bag of chips and third quart of water, but I'd live. I didn't want to get swept away in another uncontrollable firestorm.

I had cameras in every corner, thanks to Darlene. I had piles of paper documenting Vince's need for control over me. When the police said I had to wait him out, Darlene went batshit.

"Why is it on her?"

She'd been right. I was the victim, and it was up to me to live in fear until I could prove he'd done something strikingly illegal. And once the judge let him out for hitting me (no priors, show of regret, plenty of community ties), there was nothing I could do but look behind me and worry about what he was planning.

I plopped on my couch in my pink sweatpants and a tank top. I flicked through the channels. Crime. News. Drama. Comedy. Crime. News.

I stopped at the entertainment channel where musicians were being interviewed live outside the UNICEF event. I recognized the gown before I recognized Darlene. All forty grand of it sparkled and shimmered, so she subverted it with a worn-out baseball cap low over her eyes.

"Oh, Darlene." I shook my head like a disgruntled parent. She laughed at the interviewer's joke and went toward the door. The interviewer faced the camera and said something no one gave a shit about. Darlene was behind him, walking to the next bank of cameras, and behind her was Carter.

He looked like her date, if dates had a wire in their ear and looked everywhere but at her. Two fewer degrees of physical separation and he could have been kissing her on Instagram to spite her rapper boyfriend, except Darlene didn't have a rapper boyfriend any more than she had an Instagram account.

Then, in the corner of the screen, just before the show cut to commercial, I saw Carter lay his hand gently on Darlene's lower back, and I thought, *Well, she deserves a nice guy after Jinx.*

CHAPTER 7

CARTER

Three other guys could have watched Darlene at the UNICEF event. Carlos, who ran this ship, had to take care of something with actor Michael Greydon, who was apparently dating a paparazza, opening up a whole can of problems. Fabian, the workaholic, had done too many shifts that week, which was not a good way to stay alert. Bart, who did stand-up, couldn't miss a show. Jamal was driving. So even though I didn't like working nights, I was on the awards show.

Watching Darlene McKenna was my job, and I was fine, just fine. But working the event meant I couldn't give Vince Ginetti a talking-to. And that guy needed a talking-to.

This was some stage six shit. This was about controlling her responses. He'd drugged her so he could have control over her for a few hours. When she didn't call him to either thank him for the high or yell at him for the assault on her bloodstream, he was going to get pissed and plan something bigger and better.

Emily knew this. She knew not to talk to him, and she knew she had to lock herself in the house. Darlene had put a nice security system on the house, but nothing was perfect.

"She used to sing. You know that?" Darlene said through her smile, waving to the cheering crowd. "She was better than me. More range. Just better. She stopped because her success bruised his little ego."

"That's sad." I wanted to hear her sing more than anything. I wanted to hear her open up her soul, then tell her she was a star. I wanted to be the one to heal what he'd broken.

"I want you to go there and beat his ass." She was so angry she walked the wrong way.

"That's only going to make it worse." I put my hand on her back to guide her in the right direction. "I'm just going to case him."

"She hasn't had a boyfriend in two years because of him. Last guy she dated ended up with four flats and a broken nose. He got hit with a crowbar, and while he was bleeding, the motherfucker told him he was now officially single."

"And he broke up with her?"

"She left him. She cares about everyone but herself." Smiles, waves.

That guy was a pussy if he let her walk away. He didn't deserve her. Yvette, security from another firm, opened the doors, giving me a nod. I would have given her a smile or a word, but I was too wrapped up in thoughts of killing a stalker.

The sound changed indoors, and Darlene's name buzzed in my earpiece.

"Status: McKenna."

"Darlene McKenna's in the building."

In my earpiece, the buzz of names and places from every security person in the network went on and on. I located security on the balconies and in the corners, making eye contact when possible.

"What happened with the cat?"

"Ate the poinsettia and dropped dead at her door."

"Cat would die in a corner. Under the house. Someplace like that."

"See what I'm saying?" She looked past the brim of her baseball cap, flashing the fake silver lashes, her attitude as deep as the mean streets.

"When we were growing up, she lived on Lake Michigan and I lived in Shit Town. She brought me around her friends like it was nothing and let me sleep over when it got loud in my house. She never made me feel like I was poor and she was privileged. So I don't want her to feel like she's vulnerable and I'm not. But if you have a few minutes tonight, go look in on her."

"No problem."

I took two steps back as my client made small talk with other artists and businesspeople. It was my job to know who they were by face and name, memorize whom she spoke to, how they seemed and their attitude toward her. It was my job to see everyone, any sudden movements, note the employees and what they were looking at, and keep track of the time.

I didn't have a hard job. I'd been watching over people since I was in my teens. I ran my block like an enforcer. My motivations had changed, but situational awareness was a habit. I liked that I was expected to be detached. I liked things cut-and-dried. My home life was messy enough. I didn't need a roller coaster in my working life.

But I was thinking about Emily, alone in the house, a cat-killing psycho's obsession. He'd be thinking about the brownie. Scouring the news to see if she showed up on it. Probably watching the awards show right now to see if Emily was with Darlene.

I hadn't thought about my sister in a long time. The crippling grief and guilt had been locked away, but deep in my gut, something in the bolted box growled awake.

It was all a memory, but the fury was so real I could touch it.

Maybe letting Emily stay home had been a bad idea. The worry started small as we entered the building and turned into a full-on roaring lion by the time Darlene sat down and I was backstage with fifty other security guys.

The Shrine Auditorium was the safest place on earth.

I tapped Darlene a message.

—I'm going to go look at this address you gave me—

Before I was sending the first message, I knew I couldn't just case Vince then go home.

—And check on Emily—

The answer came back immediately.

—Good—

—I'll get back by the end—

—Thor can handle it—

Thor was her joke name for her driver, Jamal. His skin was as black as onyx, and his head was completely smooth. Physically, he was the exact opposite of a long-haired, blond Nordic god.

Hence, Thor.

—I'm out—

When I was LAPD, I'd developed a sense of when someone in my sight was in danger or when something was off. My mentor, Brian Muldoon, called it the Iron Eye.

I was supposed to check on Mr. Order of Protection first, then see Emily. But the Iron Eye said Emily was first, and I never questioned it. There were days I tried to remember if the Iron Eye had something to say the day my sister was killed, but it had just flat out failed me. Knowing it could fail humbled me and made me more sure that when intuition spoke, I had to obey.

CHAPTER 8

EMILY

I wasn't much of a drug user. I'd smoked a few times in the High School of the Arts. Dropped acid once. Did my share of drinking. Once we got to LA, I saw how people acted on drugs, and mostly they were fine until the chemicals reached their brain. Then, no matter who they were, they were douchebags.

I had to dance the pot through my system. Sweat it out. I got up and did Darlene's first dance in my dining room.

The first thing I ever choreographed for Darlene was one-two-three-and-up-and-turn-and-punch-and-bend-and—

I was a singer and dancer. Feeling fake euphoria or really shitty wasn't good for my performance. Smoking hurt my throat. Drinking depressed my immune system. So I just passed. The only time I felt really and truly free was when my body and the music worked together to make something new. Without that feeling of connection, I felt broken.

One-two-three-and-up-and-turn-and-punch-and-bend-and—

I wasn't prepared for how my body would react when the marijuana left it. I felt awake and exhausted. Sweaty-palmed. Confused. I was watching a show, then another, and didn't remember changing the channel. When I closed my eyes, I concentrated on the light bursts behind my lids in a way that was mentally uncomfortable.

One-two-three-and-up-and-turn-and-punch-and-bend-and—

The moves weren't connected to my pleasure centers. I did them because I could. Because I wanted to work the drug through and out of my body. Because I didn't want to eat another chip. I just wanted someone to talk to. Barring that, I'd dance.

My phone dinged, and I scooped it up.

—*Was it fun, babe?*—

Vince didn't have my new number, and I'd blocked his. But there he was. I took a screenshot of the text just like I was supposed to. Because he was admitting he was the one who put the pot in my brownies and that he'd found my number.

Except, since the number wasn't his old one and I'd blocked him, this could be anyone.

And if I engaged him, I was giving him what he wanted, control over my time and my thoughts.

I knelt down. Tried to take a deep breath, because that was what a girl did to relax. Right? Take a breath. Think. Except I couldn't think. Not clearly. I couldn't decide if it was him, and I didn't know if I needed proof or if it mattered, and my brain was all cocked up with stuff and things and the two millimeters between the edge of my nail polish and my cuticle. How all my toes had the same amount.

Would Darlene be proud of me if I texted back and proved it was Vince? Would the police say, "Good work"? Or would that open the door for him?

Just as I was obsessing over open doors, there was a buzz from the front gate.

I swallowed about four internal organs.

What was I supposed to do? I had a plan in place. What was it? The gate was modest, coming right up to the sidewalk, and had a keypad, microphone, and buzzer. The fence obscured the view of the house. I had cameras everywhere. Of all the security systems in Los Angeles, it wasn't even close to the most exhaustive, but it made sense for the neighborhood and was a good deterrent.

Brain. Fucking brain.

I had a button to push. A red button on a keychain that would alert the police. It was on my bag, which was near the door, and there was one Louisville Slugger in the car and one in the front closet I was supposed to wield in case of emergency.

But I wasn't supposed to answer the buzzer or acknowledge him at all.

I tiptoed to the front closet, wishing myself invisible so I could check the monitor and confirm it was my psycho ex.

The security closet had a monitor for each camera. The front gate feed showed a man in front, and it wasn't Vince. Not at all. There wasn't an ounce of douche on the guy. He was still in his suit. Tall and strong, looking down one end of the street, then the other, checking for danger.

I pushed the microphone button, and he spoke before I could say anything.

"Emily? It's Carter. Carter Kincaid."

His name was sexier every time I heard it.

"You nearly gave me a heart attack."

"Sorry. I should have called first."

I opened the door and padded down the front walk in my bare feet. The night was warm, and the stones were cool. The squirrels rustled the loquat tree.

I turned the lock and opened the heavy gate.

"Hey," I said. "I thought you were at the music thing?"

"Darlene's fine. Thor has her. Do you always answer this gate by yourself?" He touched the gate frame, putting his finger in the hole

35

to make sure the dead bolt was deep enough, eyeing the buzzer, the keypad, the knob.

"It's not like I have a staff."

"Yeah. Well . . ."

"You can stop looking at everything. I'll point out where the cameras are."

"No need."

He moved his eyes from the security system to my body, making me realize I wasn't dressed appropriately. I'd peeled off my sweatpants when I started dancing around, leaving me in Lycra short shorts and a crop top. He'd seen me in outfits like this a hundred times during rehearsal, but without the safety of two dozen dancers and assorted hangers-on, I felt naked.

And I kind of liked it, because it was him.

"Didn't you come to look at my security system?" I didn't care why he came. I wanted him to stay. I needed company.

"I wanted to see how you were feeling."

"It's complicated." I stepped out of the way and handed him my phone with the text open. "Come in."

CHAPTER 9

CARTER

Emily's house was on the corner of Olympic and Citrus, not too far from where I lived. The front entrance was on the smaller street, and the driveway faced the wide thoroughfare of Olympic. That must have been for safety. Desolate streets helped the stalker, not the victim. Corner properties on major thoroughfares had advantages.

She handed me her phone as I came through the gate.

—Was it fun, babe?—

"Are you sure he sent this text?"

"No. He doesn't have my new number, and I've blocked him."

I gave her back her phone, following her inside. She closed and locked the front door. The little house was clean and uncluttered. I could see where the walls met the floors.

"Did you answer?"

"No. I blocked the number so he won't text again. And I got a screenshot and uploaded it to my lawyer's server. Blah blah. Can I get you something?"

"Water?"

I followed her into the open space in the middle of the house.

"Is this—?"

"Dining room," she answered. Her eyes were still bloodshot and her lips were a little dry, but her reaction times appeared normal. She seemed to be coming down from the unexpected high just fine.

"Where do you eat?"

She shrugged. "When I'm not working? The bar, I guess." She pointed to a butcher-block bar that separated the kitchen from the living room with a single stool tucked under it. "It's nice to have the practice space right here if I get an idea, but mostly I work in the studio out back. Lemon?"

"Sure."

She stood in front of the sink with one foot bent. Toe pointed. Hands folded in front of her as if they kept her from leaping at any second. She wasn't a wilting flower when she was working. She was smart and confident. But in her own house? She had a shyness about her. A reticence that was the exact opposite of her best friend.

She handed me the glass. "The whole house is filtered. So you can drink it."

"Does the studio have a separate security system?"

"Same one."

I drank the water. It gave me a moment to figure out how I could politely demand an inspection of every inch of the house. When a woman is being stalked, a man shouldn't demand things, even for her own good. I'd learned that too late, but I learned it.

"Do you want to see it?" She read my mind. "I mean, you're here. You might as well check the security."

"If you're up to it."

She flicked on the backyard floods. When she slid open the glass door, another flood flicked on, revealing a fountain with a black stone fish leaping from the center.

"Do you like it?" She flicked her hand to the fountain. "It came with the house. It's reclaimed water."

"I do. You need fish in it."

"I'd forget to feed them, and they'd be floating when I got back from a trip or something."

We crossed the yard. The lights in the converted garage were already on, illuminating the red door. The cameras at the entrance to the studio looked like they worked. More motion-sensor floods.

She stopped when she had her hand on the knob. The light of the floods lit the fringes of her straw-colored hair as they escaped her ponytail. Her profile was perfect. Sharp. Patrician. Almost flawless except for a little bump in her nose that made her even more perfect.

"You know what's funny?" she asked.

"Old *Abbott and Costello* reels."

She laughed softly. A real laugh. Not some fake stoned cackle.

"Sure. No. It's funny that I don't know anything about you. Not really. And I let you into my house. And now the studio. I mean, what's the point of all this security if I just let Mr. Rando have the run of the place?"

"Mr. Rando? You mean the way middle schoolers say 'random'?"

"I'm not trying to insult you."

Of course she wasn't. She was trying to engage me. She had a couch in front of the television and cameras at every entrance to her house. She had access to the best parties and the most exciting people in the city, but she ate alone on a single stool set at the kitchen bar. I envied all the space she had to herself. But she seemed lonely.

"You're protecting yourself against a specific threat. Not every guy in Los Angeles."

She opened the door a crack as if I'd convinced her.

"I'm from the South Bay."

"How nice."

"Torrance, actually."

She opened the door. "Not a lot of hometown pride in your voice, there."

"It was terrible. There was nothing to do but drink in whoever's basement and get into fights. We called it Borrance."

She laughed again and stepped into the white light of the studio. The garage door in front had been walled off from the inside. Two sides of the room had floor-to-ceiling mirrors and a barre.

There was a stereo system mounted into the wall and a small table with a notebook.

"Where do you live now?" She stepped into the center of the room, reticence gone. She was all grace, curving her body so naturally I was sure she didn't even realize she was dancing.

"Not far from here."

No one but Carlos knew where I lived, and I didn't want that to change. I didn't tell her why I was there, really, or why the reason I'd bought the house was irrelevant now. I didn't tell her the size of the house or who lived in it. I couldn't answer all the questions; I could only hope she wouldn't ask.

That scared me into changing the subject. "You didn't tell me where you're from."

"Just outside Chicago, same as Darlene. You can read all about our friendship in the trades."

"I bet that makes you comfortable." I tapped the barre.

"I'm just a prop."

"That work for you?"

"Very much. How did we end up talking about my life?"

"I'm not that interesting."

She crossed her arms. "Parents?"

"Yes."

"Do you dance?" She clicked the stereo and a light, lilting classical piece came over the speakers.

"No."

"Okay, here's the deal." She was close to me in two steps and pulled my forearms forward. I let her because I was curious and because I wanted her to touch me. She wasn't my client. Not exactly. She wasn't the principal. "You answer the questions or you dance."

She pulled me to the center of the room, and I let her. I never gave anyone control, yet for those seconds, I couldn't resist her.

"You wouldn't call what I do dancing."

"Tell me about your parents."

"One male. One female."

"Wrong." She slid her hands down my arms and took my hands. Before I could react, she turned, let the left hand go, lifted the right, and spun, taking the left again.

"It's going to get harder next time," she promised.

"My father was a cop. My mother was a nag."

"Was?"

"He's not around to nag anymore, so she had to change careers."

She didn't ask a question, but she pulled on my hands as if she were going to do another move. I laid my hand open, and hers spread over it. She was so tiny against me. Her bones were short and narrow. I ran my hand along her forearm and to the elbow. All muscle, bone, and skin. I could break her but wouldn't. Not physically.

I wondered just how tight she was.

Enough of that.

I interrupted my train of thought with an answer to her question.

"Divorce," I said. "He left when I was little. Speaking of . . ." I ran my thumb over her collarbone, into the divot at the base of her neck. I couldn't help myself.

"Speaking of what?" Her eyes fluttered, half-closed. She had freckles on the lids. Everything about her made me wild.

"You're so small. I didn't realize until now."

"Why?" She whispered it.

My dick stretched against my pants. "You have great presence when you dance. You seem ten feet tall."

"You're really good at this."

"Touching you?"

"Calculating and avoiding."

I held her fingers tight and pulled her to me. She resisted enough to do a dance move. Not enough to keep me from getting her close enough to smell her peach soap.

"You're really good at this too," I said.

"Good at what?"

"Pretending you're flirting."

"I'm not," she said.

"Not flirting?"

"Not pretending."

She tried to pull into another dance move, but I held her close and kissed her before I could talk myself out of it. I gave her my tongue, and she took it willingly, letting my hands go so I could get my arms around her waist and she could get hers around my shoulders.

I hadn't kissed a woman in a long time. I wanted to eat her alive. Put my hands on every inch of her. Take her body on the hardwood. Everything. I was about to completely lose control when alarm bells went off in my head.

She's vulnerable.

So are you.

CHAPTER 10

EMILY

The kiss was such a surprise I lost control of my body, falling into it like a perfectly warm bath. His lips moved gently against mine, his tongue flicked against mine with care as if reading a foreign language he knew he'd understand if he were careful.

I'd never been kissed like that. He kissed as if he were listening to me tell a story, and I kissed him back as if I was.

He pulled back gently. He wasn't an asshole about it. He was perfectly fine. A gentleman. But when I realized he wasn't pulling away so he could breathe or kiss me at a different angle, I got mad. Defensive. Butthurt. Whatever.

"I'm sorry," he said. "I can't."

And you know, he could go screw himself. I was in no mood. I was weird from a pot brownie and tired, and I had work the next day. One-two-up-turn-what-the-fuck-ever.

"Yeah. It's fine."

He paused as if he wanted to make some other pathetic excuse for . . . what? Not kissing me longer? Not having sex with me? Not marrying me? What did I want from the guy anyway?

It didn't matter. The last guy I had kissed was named Peter. That had been a little more than a year ago. We were together for five months. I'd liked him. He'd liked me. We could have loved each other, but Vince had found out I had a boyfriend and that had been that. He snuck up on Peter in a parking lot and smashed his face in with a crowbar,

I broke up with Peter when he got out of the hospital. I was toxic. His broken nose was my fault.

He didn't say any of that. I did.

"You know the way out."

"Past the, ah . . ." He jerked his finger toward the front and took a step away, smiling. "Bank of cameras."

"That supposed to be funny?"

I was acting like a bitch, but mentioning the cameras meant I was too much trouble. Crazy ex. Superfamous best friend. The maintenance costs of a girl like me were huge.

This wasn't even the first reason I kept away from men. I was a danger magnet. Peter hadn't gotten his dick cut off, but it might have only been a matter of time.

"I think the pot made me grumpy."

"I'll see you tomorrow, tiny dancer."

A smile crossed his lips when he coined the new nickname. I didn't know if I was irritated with the name or the smile.

"Yeah. Tomorrow."

He was gone a second later, and I was alone.

CHAPTER 11

CARTER

I could have kissed her longer. At least all night and into the next day, but I'd promised to look in on Vince.

Deep in Glendale, just north of Mountain, stood a house shaped like one cracker box stacked on another. You could barely see the 1920s Craftsman it used to be. It had been built to two stories, siding removed and stuccoed over. Windows taken out and filled in to fit Home Depot standard vinyl. Bathroom tile on the steps leading into the closed-in porch. The entire property had been paved in beige concrete so two black BMWs could park in the front yard.

The garage was in the back, and on the night I kissed Emily, the rolling door was open. I could see the whole yard down the driveway. A set of metal prefab steps went up the side of the house to a door on the second floor. My guess was that was his way in and out of his room. A few guys were milling around with beers, poking sticks into a barbecue. I couldn't hear what they were saying between bold laughs and steaming vapes.

Carlos had sent me a picture of Vince, and I spotted him right away. Five ten. Shaped like a loaf of Wonder Bread. Goatee. Backward baseball cap. White sneakers. Nylon shorts falling just below the knees.

I'd figured she was out of this guy's league, but I'd had no idea just how far.

One guy kept pacing around even though there was a chair. He was about six four, maybe a hundred sixty, all bones and skin. Bald head. Adam's apple as big and knobby as his elbows. The others looked like Vince, more or less. Dressed like adolescents and built as if they'd spent time at the gym but skipped leg days.

I took license plate numbers. Checked for security. Watched as the upstairs lights in the house went on and off and stayed until the guys left and it was only Vince with his goatee and backward baseball cap. He lowered the garage door.

He looked at his phone on the way inside.

Was he texting her?

I couldn't call and ask her. Not after that stupid kiss.

That fantastic kiss.

But stupid.

When the house was dark, I went home.

———

I had a two-story Craftsman. Rock solid.

When I'd bought the house in Hancock Park, I had a single priority. The best school district in the city. And by the city, I wasn't talking about Studio City north of the hills or deep south El Segundo by the airport. I meant in the middle.

I needed a house in the middle of the city or nowhere. Being a bodyguard meant I had to travel from the water to Pomona, from San Diego to the Angeles National. I didn't want to live too far in one direction.

Also, the people I lived with had *opinions*. Irritating opinions, but in the case of the location of the house, the opinions fell into line with mine. Which was unusual.

I pulled the car up to the garage door and entered the house from the side.

The door wasn't locked.

Jesus fucking Christ, guys.

I opened the door to the kitchen. The breakfast nook was loaded with activity books, puzzle pieces, Lego creations that made their own kind of sense. A half-finished cell phone case made with a 3D pen.

The counters were clean but cluttered, and the fridge was covered with pictures, drawings, and a prescription that still hadn't been filled.

"You're late."

She stood in the doorway in a T-shirt and yoga pants. Slim for her age but well put together. She dyed her hair chestnut brown and had it blown out twice a week on Larchmont. She never had a hard time getting a date.

"You didn't lock the door, Ma."

"I thought you'd be coming through it sooner." She snapped the lock shut. "He misses you when you're out late, and for the love of Pete, call me Brenda."

"He hates me." I grabbed her and kissed her on the cheek. "You gonna get his pills?"

She waved her arm as if swatting a fly. Three fingers had rings stacked on rings.

"You're such a Boy Scout. We have three days left. Take it easy."

"You could just have the doctor call it in."

"I barely trust that guy to take his temperature."

"He's a psychiatrist. He—"

"He hacked into Jerry's Wi-Fi again."

The "he" in question wasn't the psychiatrist. It was the little coder in the house, and Jerry was our neighbor.

"How was he even sitting at a computer?"

"He had homework to do, Mr. Boss. You want him to do homework on paper, you can take him out of Swanky School."

47

"You have to unhook the router."

"I did. Ask him how he did it. Do you want coffee, or are you going to bed?"

My mother hadn't slept in fourteen years, and whatever sleep disease she had was genetic. We were night creatures.

"Bed." I kissed her on the cheek again. "See you tomorrow."

She turned the gas on under the coffeepot. "Yeah. Sweet and sour dreams, kid."

I checked to make sure the doors and windows were locked, put the schoolbag where it went, the shoes on the shoe rack, the jackets on the hooks, and went upstairs.

I checked his workroom at the end of the hall. The computer wasn't off, and the floor was coated in a spray of Legos. I knew they had a logic, and if I put them away I'd hear it. I went to his bedroom.

"Phin," I said in the doorway.

"Hey," came a muffled voice. "How was it?"

"How was what?"

"Whatever you were doing."

I sat on the edge of his bed. Phin's whole name was Phinnaeus, of course, because his mother wanted to fit into the mold of the Hollywood star. I'd had to talk her out of naming him Huckleberry.

Phin was wrapped up in a fourteen-pound compression blanket. Having weight on him made him feel contained. He'd struggled with ADHD and sensory issues his entire thirteen years. Little things like a heavy blanket and tight shirts made a big difference.

"How was school? Did you talk about inclusion and love all day?"

He rolled over until I saw his mischievous smile. I'd sent him to the well-rated public school around the corner where he did well enough on the power of his brain, but his learning style made him rebel against the structure. Mom and I found him a progressive, project-based, experimental school that ate through money like a piranha but made him happy.

"Half a day," he said. "Math in the afternoon. Then we did flower-sniffing."

"Flower-sniffing?" He was joking, but I had to get mad. That was the routine. He was doing all the geography and algebra a kid needed to do.

"And tomorrow we have 'cultural pluralism' all day!"

"Cultural what?"

"We sing 'Kumbaya.'"

He said it with half a laugh. When I got back from the first open house, I called it a "Kumbaya school," and he begged to go. None of his friends were there. He wasn't trying to fit into a group. He wanted more art. He wanted to be in a school where they worked to understand him. I figured a little squishy left-wing arm-linking wouldn't kill him.

I tickled him and kissed his face.

"What's this about Jerry's Wi-Fi?"

"I wanted to check something on the internet, and his password was really vulnerable to a brute-force attack. I emailed him and told him how to fix it."

"After you used his bandwidth."

"I needed to look something up for homework."

"We have books."

He rolled his eyes. I didn't know how to fight against Google-ization. The rock I was rolling up the hill got heavier and heavier, and the boy was getting too old to boss around. He was just starting to exhibit manly stink. The air in his room was getting particularly thick.

"Did you shower before bed?"

"Morning," he said, eyes half-closed. He held up his fist.

"Size of my heart," he said.

I held up my fist. "Still bigger."

We bumped knuckles to prove we loved each other as much as a heart could.

"I love you, Dad."

"I love you too, kid. Now get to sleep."

CHAPTER 12

EMILY

I woke up with a headache. Not a nagging pain that would go away but a dense throb that felt like a cinder block duct-taped to the left side of my head. Add a side of nausea, and bang: recipe for my morning.

After coffee and three ibuprofen, the cinder block turned red brick, and the nausea came out as the star of the show, took a bow, and wouldn't leave center stage. I showered, dressed, and got to work only slightly grumpy.

The morning sun blasted through the windows and went right into my brain. The early birds were at the craft services table or checking equipment. I grabbed a piece of bread to soak up whatever my insides were producing too much of.

"Good morning," Carter said as he poured fresh coffee into his Starbucks cup. I grumbled a polite response. I had more to say, but I didn't know what he deserved. Thanks for the kiss? An insult for cutting me off at that? Praise for a solid lip-lock?

"I went to Vince's place last night."

Every muscle tightened. I didn't expect him to mention my psycho ex. My entire body tingled with adrenaline.

"What happened?"

"Nothing." He stirred his coffee. "From across the street, he seems like a standard-issue douchebag."

"He's much worse up close."

"I bet." Pensively, he tossed the stirrer in the bin.

I had moves to practice before everyone arrived, but I couldn't just walk away.

"What?" I asked.

"Nothing."

"You want to know how I could be with him."

"You're way out of his league."

"Good to know you won't question my looks as easily as you'll question my judgment."

I stormed off before he could answer. I didn't want him to defend himself, and I didn't want to apologize. I didn't want to hear about how pretty I was or whatever he had in his mind.

Mostly, I didn't want to get to the true fact. My judgment sucked.

All the signs had been there. I was out of his league, sure. Whatever. He turned his polo collars up and wore his hats backward. He had a drawerful of sweatpants he found appropriate to every situation. He laughed at other people's misfortunes and took personal offense when someone went the speed limit in the left lane.

All that was true, and I hadn't seen it.

He was nice to me. He acted as if he were the luckiest guy in the world. He said he won the lottery with me. Blah blah. When another man looked at me, he went wild with jealousy. I had to peel him off a guy at Cat's Cradle. I blamed the alcohol. But when I was supposed to meet him at the Arclight and I ran into my uncle before Vince arrived, it stopped being cute. My uncle Jim was a fascinating guy. He worked at JPL designing updates to the Hubble telescope and played oboe in the NASA orchestra.

Vince jumped him. He had him on the ground while I screamed, "He's my uncle, he's my uncle!"

And oh, the tears. And the begging for forgiveness. And the self blame. He was a picture of contrition. Stupid me. I fell for it, but I made sure to stay away from other men in casual conversation. I introduced him to every male dancer ahead of time so he could shake their hand too tight and glare at them.

And that seemed normal enough. He was still nice to me. More or less. Kind of normal. I figured the honeymoon phase didn't last in any relationship. I'd tried to explain that to Darlene, who was the product of an abusive father. She wagged her finger at me. She said *guuurl* a lot and told me she'd be there for me when he went too far. I said I was okay a million times.

I was a frog in boiling water. Everything seemed fine, a little different but tolerable, until it wasn't. He had everything in the world to say about how much skin I should show when I rehearsed and how I touched the other dancers. His tone got angry and threatening often enough but not all the time. I kept going back to those moments when he was honored to be with me. When I needed him to be 50 percent nicer, he gave me 45 percent. I accepted that.

Then, like a frog in a pot, I realized it was too fucking hot and I was going to get eaten for dinner.

Looking back and seeing how stupid I'd been was a bad habit. Every time I had to look behind me, every time I wouldn't go on a date because I was afraid he'd come for the guy, every time I refused an unknown number, I beat myself raw. I was a stupid, stupid woman with shitty judgment who was living the life she deserved. There was no chance I could go back to singing either. He'd see me. I couldn't be seen. I'd paid a price to leave him and to be with him. I'd paid for being stupid, and the price had been my career.

That punitive loop ran in my brain all day long. Even watching the dancers, training Darlene, and trying to avoid Carter's motherfucking piercing blue eyes, I ran that loop.

I was in denial that I deserved anything good at all, and the denial was such a habit I didn't know there was another way to live.

It took a lot of concentration to berate myself and choreograph a major production at the same time. When the dozen red roses arrived, I didn't even see them. They just sat on the piano until Darlene stopped after a turn, nailing the move.

"Excellent!" I shouted.

"Whose are those?" she demanded.

Monty snapped the card off and handed it to Darlene. I assumed they were for her.

She closed the envelope and pointed to me.

"You." She pointed to Carter. "And you. My crib."

I met Carter's gaze. Had he sent the flowers? He was so good at the stone face, I couldn't tell what he knew or what he thought.

Because she was using the entire floor for studio space, Darlene's crib was the service hallway. She kicked empty boxes out of the way and wheeled a broken keyboard to the corner so hard it clattered when it hit the wall.

She handed Carter the little envelope.

He read it and didn't make an expression one way or the other. He gave it back to Darlene, who handed it to me as if serving me papers.

Babe, you're so sweet when you laugh.
Next time I'm going to see it.
I swear I changed.
Give me one chance to prove it to you.

I spit-laughed.

53

"You're not thinking of giving him a chance, are you?" Darlene asked.

"No. God no. It's funny he thinks I'll fall for this."

"He knows where you work," Carter said. "If we weren't sure yesterday, we know now."

A year and change earlier, I would have considered talking to him. I'd believed in my ability to convince Vince I wanted him to go away, and he repeatedly came back, proposing to love me more than before. Promising he'd changed. He brought flowers once, chocolate another time. Darlene said he was one visit away from bringing me a hat made of my dead cat's fur.

"There's nothing to do." I tossed the envelope and the note into the trash. Vince's attention was cyclical. He'd be insistent for a few weeks, then he'd go away.

I glanced at Carter. I cared what he thought. I didn't know why, but I wanted him to know I wasn't going back to Vince. I needed him to know I might have been a poor judge of character, but I wasn't stupid or weak. He wasn't looking at me.

Darlene folded her hands together and put them over her face.

"I'm sorry," she said. "I have to make this about me." When she brought her palms down, she slapped them against her thighs. "Yeah. True facts. The tour starts in two weeks, and we have Vegas in a few weeks."

Darlene was doing a supersecret preshow at the MGM Grand that was about to go public. Tickets would sell out in minutes. It was a way to work out the kinks, make sure everything looked good, and bump excitement for the tour. It would be my last working day on this show.

She continued. "We're not ready. The show's not ready. You know what I got riding on this tour."

"I know."

Tours were money. Big money. A good 40 percent of her income, which meant *my* income. The dancers, the techs, the publicity people—everyone depended on her tours. Sexy Bitch had to do 30 percent better than Sexy Badass to make up for the 20 percent increase in expenses.

"And I need you. I need your head in the game. Don't start, okay? Don't tell me it is. Yeah, I know it is. I know you got this. But I don't. I freak out every time I see a goatee."

I'd never felt smothered by my friendship with Darlene until she scolded me with Carter watching.

"He's not going to bother me," I lied. He'd just fed me a pot brownie, texted me, and sent flowers. The falsehood was so easily provable I shrank to half my normal size. My credibility in the matter was shot anyway.

"I'm done." Darlene cut the air with her hands. Was she firing me? "You're done." She couldn't fire me. I had the entire show in my head. "All done. You." She pointed to Carter. "You're in charge of her."

"Wait, wait . . ." He held up his hands as if anyone or anything had the power to ward off Darlene McKenna.

"No waiting. Now."

"I can't."

"What do you mean you can't?" I piped up as if I wanted him to be in charge of me. Which I didn't. I was in charge of me.

"I just can't."

"As God is my witness, Carter Kincaid," Darlene said, "I will call Carlos, and he will make this happen if you won't."

"Why not?" I hadn't even heard Darlene. I was just mad and a little hurt.

Carter's eyes went from me to Darlene and back. We'd cornered him good. Darlene with her demands and me with my questions.

"I have something to do this afternoon."

"Fine," Darlene said. "Start tonight at Club NV." She wasn't about to take no for an answer, even if I threw a tantrum.

"I'll let Carlos know." He didn't seem happy about it.

"You do that." I didn't wait for anyone to ask me to leave. I just walked out. I had work to do.

———

I'd been away from Vince for almost two years. Before that, we were together eighteen months. Moved in together three months after meeting on Tinder. Nothing in his profile indicated he was crazy.

I'd been dating a lot when we met. I expected nothing. I showed up, met a guy, nine times out of ten we didn't make it past the second date. Two times out of ten we became friends and said hello whenever we crossed at the usual first-date meet-up spots. Coffee shops. Parks. Sandwich stands.

Sex was a third-date thing. I usually didn't get that far. But I tried to like the men I met. I tried to see the good in them before deciding if they were for me or not.

Nothing about my expectations or attitudes would have made me a target for a guy like Vince. I wasn't easily sucked in by sweet words or shows of affection. I was looking for a guy who was good for me, not the other way around.

But something clicked. We met at a custard place on Sunset. The customers put the frozen custard in the cup and chose the toppings from a bar. The price was based on weight. I didn't eat a lot of dairy because it wasn't good for my voice. So even though the custard cup was huge, I didn't fill it with more than a squirt of soy vanilla and a teaspoon of chocolate chips. That was plenty.

But Vince, a guy I didn't even know, thought it would be funny to put more toppings in my cup while I wasn't looking. I thought it was funny too. As many dates as I'd been on, none had done anything the least bit spontaneous or impulsive. They'd all sat down and told me their life's accomplishments as if they were at a job interview.

But this guy was fun. Probably because he didn't have any life accomplishments. He told me he was a caretaker/dealer and couched that in funny stories. Really funny. Piss-down-your-leg funny. Fuck-on-the-first-date funny.

I thought a lot about those first three months.

Was I insecure?

I didn't think I was.

Was I lonely?

No. I'd had friends and a career. I spoke to my family often enough.

Did I want to slow down on dating?

Yes. That one was probably spot-on. I should have slowed down and dated a résumé guy for a few months.

Carter didn't want to be my bodyguard. I took it personally. I felt the same way I had the first time Vince said my tits were too small.

Unimportant. Unwanted. Vulnerable.

Both feelings created emotional acrobatics. One was a full layout and the other was a full pike, but they both left me suspended in the air with more to do before I hit the floor.

I went through the routine a hundred more times that morning, and each time I forgot the feeling of being unwanted a little more. I sweated it out, kicked it away, worked it down.

"Lunch!"

I wasn't ready to stop. I hadn't gotten rid of all of it, but I had to let everyone else break.

"Can we talk?" Carter asked from behind me.

I walked toward my bags. "I don't know. Can we?"

He dropped his voice. "Last night." He cleared his throat. "If you're my principal, that can't happen again."

"Fine." There was no venom in my voice, just exhaustion. Everything in my life was mitigated. I had to look where I went, watch what I said, make sure I was alone even if I was desperately lonely. Of course I couldn't be attracted to a decent man who found me interesting. Of course a perfectly nice kiss had to be renegotiated the next morning.

I pulled a towel off the back of a chair and walked past him without making eye contact, heading for the bathroom, slapping the black door open with the heel of my hand.

I did my business and washed my hands, looking at the sink instead of my face in the mirror.

I regretted being short with him before I even shook the water off my hands.

Darlene came in, pulling the door closed.

"Okay, listen," she started.

I didn't let her finish. "I love you. But I need you to back off."

"I'll back off."

She'd never given up a fight that easily in her life.

I snapped towels out of the dispenser. "Really?"

"Just let Carter watch you and I'll stop getting in your face."

I tossed the ball of brown paper in the trash.

"I already feel like I live in a prison."

"I know."

"I don't go out unless I'm with you. I don't date because I'm afraid someone I like's going to get a crowbar in the face. I'd love to have a cat, you know? A fucking *cat*. And now you want a guy to follow me around? Thanks, but no thanks."

"He told me."

I had to lean on the counter with my whole body bowed. There was no pretending Darlene meant anything but the kiss.

"And?" I said to the floor.

"He is really hot, Emily. He's one of the finest men I—"

I shot up. "Why are you saying it like it's a bad thing?"

"Because I trust him to watch you. Look, this is Los Angeles. I can find another choreographer, but I can't find another best friend. I can't trust anyone else, and I know I'm making it about me again. I've never been as scared as I was when you were with Vince. I felt like I was losing you."

"I was right here the whole time."

"Not like that. When he didn't want you to travel, or be onstage, or let anyone hear your voice, I thought it was only going to get worse. That's how these assholes start. When he hit you . . . I know that was the end of it. But you're lucky. Most women who get involved with a guy like that get hit a lot more often before they leave. So now, I keep waiting for you to go back and finish the job with him."

"You know this has nothing to do with me. This is about your mother."

"Goddamn it is, and you know it. And I know it. So, girl, let me sleep at night. Let me give you Carter."

"There are four other guys you can assign me."

She shrugged. "The other guys are fine, but he's the best."

I looked back into the mirror and twisted my hair up into a high bun.

"And I have to keep my hands off him?"

"He's really clear he can't protect someone he's involved with."

"You're really sadistic, you know that?"

"If you want to start dating again, girl, I can get you dates. Lotta dates. You know my agent?"

"Gene? With the pink-gold watch?"

"He thinks you're hot. Told me so. He'll be at the party tonight."

Party? Was there a party? I went deer-in-headlights.

"Tonight? Is it Wednesday?"

Darlene opened the door. Music wafted in over the clatter of the caterer packing lunch away.

"Yup. What are you wearing?"

"A dress and a bodyguard, apparently. Except the dress part. I don't have a dress. I can't—"

"Simon!" Darlene called out his name midsentence. He came to us, every step a dance. He had the strength of a man and the grace of a woman, with dark-brown skin and supershort hair he dyed white.

"You rang?"

"Emily needs a dress."

He eyed me from head to toe without a bit of sexual interest, as if taking inventory of possibilities. Resistance was futile. I held out my arms.

"I was thinking something black," I said. "So I can hide."

"I don't think so." He wagged his finger at me. "We'll meet right after work. I'm going to get you some attention."

CHAPTER 13

CARTER

I had the afternoon off. I got Phin from school. He threw his bag in the back seat and hurled himself in the car.

"Hey, Dad. Size of my heart." We fist-bumped.

"Size of mine. Did you shower this morning?"

"I forgot."

He forgot a lot of things. If we didn't remind him to brush his teeth and hair, put on matching socks, close the damn door, none of it got done. I understood this was normal for kids his age, but I also knew that after a certain point he might not improve. For an orderly man, a child with ADHD could challenge every fiber of patience.

"When we go home, then. Before I leave for work tonight."

He used to get upset when I worked nights. Not anymore. Either he'd accepted it as his reality or he stopped caring. I got onto Olympic, right into a knot of traffic.

"I have homework," he said, turning the radio to a station he liked. "I need you to help with it."

"If it's precalc, we can call Sean."

Sean was his tutor. We called him only for math emergencies.

"It's humanities." He shut off the radio. That was weird. If we hadn't been at a full stop, I would have pulled over. "I have to do a family tree."

Ah.

Don't make a big deal about it.

"All right."

"I need to know about my mother's family."

"I'll tell you what I know."

The light turned green.

Look forward. Pressure off pedal.

"I need at least three generations to get an A, and I'm so close, *this close* to getting a perfect score in this class."

His eyes were open a little wider, his body thrust toward me a few inches. His mouth was tense. He wanted that score. He could taste it. He wanted to prove them all wrong. He was smart; he just needed to be taught differently.

"I can't tell you what I don't know."

"Please, Dad. I know you know. You just have to do what you always tell me to do. Focus and pay attention. Put in a little effort." He said the last sentence in a singsong to lessen the force of my words coming back at me.

"When is it due?"

Translation: How long can I stall?

"The twenty-fifth."

"That's plenty of time."

"Maybe we can do some research?"

"Google it?" I felt safe with Google, as long as Phin stuck to the information I'd given him.

"Sharon says birth records are at city hall."

I almost slammed into the car in front of me.

"No," I said, once I knew I'd avoided an accident. "I think you have enough without going to the county registrar."

"I have to show you the thing I made in animation class." He'd moved to the next subject fluidly and quickly. For once, I was grateful.

CHAPTER 14

EMILY

Simon held up a pure-white sleeveless dress. It matched his short, bleached hair and contrasted against his dark-brown skin. His tongue clucked against the roof of his mouth, and he shook the dress until the skirt waved.

"What if I spill on it?"

"Spill what? It's not like you've had a drink in your life."

"Not true." I snatched the dress from him.

Something about it jolted me. The color. The shape. I couldn't place the memory it called up.

A salesgirl appeared out of nowhere.

"Can I start a dressing room for you?"

I handed her the dress, and she passed Bart, my bodyguard until Carter came back from whatever. We'd just gotten to Nordstrom, but I was ready to leave.

"Atta girl. You'll knock them over in that. Trust me. Club NV will be your bitch."

I doubted that. Club NV was way above my pay grade, but I always had a good time pretending I was a star.

"I'll just buy it."

"I need to see it." He dragged me to the fitting room, trying to come in with me so he could make adjustments, but I pushed him out.

I got the white dress on and stood in front of the mirror.

"Well?" Simon called from outside. "Do you need me to zip it?"

"No."

I turned and checked it from the back. It was everything Simon promised. I stood in front of the mirror. The wide neck revealed my collarbone, and the narrow straps showed off my muscular shoulders.

"Are you fabulous?" he called from the other side of the door.

"I think I might be."

The dress didn't make me anxious the way it had when Simon held it up, but there was something about it that opened my brain to things I hadn't thought about. I put my finger on my collarbone and drew it across, tracing the line the way Carter had.

High school graduation. All-girl's college prep. We'd worn white, and I had a dress almost exactly like this one, with my collarbone and arms showing. The skirt went to the floor, and I'd worn a white cardigan over it, but it was otherwise the same.

I'd had a solo at graduation.

What had the song been?

I took a deep breath and sang the first word in a key I barely remembered, stretching the note as long as I could.

"Amazing graaaace . . ."

I sounded like a frog. I'd never sing again. Not really.

My voice didn't work anymore, but the dress did.

CHAPTER 15

CARTER

Los Angeles was stuffed to the gills with beautiful women. You couldn't swing a dead cat without hitting the prettiest girl in her hometown or the product of two attractive actors.

Emily laughed with Darlene, who could relax at a VIP-only club. Emily wore a pure-white sleeveless dress that ended right over her knees. Her shoes were bright green. In the flashing colored lights of the club, the dress looked like a rainbow and the shoes looked black.

Speaking of beautiful women.

Even in high heels, she navigated the chaos of the party with grace. I couldn't take my eyes off her, which admittedly was my job. Fabian, who was on Darlene for the night, made his way to me across the room. He was huge, six five, and built like a bookcase.

"Yo." I could hear him only in the earpiece. "Gotta whiz."

"Don't forget to shake it."

"Fuck you, man."

He gave me the thumbs-up and disappeared down the hall to the men's room. I put my eyes back on my principal, half a room away. Easiest job I ever had, until Darlene's agent sidled up to her. Hugo Boss suit and a forty-pound pink-gold watch he wore on the same wrist with an Apple Watch. His left cuff was rolled up so it wouldn't be missed, and when he spoke to her, he made sure to put his arm up and check the time.

She cradled her drink and moved her hips slightly to the music, as if she couldn't help herself.

I watched as she spoke to Gene. She was special. Like I said, a million pretty girls in Los Angeles, but the tiny dancer was something else. The way she pursed her lips. The way she smiled. The way she took one hand off her glass and rubbed the fingers together to spread the condensation. Nodded. Looked up at him. Laughed a little.

Was she flirting?

He touched her shoulder. Just a fingertip. She moved away half an inch. The signals from both of them were unmistakable. She was talking, biding time. He was circling like a shark.

He took her glass away and led her to the bar.

Guy like that?

A guy like that would buy her a drink and think that entitled him to something.

I looked away. The room was full of stars and no threats. Darlene was at a table with two executives and the actress Claire Contreras. Fabian was back. Hollywood bad boy Brad Sinclair was by the bar, talking to a guy who dropped his sunglasses to ogle two German models. Emily was more beautiful than both of them put together, not that comparisons mattered. But I couldn't help it.

Neither could Mr. Sunglasses, because he looked past the girls and right at Emily.

I knew the guy. Not personally, but security people exchanged information, and the intel on him was that he was enjoying his friend's stardom with a hell of a lot of women.

He wouldn't go near Emily. Not if I had anything to say about it.

I didn't want to look back and find out how far Gene had gotten with her. The flirting shouldn't have bothered me any more than Brad

Sinclair's roving eye. And it didn't. She wasn't mine to get bothered over. But Gene Testarossa was a douchebag, and Brad Sinclair was a promiscuous little shit.

So yeah, it bothered me. I couldn't have her, but if someone was going to be with her, he wasn't going to be an asshole. He wasn't going to be another Vince. I didn't want that for her.

Jealousy looked shitty on a guy, and as I watched Gene, then Brad, then Gene, then Brad, I was wearing it like a cheap suit. The movie star was really checking her out and sliding toward her. He was going to make a move. I couldn't take my eyes off him because I wanted to find a reason to stop him.

My job was to watch her, so I forced myself to look to where she was at the bar.

She wasn't there.

Gene was on the balcony talking to Michael Greydon.

Darlene was at the table with a suit from Overland Studios.

Claire Contreras was gone.

Emily was . . . ?

"Fabian," I said into the mic.

"Yeah?"

"Emily? What's her twenty?"

"Saw her head to my eleven o'clock."

"I'll go look."

There was only one hall, then a choice between two, and as I cut around a corner, I heard a woman weeping before I saw her.

Emily stood in the center of the narrow hall, looking down, arms out. Red gashes slashed across her chest.

Blood. I couldn't see anything but blood in my vision.

I was there in an instant, holding her up, mentally beating myself to a pulp with lightning one-two punches for letting her out of my sight.

"Nine-one-one," I said to Fabian as I held her up. She was weeping, yes, but not screaming from chest wounds.

"No," she choked out.

The blood was flat and dry.

And her dress wasn't torn.

The red gashes were ink. Sharpie.

She pushed me away. "I don't want you. You have to hear me. Hear me." She wasn't even talking to me. She was talking to whoever had attacked her thirty seconds ago.

"Fabian. Abort. No call."

"I hear you." I knew she wasn't talking about me, but I had to answer her to calm her down. "Who was it? Vince?"

Her eyes cleared for an instant, and she nodded. I recalled his car and where the nearest exit led. "Fabian. Douche running out on the Venice Avenue side. Black BMW."

"Copy," Fabian replied into my ear. "We got particulars?"

"He did . . ." Emily looked down at the red marks on her dress. Her lashes were wet and her lips quivered. She covered the slashes of Sharpie as if they made her naked and ashamed.

"It's okay, Emily. I'm here. What was he wearing?"

Her brows knotted. She was in some kind of shock, clutching bunches of fabric at her chest as if she'd been stabbed.

"What was he wearing, Emily? So we can chase him."

She shook her head slowly.

"Carter, man, what do you got?" Fabian said through the earpiece.

I wasn't going to get anything out of Emily. Not in time to chase after the only guy in the world who wanted to mark her.

She was fully clothed, but I took off my jacket and covered her. Still looking down, she crossed her arms over her chest and held the jacket closed with her thumbs.

I didn't have to ask who had done it or how it had happened.

"Forget it," I told Fabian.

"Everything copacetic?"

Was everything copacetic? Everything was fine. No one was hurt. He was gone. There was no immediate danger. The worst thing? The dry cleaner was going to have his work cut out for him.

Right?

My skin ran hot, and my blood thrummed through my veins like a team of horses. Every joint in my body wanted to do violence, break shit, run hard and fast until I found him, then throw him into the air until he was a speck in the sky.

A second had passed. A second too long. A second where she held my jacket closed over the gashes as if they were humiliating.

No. Nothing was copacetic.

I wasn't supposed to touch her. I was supposed to call Darlene and the cops and go home. But I didn't. I took her in my arms and held her so tight she couldn't move. When the weight went from under her knees, I held her up, and when she started crying so hard her body shook, I held her together. Her mascara and lipstick were getting all over my shirt. I wished I had another shirt to give her. I would have given her my entire closet to cry on.

Fabian rounded the corner at a run and stopped short.

"What the—?"

"Did you see anything?"

"Black BMW booking. Couldn't get a plate."

"Don . . . Don't . . ." Emily's chest hitched against me.

"It's all right."

"Don't tell Darlene."

It was my job to tell Darlene. On top of that, she paid a nice salary, showed me respect, and cared about my new principal.

Emily looked up at me with glassy sludge-rimmed eyes, and I knew that the best way to protect her was to protect her from her best friend's love.

"There's a back exit."

Down the stairs, around the corner, and out to the underground parking lot. She nodded a little, and goddamn if I couldn't let her go enough to make that trip. Vince could be anywhere, but that wasn't what I cared about. I'd get to him soon enough. Once the rage filtered out and I could think, I'd sort his ass out. But for now, I wanted to be her crutch and her cast. Her splint and tourniquet. I was going to be the bandage over her shame until she could take her hands off the red marks on her dress.

I bent down and got my right arm under her knees, lifting her into my arms. She gasped, and the jacket opened a little. She put her hands between the lapels, which made me want to rip Vince a new asshole.

"I have you," I said.

She blinked once, hard, as if she wanted to get the last tear out.

"You don't have to carry me."

"I know."

She relaxed, putting her arms around my neck and her head on my shoulder.

She didn't weigh a thing, and carrying her calmed me. I was doing the right thing. The only thing. I was exactly where I needed to be. Protecting her.

CHAPTER 16

EMILY

I'd gone to the bathroom without telling Carter or Darlene. Why? Because I was an adult with a full bladder. And I wanted to get away from Gene. I wasn't used to telling guy one I was going to the bathroom, then having guy two follow me in so guy zero wouldn't do what he did.

Or whatever. Switch the numbers around. It didn't matter. Someone had come from behind and pushed me around the corner. I didn't resist because I thought (hoped?) Carter was coming to the back hall to get me alone. I thought he'd come to kiss me again. I was mentally preparing myself for that kiss when it happened so fast I didn't have a second to scream. He put his hand over my mouth.

Not Carter. Vince. He'd finally come for me.

I didn't switch immediately from sexual anticipation to fear. I got annoyed. Maybe I should have been scared instead, but I'd been conjuring Carter in the back hall only to be interrupted.

"Say you miss me." He moved his hand away from my mouth just enough for me to talk.

"Did you not hear me the first time?"

"Say it again, babe." His breath stank of Long Island iced tea.

"I told you in court. Go. Away."

I tried to push him, but he pushed back and trapped me in the corner. He smelled of beer and whiskey sour with extra cherries. The edges of his goatee had a crisp edge against newly shaven skin.

"That guy? He wants to fuck you."

"How did you get in here?"

"I always find you." He pressed me up against the wall and talked low in my ear. He was too close to knee in the balls or head-butt. "You're mine, babe. I'm the only one who can make you happy."

"Listen to me."

"You like the brownie? Did you laugh, babe?"

God. This asshole was acting as if we'd just started dating. As if none of it had happened. The punch in the face. The crowbar. Socks in a ball of fur at my front door.

I knew what to do. I had to wait for him to put enough distance between us for me to hit him. Keep him calm until then. Not let him take me to a second location. But he was so composed. I was worried about getting killed, and he wasn't hurting at all.

"I laughed thinking about your tiny little—"

He pushed me against the wall with one hand and got something out of his pocket with the other. I swore it was a knife. I tried to scream, but I just squeaked. I flailed my arms at him, but they were like palm leaves in the wind. My knee connected with nothing. I couldn't see what he was doing, but I felt a pull at my dress.

I was confused. Disoriented. Time skipped backward a little. *Back-one-two-and-over.*

I pushed against the arms that held me even though the part of my brain that kept time knew he wasn't there anymore. I knew he was gone, but I was *back-one-two* steps behind, catching up when Carter asked if it had been Vince.

You're safe, one side of my brain said to the other as if calling behind.

Something about a black BMW.

Red. Marked. An *X* of ownership over my heart.

How could he?

How did he?

Did he not hear me?

Of course not. I wasn't supposed to talk to him.

Don't chase him.

What did bodyguards do? Chase or stay? Arrest them? Beat them up? I had no idea.

Please stay.

I wanted Carter to stay with me, but I didn't want him to see me. I covered the red gashes as if they were my naked body and looked at the floor.

Stay with me.

His arms went around me. He spoke, but I didn't know what he said. I covered the red *X*. I couldn't let Carter see. I was marked. I knew it was just Sharpie. I knew it wasn't me or anything about me, but if he saw, he'd be disgusted. He'd think Vince owned me.

I knew the fear that Carter would think I was marked and owned by Vince wasn't rational. But my rational mind wasn't in charge. People would think I gave up. I didn't want to be the girl who gave up.

Carter took off his jacket, exposing his holster and gun. He put the jacket on my shoulders. I closed it around me, covering the *X*.

"Don't tell Darlene," I heard myself say.

Carter picked me up, and I let him carry me down the stairs like a child. Not having to hold myself up broke something in me. Some defiance about letting another human being see who I was and what I'd been through. I didn't have to be strong for that minute. I took my hands away from the marks and put my arms around him.

They were just red lines, after all. Not a tattoo. Not a permanent smear about who I was or what I was worth. They were just a madman's marker.

"Tell Jamal we're getting in a cab," he said. I thought he was talking to me, but I could hear a garbled response from his earpiece.

Cabs hung around outside the clubs on most nights, and Carter had me in one in a few seconds.

"She sick?" The cabbie looked at him from the rearview mirror.

"No," I said.

"She's fine." Carter closed the door behind him.

"You puke, you pay," the cabbie responded.

"Deal." He gave the guy my address, and we pulled into Sunset Boulevard traffic. He turned his body around to face me and looked right into my face. I was vulnerable and frightened. Even in the dark with the cab jerking to a stop at a red light, I found strength in his eyes. A calm in the storm. A stability when everything around me was unsure and dangerous.

"Thank you," I said.

"I shouldn't have left you alone."

"You can't be on top of me all the time."

His eyebrow raised slightly as if he wanted to disagree but couldn't. I got the joke and let myself smile.

"Can you make sure I've locked up before you go? Just check everything?"

"I'll stay with you."

Was he staying? It was too much. Where would he sleep? Would he keep his hands off me? Would I keep my hands off him? In my emotional state, I didn't think I could.

"You can go home. I have the best security system money can buy."

"Yeah. And his name is Carter Kincaid."

He said it with such confidence, I let a few more layers of fear and insecurity drop off me. We were in a tight space together, behind locked car doors. I leaned into him and let myself relax, watching the night city streak by the window.

"I feel so stupid."

"Why?"

Going to the bathroom. Letting my guard down. Buying a white dress.

"Everything."

"What happened tonight is seventy-five percent my fault."

I turned away from the window to look at his profile.

"I went to the bathroom without telling you."

"Doesn't matter. I thought the back hall was secure, and that was lazy and stupid. Now it's personal. Now if anything happens to you, it's on me. Trust me, that marker he put on you? It's not harmless. It's where he wants to hurt you next."

Suddenly exposed and weak again, I closed his jacket over my dress.

"I'm sorry," he said. "I wasn't trying to scare you."

"Yes, you were."

"These guys, they go quiet for a while, then they pop back up like ducks on a shooting range."

"Ducks on a shooting range?"

The comparison struck me as funny. It poked me in just the right place, or wrong place.

"Yeah, they go around and come back and . . . What? What's so funny?"

"That's the worst analogy I've ever heard."

"Why?"

"The ducks just, I don't know. Move across slowly. They're a little more predictable."

"All right, well . . . It's not that funny."

I couldn't stop laughing.

"Poor ducks." I spoke between breaths. "Not bothering anyone and . . ." I tried to catch a breath. "Evil, deadly ducks. A horror movie of poultry. Donald . . . Donald . . ."

"Did you eat a brownie?"

I shook my head and rubbed the tears from my eyes. "Donald Duck. Evil mastermind." I made a throaty quacking noise.

He smiled and did something shocking. A perfect squicky Donald Duck impression.

"Kill them all."

We both laughed all the way to the house, and it wasn't even funny.

CHAPTER 17

CARTER

She was releasing tension. Her nervous laugh was no more than a response to being strung too tightly. So that was what happened when she let go a little.

It was all right. I loved watching it get released. I figured by the time we got to her house, she'd be thinking straight.

I needed her to have her head on her shoulders, because mine was getting spun around. Seeing her hurt and humiliated had awakened *feelings*. Admittedly, I'd been attracted to her before. Not a big deal. I'd been attracted to plenty of women. I'd even dated some of them.

But she was my principal, and she had an active stalker.

Feelings kept a bodyguard from thinking clearly.

Feelings got in the way of good judgment.

Feelings made a guy look in the wrong direction.

Most of all, feelings could rearrange a guy's priorities. That couldn't happen.

"Can you check the back?" she asked as we went up the three steps to her gate. "I get nervous going outside."

I was going to do more than check her back door.

I was going to stay for the remaining two hours of my shift. We could talk or whatever. Then I'd lock her in the house and away from danger.

She punched in her code and opened the gate; I followed her in, covering her back and snapping the gate closed behind her. Walking behind her, I could take in her perfect shape. She was insanely feminine. Graceful even when doing something as simple as stepping up her pace. The motion-sensitive light went on as if applauding her presence, and the camera clicked on, following her as if it couldn't help itself.

I could almost sympathize with Vince's obsession.

Almost.

She pressed her thumb to the glass pad in the door, and it opened. The lights in the house went on automatically. She looked at me over her shoulder.

"I'm going to change. Kitchen's over there if you want anything."

"No. You stay here for a minute."

I checked the house. In corners and under furniture (meticulously clean). Behind curtains and in the cabinets (neat and organized). Her spare room was unoccupied. Bed (made), night tables (ballerina statue and lamp) where they should be. The closet was empty of anything but winter coats and shoes. I checked the safety of her bathroom. Jack and Jill. Accessible from both bedrooms. Bathtub empty. The window was locked. The shower rod had underwear hanging from it. Her underwear.

Was it normal that I wanted to sniff her panties?

No, that was not normal.

I backed away from the underwear and into her bedroom. It looked exactly like her bedroom was supposed to look. Queen-size bed with a blue floral duvet. Thick area rug. Pale wood dresser. Closet that smelled like lemongrass. Locked sliding doors that led out to the little yard. I could see the bed in the glass's reflection.

I could really fuck her senseless on that bed. I could make her grip those blue flowers so hard the petals fell off.

In the reflection, I saw her peek in the door. "Well?"

I felt as if I'd been caught with my pants around my ankles and my hands around my dick. I cleared my throat as if that would get the filthy thoughts out of my head, but it did nothing at all but rattle my throat.

"You're all locked up."

"Good." She kept her gaze everywhere but on me, tucking her hair behind her ear. The cuff of my jacket brushed up against her cheek, and she reacted with a smile. "I forgot." She slipped off the jacket. "Thank you."

She held it out for me. We met in the middle of the room, both our hands on my jacket. Her bed was behind her, and her brown eyes were wide and expectant.

"Can you unzip me?" she asked with her hand over the red marks on her chest.

"Sure."

She turned, pulling her hair to the front. My hand on her shoulder, my other hand clasping the zipper, I opened up a V of skin to my touch. I couldn't help what I did next; or I could have but didn't know how, or didn't think of it, or just kicked my good habits to the curb and locked the door. I drew the zipper down slowly, letting a finger drop below the teeth to stroke the skin.

I don't think my dick had ever been that hard. Ever.

"Carter," she said. I'd gotten to the center of her back when she said my name.

"Yes?"

"Did you want to check the back gate?"

"Yes." I laid my lips on her shoulder. She tasted like her closet. Sweet lemongrass. Yes, I had to check the back gate, but the texture of her skin was like a magnet, and the way she put her head back and

79

sucked in her breath, pushing her body against me, got my cock thinking instead of my head.

I pushed her dress over her shoulders, and she turned. All my alarm bells went off. She was a yes. It was go time. Eyes open wide. Lips slightly apart. Chin tilted up. Hands keeping her dress barely over her breasts.

"Kiss me first," she said.

CHAPTER 18

EMILY

The first time he'd kissed me, it had been unexpected, unformed. It had been a first practice before we knew all the steps. This time he took it slow, brushing his lips over mine, only enough to waken the nerve endings. I pushed harder against him until I could feel the shape of his jaw when he opened his mouth, prying mine open to meet him.

He was a wave, a tsunami drowning me. My whole body tingled for him. My blood pumped fire from heart to fingertips, igniting on his gunpowder smell. Smoke and electric air. Fifth of July. New Year's Day. The air after the fireworks at Santa Monica Pier. The explosive potential of combustion and danger. His tongue probed the mouth of a body alive and crackling for him. My resistance went *pop pop pop*, leaving the white smoke of desire in the air.

My arms were around him, and I was lost. My dress was around my waist, held up between our bodies. His hands were at my lower back. I shifted my body so I could feel his erection. I groaned into his mouth.

A sound outside. A *crack* or a *snap*. He pulled away violently and pushed me down. I hit the rug with the top of my marked dress bunched around my waist.

Carter shut the lights. I could see the entire backyard.

"Stay down."

In half a second, he was gone.

I didn't know what was going on. He'd left the bedroom sliding doors locked and gone out either the front or side door. I couldn't see him in the yard. Just the leaves on the lawn furniture and the shadows of the big ficus that took up half the space. The front door of the garage was bright red and made me think again of the *X* on my white dress.

Nothing happened. I laid there forever, listening to my breath against the rug, waiting.

Carter was outside because of me. I didn't have to be afraid for him, but I was.

I'd met Peter in the ER after Vince broke his nose. He wasn't an asshole about it. He didn't blame me, but he was a guy in glasses who'd worked his way up to the executive offices at Overland Studios from the mailroom. He had a communications degree from Michigan. He wasn't an athlete or a fighter. He was the kind of guy who would make you laugh, put you at ease, and move so slowly to get what he wanted that by the time he asked for it, you threw it at him. And that was just what his boss at Overland said. I was pretty sure everything I liked about him had made him an easy target.

Vince had come from behind Peter with no warning. Carter wouldn't let that happen. But if Vince was prepared to attack and Carter was distracted? That was an ambush, and it wasn't fair.

And if Vince thought Carter was that much more of a threat than the sweet, artsy Peter, he was going to hit harder.

The motion-sensor lights flicked out, and the room was totally dark again.

My heart started pounding as I thought of Carter's head snapping back from a crack to the face or him falling forward from a surprise blow from behind.

And. No.

No, not again. I wasn't going to be the reason someone got attacked.

I got up and darted for the back doors. My dress fell, exposing me. I got my left hand through an armhole while I used the right to slide open the door.

I stepped onto the patio in my stockinged feet. Twigs and leaves snapped under me. The light from the studio went back on.

This was stupid. I was walking right into danger.

I put my hand through the right armhole and took a step down, leaving the glass door open in case I needed to run back inside.

On the other side of the hedges and cinder block wall, the traffic on Olympic was quieter than usual. I pushed the dress back up. Without the zipper to hold it, the shoulders kept sliding down.

"Hey!" A male figure on the edge of my vision.

My heart stopped. Or maybe it thumped too hard. But it hurt, and I sucked in a bunch of air as if it was my last breath. I snapped my head to the sound and stepped back.

"Carter! You scared the hell out of me."

He was smiling. I was having a heart attack and he was smiling. His arms were crossed in front of him, and something furry poked out from between the folds of his sleeves.

"It was a cat." As if she knew when she was being called, the cat poked her head up and meowed. She was a gray tiger stripe with green eyes. Either young or a runt. "I think she's hungry."

"Are you trying to get me to keep the cat?"

"You can't leave her out here."

"Carter. The last cat I had was named Socks. She wound up dead on my front step."

The stray jumped out of Carter's arms and hopped up on a lawn chair.

"Do you have any cat food around?"

Did I? And did it matter? I didn't want a freaking cat.

But what was most disconcerting was Carter. The hard-ass man of few words softened like putty at the sight of a little gray cat cleaning her paws on my lawn chair.

"I think I have some under the sink."

He snapped his fingers.

"This doesn't mean I'm keeping it."

"What should you name her?"

"Carter!"

He brushed by me and went into the house. The cat didn't even look at me. She just ran her wrist over her face, over her tongue, and back again.

"You're not staying. For your own good."

She sat up straight and flicked her tail. Yawned as if my expensive bodyguard hadn't just rescued her from starvation or whatever.

I waved my finger at her and went inside, closing the door behind me. Maybe she'd leave if I shut her out.

I got out of the dress and put on a shirt and jeans. Carter had made himself at home in the kitchen, pouring Meow Mix into the bowl that had been next to it, as if I wanted to feed a cat in the first place.

"I hear they need wet food once in a while," he said, rolling the bag closed.

"You can feed her whatever you want when you bring her home."

"I can't." He put away the bag of cat food. "You still have a litter box and litter under here."

I'd thrown away Socks's toys, but I didn't have the heart to toss the practical things. Maybe I thought she was coming back.

"Why can't you take her?"

"Come on. Let's see if she likes it."

He swooped up the bowl, put his arm around me, and we all went to the back through my bedroom.

The cat was still there, waiting like a customer in a fancy restaurant.

Slowly, showing both hands, Carter made his way to the cat and put the bowl on the floor next to the lawn chair. Then he stepped back until he was next to me.

"What should we name her?" he asked when he was beside me.

"Carter's cat?"

His face, when he looked down at me, was a side of him I'd never seen before. He wasn't an ex-cop or protector. He wasn't Mr. Business. He was just a guy who wanted a cat.

"Are you going to tell me why you can't have a cat?" I asked.

"No."

The cat had slinked down and was getting her fill of Meow Mix.

"Then her name will be secret."

"You're naming the cat after a deodorant?"

"That was not even a joke."

I kneeled down and ran my hand along the soft length of the cat's spine.

"Emily." He sat on the lawn chair with his legs spread and his elbows on his knees. He tapped his fingertips together and bowed his head. "I'm going to be honest. My life is complicated."

The first thing I thought in that unguarded moment before bad news dropped was that he was married. Engaged. Otherwise attached. The thought cut through me so deeply it landed like an inevitability.

"Really?" I didn't look at him. I kept my voice noncommittal and flat. I didn't need to say it for him. If he was going to tell me he was married, he was going to say all the words without help.

"And you. You're . . ." He paused as if he were looking for words. The space annoyed me. He was softening some kind of blow, and I was in no mood. I'd had a shitty evening already. "You're amazing and beautiful. You're—"

"Stop it." I said it definitively. I had no time for this line of bullshit. He was putting camphor on a muscle that hadn't been pulled yet.

"I want you to know—"

"Carter Kincaid." I stood, putting my feet apart and my hands on my hips. "Just say it. Say the thing without stroking me. Neither of us has the time for this."

Say you're married.

He looked up at me, elbows still on his knees, big blue eyes asking forgiveness for a sin he wouldn't confess.

He took too long. I'd been jerked around before, and I wasn't playing this time.

"Time's up." I spun on my heel and crossed the deck, grabbing the handle of the sliding glass door and using my torque to close it. I didn't look back, but I knew the door didn't meet the jamb. I didn't hear the satisfying *snap* behind me.

"Emily," he said, but I kept walking. I grabbed the stool and went for the front door. He caught me by taking a wood leg and jerking it toward him.

"I want you," he said. The statement melted me just enough to encourage him to continue. "Every time you're near me, I stop thinking. I stop making sense. But I can't have you."

"How dramatic. What's the actual problem?"

"You're my principal. I can't protect you and let my guard down with you at the same time."

"Bullshit."

"What do you think happened back there? How do you think you got attacked? I wasn't watching you. I wasn't protecting you. I was thinking about getting my face between your legs. I was giving you a dozen orgasms. I failed because I was worried about another guy touching you on the dance floor. I wasn't paying the right kind of attention, and next time it might be more than a dress."

I yanked the stool, and he let it go. "I won't be jerked around. I won't be toyed with. If your life is so complicated and you can't tell me the real reason, then maybe you shouldn't be protecting me." I opened the door and put the stool on the front step. "Hour and change left in your shift. Go for it."

He went outside and turned around at the doorway, as if he wanted to say something. The next step was for me to close the door, but he was so close to the edge that no matter how softly I shut it, I'd look as if I was slamming it in his face. That was too much. I didn't want to do anything I couldn't take back.

"I'm closing the door," I said.

"I'm driving you in the morning."

"I'll see you then."

He nodded, head tilted at the angle of kindness, but his eyes were elsewhere, as if he was thinking deeply about something. He snapped out of it and reached into the house, toward me. A twitch of hope flicked in my chest. Was he going for me? Trying to touch me? Or was I just all turned around from the horrible night?

Where Vince had marked me.

What was I doing?

He rested his fingers on the doorknob as if he wasn't ready to go just yet.

"You know what?" I said. "You're right. This won't work. Not because I don't like you but because I do. Tonight reminded me that I'm damaged goods. I have this crazy person obsessed with me, and anyone I bring into my life is going to be in his sights."

"Don't insult me. I can handle him."

"Carter, you just said we couldn't be together, then I agree, and now you're insulted that I'm agreeing so we can keep you off his radar?"

I crossed my arms.

"I'm going to figure it out," he said, "and when I do, Vince isn't going to be part of the equation. Trust me."

He closed the door.

CHAPTER 19

CARTER

The problem, as I saw it, was that I had two areas of concern with Emily. One was the fact that she was my job. My specific job. She was what I did for a living to support my family. Phin's mother's residual checks got smaller every quarter and did little more than cover his education. So I had to work. If I started fucking Emily, I wouldn't stop. I couldn't protect a woman I was sleeping with. If I was doing my job, and I always did my job, we'd both be vulnerable at the same time.

The second concern was Phin himself. He was everything, and a relationship would divert me from the attention he needed. I'd made the decision long ago that my mother had raised my sister and me already, and it was too much to ask her to raise Phin full-time.

I had two hours to really think about it.

Two hours of pacing the property inside and outside the gate, getting angrier with every step. Who was I pissed at?

Yes. I was just pissed. Me. Vince. The lapsed order of protection. The circumstances. My decisions. Darlene for putting me on as principal. Me and, again, myself. I spent an extra five minutes standing outside her dark bedroom window. Was she sleeping or hiding from me?

This really didn't have to be so hard. I didn't have to tell her about Phin. Not yet. He could stay an anonymous Los Angeles kid for another few years. As far as her being my principal, that could be rectified.

And Vince?

He was going to have to get rectified too. Every time I thought about all the things keeping me away from Emily, my brain held up a picture.

Emily clutching the fabric of her dress, hiding the *X*.

The look on her face.

The shame. The humiliation.

The fact that he'd gotten close to her.

He could do it again.

Everything else got pushed out.

Vince had to be rectified.

———

"You fell down a flight of stairs." I turned Vince over with my foot. He flopped onto his back. I'd taken out the light at the top of the garage door, but the streetlights filtered in through the trees. The blood bubble forming at his lips looked black. I crouched by him when he tried to get up and pushed him down.

"Once your face is healed," I said, "it's time for you to find yourself a girlfriend. A new girlfriend. One who likes you."

I might have gone too far on him.

"Fuck you, man."

I kept my voice low so he had to keep quiet to hear me.

"I want you to consider me her order of protection. If you're in my eyeline, I'm going to assume you're there to hurt her. There will be consequences."

He smiled, and his mouth was so blood-soaked he looked toothless in the blue-cast light.

"Sucks dick like a champ, doesn't she?" His smile was blood red. "I taught her that."

I stood up. The heel of my shoe could come down on his face so hard, I could break his jaw before he could even think about another dick-sucking comment. But I got control of myself. If he wound up in the hospital, I'd have to answer questions.

"You really should hang on to the railing when you come down the stairs. Good habit."

I turned to go without looking back.

"She's always mine. No matter how much you bang her. She's mine."

I almost turned around and gave him a final kick in the face. Emily wasn't his. Not even a little bit. And she wasn't going to get "banged" by me. She was better than a quick knockoff.

I hurried to the car. My right fist ached and the knuckles were raw. They'd be so stiff in the morning I probably wouldn't be able to move them. Worth it. All worth it.

But not to be repeated. I couldn't do this again. Not unless she was in immediate danger. I'd avoided a life of violence, avoided prison, the wrong side of the system. I could just as easily get sucked back in.

I'd had a rough time in high school, getting into more fights than I should have. Detention was my stomping ground. My sister was busy getting eaten alive by Hollywood, and my mother was busy crying over my dad leaving. Detention meant I didn't have to go home to see it. Mom's tears made me want to kill my father and any man who ditched his family. Getting into fights kept me from going home and gave rage a release. By the time I was old enough to come and go as I pleased, I was just getting into fights because anger was a habit.

My sense of injustice and entitlement started with my neighborhood. Torrance sat on top of swank Rancho Palos Verdes and right below Redondo Beach, but Redondo was cut into a weird shape so it got all the beachfront. Torrance got a token mile of beach, but the rest was landlocked. Not that we couldn't go to Redondo and cause trouble. But I felt a kinship to Torrance. Like the shape of the world had been cut to my disadvantage.

I made my own way. I was the king of Borrance and Crenshaw. At sixteen, I'd avoided getting arrested. I was ready to drop out of school out of boredom, and yeah, I was obviously as dumb as a box of rocks.

Devon Muldoon was a classmate on the days I showed up to school. He was as much of a little punk as I was, but he didn't have the chops to back it up. He came around the parking lot I pissed in and talked trash in front of all of us, and I took him down. Not too hard, but enough to send a message.

His father showed up at my door in full uniform and punched my clock before I'd even swung the door open all the way. My mother screamed and clawed at him. He brushed her off like a gnat and stood over me. I knew exactly who he was. His son had his snarl. He took me by the back of the collar and dragged me to the police cruiser. Threw me in like a sack of potatoes.

We were driving ten minutes before I could shake the stuffing out of my head.

"My son tells me you're quite the tough guy," he said from the front. There was a metal screen between us, but I heard him as perfectly as if he were staring right at me.

"He's a little bitch," I said, because you don't back down, even when your life depends on it.

"That may be." He wasn't mad at all. I thought he'd pull to the side and work me over for calling his son a bitch, but he didn't seem flustered. His calm unsettled me. I didn't know what to expect. "But he's mine, and I protect what's mine."

I had plenty to say about how well he protected a son who got close enough to the likes of me to mix it up, but I didn't answer. Just looked out the window, watching the night city. He'd book me for assault and resisting. Mom would cry and blame Dad. My sister's last acting job would pay the legal fees. I'd want to die, but instead of dying I'd just wake up and do whatever/nothing/the same.

"I'm going to make you a deal, kid."

"Oh yeah?" I acted bored, but I wasn't. I was curious.

"You go two rounds with me, and you can go home."

"Two rounds? You mean boxing?"

"Yeah. Boxing."

"With gloves?"

"You ever use gloves before?"

"No. What do I look like?"

"No gloves, then."

Two rounds. Six minutes with this old fart who got in a single sucker punch? And for that I could just go home without a record?

I had no illusions about turning my life around, but why get a jump on a criminal record? Why not put it off until the next time I did some inevitable bonehead shit? I'd rather go home and go to bed. Give Mom a night off crying. She could use a break.

"I'm not going to take it easy on you just because you're a cop."

"Don't expect you to."

"Or because you're old."

"That's the spirit."

He pulled into a parking lot off Madrona, right in his police cruiser like he had nothing better to do. Like his time was his own. He opened the back door for me.

"Great gig," I said. "My mom leaves the register five minutes every three hours to piss. You just park wherever and go to the gym whenever."

"Benefits of not being an asshole, kid."

He indicated an open door at the other end of the lot. Men shouted from inside. Above the doorway was a hand-painted sign. ACE OF SPADES.

"Name's Carter."

"You can call me Officer Muldoon."

I went up the stairs and stepped into manhood.

———

Phin wasn't in bed. He was hunched over his computer, freckles glowing in the bright light.

"Where's Grandma?"

"Bed." He didn't take his eyes off the screen. He filled in little squares with color, clicked shit I didn't understand, moved boxes around. "Wanna see?"

"What is it?"

He hit the spacebar, and a little green snail undulated up and down as if it was moving across a leaf. Its smile went from a straight grin to a toothy *D* when it was highest.

"Cute," I said, putting my hand on his shoulder. I moved it off when I saw my torn knuckles. I didn't want him to notice them. But Phin didn't miss a goddamn thing. Ever.

He put up his fist. "Show me the size of your heart, Dad."

I put up my left fist. "This big."

He put up both fists. "Double bump."

Too clever. I couldn't say no to a double without it being called out. And it wasn't like he hadn't seen my knuckles anyway. I put up both fists and we bumped.

"What happened?" he asked.

"Nothing."

"Did you not tape your hands?"

He thought I'd been boxing. I hadn't. I'd been fucking shit up. My life revolved around being a good example for him. Beating the hell out of a stalker and lying about it wasn't going to cut it.

So I made it worse.

"Just a scrape. How was school?"

He shrugged.

"What? Not great? Not the best ever?"

"Today was twins day."

I kicked my shoes off and sat in the chair by his desk.

"What's twins day?"

"It's for spirit week. Everyone dresses like someone. Never mind." He turned back to his computer, changed windows, and started working on some gobbledygook of letters and symbols. The chattering kid had disappeared with his first growth spurt.

"Did you wear your Emperor Palpatine costume?"

"No, not like that. Like someone else in homeroom."

"Ah."

He typed like lightning. I let him code. If I pressed him, he wouldn't tell me shit.

"Everyone had a twin but me."

"There is an even number of kids in the class."

"Cooper, Leshawn, and Jarred went as triplets. I was no one. I called five people, and they all said they had a twin already."

I clenched and unclenched my fist. It was getting tight already. The wrist ached. Going after that douche had been a huge mistake. He could go away, but he could come back harder. I was going to be responsible for Emily whether she was my principal or not.

I'd known it, and even as I said I didn't want that, once the anger cleared, I knew she was the size, shape, and intention of my heart whether I liked it or not.

"It's hard to find people who understand you," I said. "Not just you. Anyone."

"Everyone else had someone who understood them."

"They had someone to dress like them. Not the same."

He shrugged. All the explanations were in that shrug. He wasn't complaining about how people understood him. He just wanted to belong. That was all any middle schooler wanted.

"Do you want to switch schools?"

"No. I'm fine."

I watched him for a minute. Coding had predictable outcomes. If he made a mistake, something went wrong. If he corrected the mistake, the code worked. There were no secret social cues. No people calling themselves your friend, then excluding you. No stalkers hiding behind people who said they loved you.

He went back to the black screen and hit the spacebar. It exploded in orange bubbles, which popped, creating yellow bubbles, which popped and became green, and on and on.

"You're going to be okay, kid."

"Yeah."

"If you get to bed. It's late."

"What time is it?" He'd gone back to the code to correct some flaw I hadn't seen.

"Ten thirty."

"Ten minutes."

"None." I reached over to the keyboard, he fought me, and we wrestled for control of the computer for a few minutes before I declared victory.

CHAPTER 20

EMILY

I'd gone to sleep with Carter's kiss still on my lips and annoyance in my bones. Once I slept off the annoyance, the remnants of the kiss remained. I woke up the next morning with an unbearable heaviness between my legs.

I rolled onto my stomach and slid my hand under my panties. I was slick everywhere, and I gasped at my own touch. Forehead to mattress, I spread my legs and thought of him, his taste, the pressure of his lips, the fifth of July smell all over him. His hardness on my hip. He'd felt huge. Monstrous. Maybe my perception was off, because I hadn't shared myself with a man in ages, but still. When I slid my finger inside, the space seemed completely inadequate for the size of him.

And that hard cock was because he kissed me and I wanted it. It was for me. When I let myself come, I made it slow so I could think of him losing control on top of me, a grunting mess of unpracticed pleasure.

I dropped to the sheet, relieved. Physically I'd let go of a building tension, and mentally I'd had a realization. As I'd imagined him letting go with me, I let go of the idea that Vince could hurt him. He was tougher, smarter, more in control than Peter. He could outsmart Vince in a heartbeat. I didn't need to be scared for him. He could handle my brand of trouble. He already had. He'd wiped away the sting of the humiliation in the hall and turned it into no more than a stained dress.

I sighed to myself. All that was great, but I still had the sneaking suspicion that despite the bare ring finger, he had a wife, or an involved ex-wife, or a fiancée.

The sun was just rising, making the white curtains glow. Behind them, at patio level, sat a little blob of a shadow.

The shadow meowed, and I groaned.

I got a bowl of Meow Mix and put it in front of her. She went right for it before I even backed away.

"Don't get used to it," I said, giving her a bowl of water. "I just want to get rid of it. Once I'm out, I'm not buying another bag."

I took a shower, got dressed, had some yogurt. There was a ring at the gate. I checked the cameras and buzzed in Carter. I opened the door to a freshly shaven, nice-smelling bodyguard with a huge cock.

I smirked and looked at the ground, trying not to think of the last part, but failed. We'd argued about something, but I'd forgotten it for a minute.

His inability to be with me, overall. That was the argument. Protecting me from Vince while we were together. Walking and chewing gum at the same time.

"Hi," Carter said. "You ready?"

"Do you sleep?"

"Not much. We're taking my car."

There really was no working around it. Not that I wanted to. All my resistance was out the window. His lips had done it. His tongue. I could still taste it where the toothpaste was wearing off. Could still feel the way it pushed into my mouth.

He opened the back door of a black Audi. I was sure I'd seen his car before, but I didn't realize it was that low and sexy.

"How's the cat?"

"Hungry. You're going to have to take me back here in the afternoon so I can feed her again."

"My pleasure."

He smiled on the left more than the right, and I had to look away from him.

I got into the back seat, and he *thupp*ed the door closed. He walked around the front, unbuttoning his jacket. His pants sat flat against his abdomen, and his tie flip-flopped in the breeze. I touched my chest. I'd worn red. I wasn't sure if it was a reproach of the red *X* from the night before or a challenge to try a red pen again.

He slid into the driver's seat and twisted around.

"Are you all right?"

"Mmm hmm."

He turned back around and started the car. A half-eaten Danish sat on the passenger seat.

"Are we going to have another 'about last night' conversation?" I asked.

"If you want to."

What did I want to say? Everything, but mostly, I wanted to tell him how much I liked kissing him and how conflicted I was. I wanted to demand answers immediately and give him space at the same time.

All the words tried to jump forward, but when he stopped at a light, our eyes met in the rearview. The words landed in a tangle, unsaid.

He tapped the steering wheel when he turned it, using both hands for the first time since I'd gotten in.

"Hey," I said.

"Yeah?" He briefly looked at me in the mirror.

"What happened to your hand?"

"Burn." He brushed his left hand over the bandage at the top of his palm, right where you'd burn it if you were picking up a hot pot handle. He caught my eye in the rearview again.

I didn't know if I believed him.

"What were you cooking?"

"Breakfast."

"And you still went to get a Danish?"

He rubbed his upper lip with his left hand and tapped the wheel with the bandaged one.

"I burned my eggs."

Right. Hot pot. Burned hands. Smoke-filled kitchen.

"You know what's funny?" I said.

"*The Three Stooges.*"

"I don't know anything about you. You could live in your mother's basement."

"That's just where I bury the bodies."

Blatant avoidance. It had been cute before; now it was getting on my nerves.

"Are you married?"

"No!"

He could have been lying, but lying liars always lied. There wasn't a thing I could do about that except make sure I asked.

Something was wrong. We'd kissed twice, and twice he'd shut down. I should have been the one shutting down. I was the one with all the ex-boyfriend baggage. Why was I the one who was always so willing?

But there he was in the front seat, driving with both hands on the wheel, glancing at me once in a while to make sure I wasn't choking on my tongue in the back seat. Discomfort radiated out of him.

Here I was with my hands in my lap thinking about ways to kiss him again.

He pulled into the little lot and wedged into a space. He turned off the car, popped his seat belt, and stared at the wheel for a split second too long. I was about to open the car door myself when he turned all the way around, arm over the back of his seat, bandaged hand on the back of the passenger side.

"Kissing you . . ." He stopped and looked at my lips so intensely I folded them back and bit them. "You're dangerous. I can't even see your lips, but I can taste them. I couldn't brush the taste of you out of

99

my mouth this morning. Right now. The honey. I can taste it but not enough. I want to kiss you again, and I can't. I lose my shit around you. I can't do it. My job is control. Do you understand what I'm saying?"

My jaw loosened, and I let my lips go.

"No. I don't. I've met bodyguards before. You're a stoic bunch, but you're not all celibate. And if you think this is easy for me, you're wrong. I'm afraid too. I'm afraid you're going to get hurt because of me. Last night . . ." I put my fingertips to my lips as if that would keep the choking sob from coming. I kept it back. "Last night just showed me he's back, and if he'll hurt me, he'll hurt you."

If I thought the seats would be a barrier between us, I was wrong. He launched himself between them and planted his lips on mine. Our third kiss was unexpected, uncomfortable, with him stretched between front and back. I wove my fingers in his hair, giving him my mouth and taking his.

I wanted that kiss to tell him it was all right. He could lose control. He could be more than a protector. He was as safe with me as I was with him. But I couldn't without lying to both of us.

He yanked his lips away.

"Trust me." He leaned his forehead on mine.

A *clack* at the window made me swallow my words. It was Fabian, looking at the scene through the side window. He tapped his watch as if he wasn't seeing anything out of the ordinary.

"Stoic bunch," I said.

"He's right." He crawled back to the front. "You're going to be late."

He got out and opened the door for me, taking my bags as I stepped onto the cracked asphalt.

"Let's just act normal for today." I stood in the unflinching sunshine.

"Later, then." He smirked with one side of his beautiful face, and it took all my energy not to kiss his dimple.

CHAPTER 21

EMILY

He was there all day, standing in the corner, by the door, watching me. I tried not to be self-conscious, but it wasn't easy. He took up more room than his height or mass, and the weight of him created its own gravitational pull.

I wasn't in the zone until midmorning. Darlene was keeping up with the pros on her feet and singing at the same time. The whole team was hitting their marks. It was a beautiful thing whenever we got to the point where we were improving the show rather than learning it. By the time the lunch bell rang, I had an involuntary smile plastered on my face. I was jumping higher and thinking to the beat of every song. My soul was lubricated with endorphins. My brain was so crowded with joy I didn't have the space to imagine anything but a constant upward trajectory.

Darlene pulled me to her table at lunch.

"How are you doing?" she asked, shoveling a kale and chicken salad in her face.

"Fine. Why?"

"I can't care about how you are?"

I took a bite of sushi before answering. I was too hungry for small talk. Glancing around for Carter, I found him in a corner with Fabian, who was taking notes in a spiral book.

"You heard about last night, I guess."

"Yeah. So. You all right?"

"I'm good. Carter was . . . Having him there was perfect. Thank you."

"You don't have to thank me. I gotta apologize for something." She cleared her throat, and I ate another piece of California roll. I didn't want to react to the apology before she made it. "I've been a bitch about Vindouche. All yelling and up in your face."

"You're a bossypants. I knew that coming in."

"It's because I love you."

"I know."

"We're the sisters we never had."

"It's okay. Really. The act's coming along great, don't you think? 'More Than a Sister' is really tight, and that's the one they want to hear. I'm going to work on punching up the bridge in 'Make Him Yours' this afternoon. But I feel good."

She nodded, flicking the cashews in her salad to the side. She was still a ball of energy and intensity, but she was more still than usual. As sure as a stress fracture, she had something on her mind.

"Spill it," I said.

She wiped her mouth at the corners with slow deliberation. Timing perfect. Pure drama. I knew her so well, I knew when she wanted to land a statement.

"How's he kiss?"

I released the tension in a shock of a laugh. The room silenced for a second. I snapped my eyes to Carter, and he met my gaze quickly before turning back to Fabian. I wasn't much of a blusher, but I was sure I was another shade of pink.

When the ambient noise picked up again, I leaned into Darlene so no one else could hear.

"How did you know?"

Her big brown eyes got bigger, and her mouth stretched in a conspiratorial grin.

"Tell me first."

"Pretty great." I sipped my soup. Was that the only adjective I had? It was lame. "We haven't done that much kissing, but it's like when you're doing a really tough lift and know your partner's not going to drop you, but at the same time, you feel like you're flying without being held."

"Girl, as your friend, that's music to my ears."

"And I think he can handle Vince. Like, I don't have to be alone while I deal with this. And maybe he'll get scared away now."

Darlene pushed away her tray. "Maybe."

"What? You have that look like you're about to storm on me."

"Nah. Just thinking you got attacked last night. Physically attacked."

"He attacked my dress."

"Don't minimize. You know what he did, then you fall into sucking face with your bodyguard."

"God, Darlene." It was my turn to push away my tray. "That's such a bait and switch."

"Tell me I'm wrong. Tell me it wasn't a reaction to feeling safe."

"Of course it was. So? Why invalidate it? Why not just call it by its name and enjoy it?"

"I'm not saying not to. I'm sorry. There's too much stuff. Listen." She folded my hands in hers and leaned into me. "He can't watch you."

"What do you mean?"

"Fabian's on you now."

"What? Why? You're a singer, not a security expert."

"He requested it."

Her expression wasn't confrontational. Actually, she looked as if she hated saying it. I stood so quickly, my chair nearly fell.

"I got this."

"You go."

I stomped to Carter and Fabian, who was putting his little notepad in his pocket.

"What the fuck?" I said to Carter with my arms crossed.

"That's my cue," Fabian said. "See you at six." He nodded at me and walked away. There was nothing wrong with him. He was a fine bodyguard and a decent human being, but he wasn't Carter, who had the nerve to smile up at me as if I were amusing the hell out of him.

"I would have told you, but Darlene insisted."

I pulled the chair out to sit so the table could keep me from strangling him.

"Don't get comfortable," he said, standing. "You have to go feed your cat."

"No, I don't. It's a stray. It'll be fine."

"Have you named her yet?" He piled up the empty food containers.

"Shouldn't Fabian be taking me?" I practically snarled it.

"We couldn't revise the schedule before tonight. I'll take you."

He dropped the garbage and waited for me to follow him to his Audi.

"I have to be back by one," I said.

"No problem."

I felt as if I'd been dumped for no good reason. I shouldn't have taken it personally. He was trying to do his job, and I was in the way. But to reject me outright, to deny me of his company, hurt to the core. So I stormed and seethed, even when he opened the front passenger door instead of the back. I threw myself onto the leather seats as if that would somehow teach him a lesson about how to treat a girl.

He didn't say anything until we were out of the lot and on the street.

"You're scary when you're mad," he said. He didn't look scared at all. He looked charmed, if anything, which made me angrier. I felt like crap. Useless. Dispensable. And here he was with half a smirk looking in his rearview and driving the speed limit because he had no emotions at all.

"I'm mad at myself."

"Why?" He flattened his hand, steering with the heel. The bandage had shifted over the course of the morning, revealing a scab on the top of his knuckles.

"For believing what you said this morning."

"About?"

About how much he liked kissing me. How the taste of my lips made him wild and impulsive.

"About burning your hand on a frying pan."

That wasn't the answer he expected. He didn't look away from the road but tilted his head as if recalibrating. There had never been a hot pan. I didn't know why it mattered, but it did.

"Unless you grab a handle with your knuckles," I said. "But even I'm not that double-jointed."

He stopped at a red light with a jerk. "You're double-jointed?"

I reached over and flicked his bandage with my nail. I did it harder than I expected, and he flinched.

"You know what?" I said. "I'm glad you dropped me. You're a liar."

"Wait a second." When he held up his index finger, the others didn't fold all the way down into a fist. I'd seen a lot of sore and bruised muscles in my life. If his hand wasn't recovering from a recent trauma, I'd eat a roll of toe tape.

"Just say you didn't burn your breakfast this morning and I'll stop calling you a liar."

"I was—"

"Liar."

"This isn't—"

"Liar."

"Are you kidding?"

"Are you lying?"

I was almost smiling at that point but not quite. He hadn't earned a full smile, and he knew it, because he stopped talking. Ten minutes went by without denial or reprisal. Neither of us said a word until he parked the car in front of my house.

"Last night," he said after a deep breath, "I found Vince—"

"Wait. You *found him*? Like you tripped on him, or you were looking for him?"

"Does it matter?"

When he turned to me in defense of his stupid semantics, I could have broken and said it didn't.

"It does."

"Fine. I went looking for him."

"Carter! Are you crazy?"

"You think I can't handle myself?"

"He doesn't play fair. He and his friends are drug dealers. There's one of you and dozens of them."

"Memorize the following . . . Carter can handle himself."

I thought I trusted him to be safe when he was with me. I thought all I had to do was let go of the fear that I put men in danger. I thought if we were together, Vince would just realize he couldn't get to me, and he'd go away. I had no idea Carter would go running into a fight to make some macho point.

"You know what? I'm going to just stay home. Tell Darlene I'll work on 'Make Him Yours' here."

I popped the door open and went to my gate. Punched the code like a prizefighter. Swung it open like a home-run hitter.

He caught up to me at the front door.

"First of all," he said, "don't leave the gate open behind you."

"Go away."

"I can't."

I put my back to the door. He stood with me on the narrow step, our bodies practically touching.

"Then why did you drop me?"

"Drop you?"

"Gave me to Fabian. Whatever."

His face went full confusion. Open mouth. Knotted brows.

"What? Cat got your tongue?"

"I switched with Fabian so I could be with you."

Now I was the one who went full confusion. The traffic in my brain stopped short, creating a ten-car pileup of reactions.

"What did you think?" he asked. "I kissed you in the car so I could get away from you an hour later?"

"No, I—"

"You think I hunted down the douche who crowbarred your last boyfriend's face because I wanted to dump you?"

I clenched my fists and shook them. I was so pent up. So annoyed with him and ashamed of myself that I couldn't even speak. Because goddamn if he didn't make perfect sense. And he'd never said or indicated that he didn't want me around. All he'd done was make a decision about his own life so I'd fit into it. And I'd yelled at him.

"Look," he continued, "I'm not going to feel right about taking you as my principal if all I want to do is get my hands on you. You're too distracting. I'm not going to do either job right if I try to do both. So I made a choice. It's not a big deal. Carlos said I could do it if Darlene said it was all right, and Darlene wanted to make sure you didn't feel pressured, so she told you instead of me."

I felt a tickle on my ankles and a soft vibration. We both looked down. The gray cat twisted between my legs.

"She likes you." He picked up my chin with two fingers, making me look into his ocean eyes. "So do I."

"I shouldn't have gotten mad about you switching without talking to you first."

"It's okay."

"But about you going after Vince?" He dropped his hand, but my head stayed high. "That was stupid."

"Thanks, Mom." He scooped up the cat, softening with the presence of the purring animal. "Now open up before Mrs. Grey starves."

"Mrs. Grey?"

"Good a name as any."

I ran my finger along the soft fur of her head. She purred. When he petted her with me, it felt as if we'd decided something.

"She looks too young to be married."

"It's easier to say than Miss Grey."

"Just Grey, then?"

He picked her up and held her high. Her legs stiffened, and her claws came out.

"How's that work for you?" Carter asked the cat. She made a noise that wasn't quite a meow, clearly stating she wanted to be put down immediately. "I'll take that as a yes."

I opened the door, and Carter put the cat on the ground. When we were both in, I turned and found Grey sitting on the step with her tail flicking.

"Are you coming in?" I asked.

She meowed with force, as if I were a stupid woman asking a stupid question.

"She's hungry, and she eats in the backyard," Carter said, on the way to the kitchen already. "Coming inside has nothing to do with eating."

It felt weird closing the door on the cat, but I did. As soon as it was shut, she scampered over the fence that led to the back. Carter had been right. He knew cats, or maybe he just understood how animals, including people, behaved.

When I got to the kitchen, the bowl was full, and he was already sealing the bag of Meow Mix. I took the bowl to the back door and peeked out. Grey was waiting outside my bedroom, where I'd come out the last time she was fed. She was going to have to get a new habit. I wasn't walking through my bedroom every time.

I put the bowl down, and she hustled over.

"You're welcome," I said as she ate.

I caught the scent of Carter before I felt his fingertip on the back of my neck. The pressure woke my sleeping skin, like the first move of a dance across still air. I let my eyes close.

"You're my principal for the rest of the day," he said into my ear.

"And then?"

"Then I'm going to take off your clothes and kiss every inch of your body."

I sucked in a breath. Closed my eyes. A tremor of arousal went down my spine. I bent a little from the shock of it.

I tried to turn, but his arms went around me.

"I want to do stupid things when I'm around you."

"How stupid?" My voice broke.

"I want to make you come."

His fingertip slid under my waistband. His lips brushed my neck. My body went wild. Every drop of blood and fluid, every zap of electricity, was immediately rerouted to the space between my legs. The conduit that ran from brain to mouth was rerouted. I couldn't say the word *yes*, but my hips thrust forward, pushing his hand another half an inch past the edge of my waistband.

"I thought you couldn't. I thought as long as I was your principal . . ."

"I know. I can't. And I can't stop wanting you either. Do you want to come?"

Such a simple question, and such an array of answers.

Yes, I wanted to come. But I was just over being angry with him, and it seemed as if there were too many unanswered questions. I wanted to have a date, dinner, a little cuddling in front of a movie before I gave him my orgasm.

But his hand was so warm, and my muscles under it twitched and shuddered.

I nodded before my brain could engage my throat to make an answer.

His hand slid down my triangle and between my legs, pushing me against him. He was hard against my bottom, grinding against me as his fingers found where I was wet.

"Yes," he said with deep satisfaction, sliding his other hand up my shirt to find my hardened nipple. "You're so ready."

He drew two fingers across my clit, holding me in the vise of his arms.

"Yes," was the only word in my vocabulary.

He gently swirled my clit in my juices, gathering warmth, circling the pleasure to a central spot at the tip. My hips jerked with him, and he held me so tight I felt as safe as I'd ever felt.

"I knew you were this hot," he said into my ear. "I can't wait to get my dick in you. I'm going to fuck you blind."

I answered with a series of short breaths. I was on my tiptoes, bent like a letter of the alphabet, muscles taut and ready for release.

"Say my name when you come."

"Ca . . . ah . . . ah . . ."

"Whole word."

"Carter." I spit it out, the last *R* sounding like a freight train as I bucked in his arms. He held me up while I came, pushing his erection against me, lightening the touch of his fingers to extend the orgasm past any reasonable length.

He stopped, cupping where I was now sensitive without moving, as if he still wanted to touch it but didn't want to hurt me. I went limp, and he held me up.

"Thank you," I gasped, getting my bearings.

"I don't want to freak you out, but the cat was watching the entire time."

Grey sat next to a mostly empty food bowl and washed herself as if she hadn't seen a thing. I flattened my feet, and once they held me, Carter let me go.

"You should have named her Perv."

I straightened myself. Waistband up. Shirt down. Deep breath. I was going to have to reciprocate.

I couldn't wait to get to it.

The feel of his cock against my bottom had sent me over the edge. I wanted to touch it, but when I went for his belt, he gently stopped me.

"I need to use the bathroom," he said, then kissed my knuckles.

"Sure." I wove my fingers in his and guided him inside.

CHAPTER 22

CARTER

I didn't want to wash the smell of her off my fingertips, but I had to get rid of my hard-on, and the full bladder wasn't helping. I washed her off my hands and looked in the mirror, brushing my wet fingers through my hair.

In a few hours, Fabian would start working with her as his primary client, and I'd go home, have dinner, put Phin to bed, and watch a little TV before crashing. Almost like normal.

Was normal going to cut it anymore? Was maintenance enough?

I'd worked hard to maintain a steady schedule for Phin's sake. I made sure he didn't have anything else to cope with except growing up. Not bringing a woman around the house for him to get used to was a conscious choice.

My choices were becoming less and less conscious.

I didn't have any control around Emily. I knew plenty of beautiful women and plenty of smart ones. She had real talent, but in Hollywood, talent was cheap. My reaction to her came from the gut. My body over-rode my common sense. I had to have her. I'd never been addicted to anything, so I was unprepared for what an addiction did to a guy.

I didn't know if I liked it, but I knew I couldn't do anything about it. Like any addict, I felt powerless in the face of my addiction.

She'd left the studio door open for me, and Grey stood guard in front of it. The tick of a metronome came over the speakers, much louder than the ambient volume of Darlene's singing voice. Emily stood in the center of the room in tight black shorts and a crop top, facing a wall of mirrors.

"Stop," she said, and I froze halfway in. Grey wasn't as obedient, hopping onto the chair and folding herself into a sphinx. "Back five."

It took me a second to realize she wasn't telling me to stop. The speakers beeped and the song started again from a different point. She stepped, bent, threw her arms up, spun, and landed.

"Stop. Take notation." She saw me in the mirror. "Hi, Carter." On a screen above her, the words *Hi Carter* appeared below a musical staff. She shook her head quickly and said, "Pause." The dictation stopped.

"Sorry," she said to me.

"It's all right."

"I owe you one," she said. "For the . . . um . . ." She wrung her hands together and went a little pink in the cheeks.

"Orgasm?"

Grey meowed behind me.

"Yeah."

"It was my gift. And I'm still on duty. You can lose control that way, but I can't."

She seemed disappointed, looking down at her bare feet.

"Another time, then."

"Soon. Are you going to stay here or go back to Citizens Warehouse?"

I was just doing my job, but I wanted to stay. I wanted to give her security system another run-through to make sure Vince wouldn't use my visit as an excuse to drop in on her.

And I wanted her to myself. Even if she didn't say a word to me, I wanted to be the only one in her orbit.

"Can we stay?" she said. "I get more work done when I'm alone, and this thing really needs work."

"Absolutely. I'll call the studio and let them know you're working from here."

"Tell Simon I'm giving my dancers the afternoon off. They deserve it."

"I will. I'm going to check your closed-circuit monitors, then I'll be back."

"Good." She went to her laptop and turned on her system, but just as I was about to leave, she called out.

"Carter?"

"Yes?"

"Thank you."

She was thanking me for more than making a phone call and checking the security system. I nodded and backed out before I kissed her again.

CHAPTER 23

EMILY

When I let my hips move to the music instead of directing them, my thinking got very clear. I heard only the music and moved. My body served the music and let my mind work.

My worry, my fear, my deep neuroses about Carter, stopped nagging at me. He could get hurt by Vince or he could be as bad as Vince. He could hurt himself trying to protect me. He could get sick of the way I lived and leave me.

All those things could happen, but while I danced, they didn't bother me.

My first boyfriend, Noah, had dumped me when I was seventeen. He had curly blond locks that reached his shoulders and blue-gray eyes as big as classroom globes. We'd had awkward sex in his parents' garage a few times, exchanged sweet words, and held hands in the courtyard at Lincoln Park High. A week later, he changed. He denied it, but adolescent girls are pretty intuitive. He didn't meet me by my locker in the morning, and he didn't break away from his friends to kiss me on the lips. He sat with Stu Marren in physics lab instead of me and said it was because Stu was just better at physics. He didn't save me a seat at the basketball game against Lake View because there was no room.

I sat with a few girls I knew, but my close friends were the performing arts kids and Darlene, who lived on the other side of the river. Besides gymnastics, I saw her only when she could take the bus to me or when she was having a hard time at home.

Noah was respectful enough to not go out with Tammy Winston for a few weeks. But by spring break they were a thing, and I'd had no closure.

There had been men when we got to Los Angeles. Darlene and I tore up the town. Men swarmed around us. Managers. Agents. Record-label guys. Other musicians trying to latch on. Was it because we were both talented? Or just Darlene? I never knew, and I never questioned it until Vince.

Until Vince, I was in control. I felt little, worked a lot, never lost focus.

I never figured out what happened with me. Why I let him in emotionally. I'd met better men. Vince had every hallmark of a loser. Legal drug dealer. Living with his mother, who waited on him hand and foot. His friends were assholes. He didn't have any interesting hobbies or talents.

Yet he said all the right things. He told me I was special and wonderful. Had no one ever said that to me? My parents had, but it didn't sink in. Or maybe they were the only ones who had said it, and I yearned to be told again.

It was nice to have a guy who didn't play it cool all the time. A guy who wasn't afraid to tell me I was important to him. And only him. I was perfect for him, and I spent so much energy believing it, I didn't see him chipping away at my confidence.

Once he was gone, he wasn't really gone. I got wary of any man willing to say he wanted me. Even Carter.

Working on the steps for "Make Him Yours" in my garage studio that afternoon, the shell of fear started to crack.

No one was going to hurt Carter.

Under the shell was another raw, red fear I hadn't acknowledged.

Was Carter going to hurt me?

CHAPTER 24

CARTER

Grey followed me as I ran the perimeter of the property. It was small, which made it easy to surveil and protect. The size also meant anyone coming in didn't have far to go to get to her.

The cat must have found small, dark rooms boring. She left me when I checked the closed circuit. Nothing seemed out of order. There wasn't visual coverage inside the garage, but the camera followed the movements of the cat as she walked through the open door with her tail straight up. Emily's form crossed the rectangle of the doorway, dancing to music I couldn't hear. She stopped, said something, did the move again. Even seeing that little of her on a two-dimensional screen, I loved watching her move. Her body cut the air so naturally I could tell where she was going before she went there. Her movements were perfection, and I watched the screen in awe until she stopped dancing where I could see her.

I'd crossed a line with her. I had no choice.

No. I corrected myself as I walked back to the studio.

I did have a choice. I was a grown man. I'd made a conscious decision to want her, and I'd made a conscious decision to have her.

Partly true.

It was all conscious except for the parts that were complete instinct.

Back in her little studio, she was taking a break. Her legs were spread wide on the floor in a split, and her forehead touched the hardwood. The speakers were silent, but she was not.

Her voice bounced off the white walls, singing. She was on key, and she had real power, but what attracted me was her emotion. As if she were putting more into the song than her voice.

"Amazing grace, how sweet . . ."

She stopped and picked up her head.

"Don't stop on my account," I said, reaching my hand out to help her up. She didn't take it.

"Not your account." She got up from her knotted position with poise and balance.

"I like the way you sing."

"No. You don't. You heard me. The cat sings better." She indicated a chair next to a little table with a glass of water on it. The cat sat on the chair, wiggling her haunches and purring as if digging in on her position.

"I got you somewhere to sit, but . . ."

"I don't sit when I work. Tell me about the singing."

She turned away but wound up facing the mirror, where I could see her anyway.

She had a dot of red on her forehead from touching the floor, and the rest of her face was red from being upside down. Her blonde hair was coming out of the pins as if she'd just had an electrical shock.

I walked toward her. I couldn't help it. She was beauty and movement. I came behind her, and our eyes met in the mirror.

"I need your help," she said.

"Yes?"

She swung her legs around until they were both pressed together in front of her. She pointed the toes for a second, then got her feet under her. I held my hand out to help her stand. She took it and kept it there.

"Do you know how to dance?"

I laughed. "No."

"Do you know how to pretend you know how to dance?"

She pulled away, keeping our hands clasped.

"I'm not a fake-it-till-you-make-it kind of guy."

She raised her arm and twirled under our hands. Pulled away again.

"You can fake it, or I can call Monty to come partner with me."

She rolled on the length of our arms until her back was to my chest. She fit like a gun in a holster, sliding into me as if we were cut to fit.

"He's a better dancer."

Against my body, my arms around her, she took a step left and I took it with her.

"I don't need a better dancer," she said. "I need someone to follow along."

"I don't follow along."

She stuck her left foot out and leaned. I leaned with her. She turned to face me.

"You've been following along this whole conversation."

She squeezed my hand and spun away. I pulled her back into my arms. Her lips were parted, her cheeks had a sheen of sweat, and her hair stuck to her skin. This was what she'd look like under me, when I was fucking her raw. Sweaty. Messy. A little dazed. Just like this. I'd move her hair off her lips. Kiss the sweat off her skin and lick away the tears I'd make her shed.

My dick pressed against my pants.

"What do I have to do?"

"Pick me up when I tell you to." She raised her arms and twirled to face the mirror. I was behind her, waiting. "Can you take off your shoes?"

I pulled them off and put them against the wall.

"And your socks."

I leaned on the wall and peeled off a sock.

"Anything else?" I asked.

"Um, yeah." She put her hand on her chest. "Probably hard to move in the shirt and tie. Do you have an undershirt on?"

"Yes."

"Wear just that."

I got down to my undershirt and walked toward her. Her eyes lingered over my torso and waist, settling on my feet.

"What?" I asked. "You want me to put the socks back?"

"You have really nice feet."

I looked at hers. She'd put one foot over the other as if to hide something, but I'd seen them already. They were gnarled and calloused, intermittently taped. Pure muscle and fight. A dancer's feet were a boxer's fists. I instinctively flexed my bruised right hand.

"You ready?" I asked.

"Yeah." She got in position in front of the mirror. "Stand right behind me. When I tell you, grab me under the rib cage, right here." She put her thumbs where she wanted me to grab. "Lift straight up and follow along. We'll go without music for now."

"Okay. Got it."

I was sure I didn't have it. We'd need to call Monty so she could get her work done. But at least she couldn't say I didn't try.

She snapped her arms up, then down. The only sound in the room was her feet on the floor and her sharp breaths with each move.

She backed into me, spread her arms, and said, "Now."

I picked her up. She leaned left, and I moved with her as she bent one leg and went on her side as if she were flying.

"Left-one-two," she ordered, and I took two steps left. "Down."

I set her down.

"You really are terrible," she said. "But I can work with it."

I laughed. She'd defined who I knew I was and improved the meaning of the definition at the same time.

CHAPTER 25

EMILY

I didn't know what I was trying to prove by working on lifts with him. I wanted to trust him, but his ability to pick me up without dropping me had nothing to do with how much of my heart I could give him. Being able to read each other in a dance didn't mean we'd be able to follow along emotionally.

I needed to know it was possible. I needed to know if he'd respect what I did, if he'd help without calling it girlie. I needed to know if we could talk with our bodies. I wanted his hands on me.

And I had work to do.

He didn't have a lick of talent. Not for dancing. But for predicting what I needed and giving 100 percent commitment to listening? He was a prodigy. He even kept his hands where they belonged.

This helped less than I'd hoped, because over the course of that first hour, his hands weren't where I wanted them. He was so close, and his touch was so firm and masculine, that I had to make a concerted effort to keep my mind on the job.

"Do I have a future in dance?" he asked during the first break.

"Not really." I tossed him a water bottle. He cracked it open and drank, squeezing the bottle with his huge hand. "Lifts are hard, but these are easy. Darlene's not much of a dancer either."

"Ouch." He wiped his lip with his wrist, looking at me as if he were burrowing inside me. In that moment, the usually poised and in-control gentleman looked like an animal.

"She knows it." I sipped my water and looked away from his feral gaze.

His phone beeped and he looked at it. His brow furrowed, and the spell was broken for a moment.

"Bathroom break," I said. "Give me five minutes."

He nodded without looking at me.

I slipped into the studio bathroom and breathed. He'd been touching me for an hour, and I'd been such a good girl. But once I was alone, the cumulative effect of his hands hit me all at once. My pelvis felt heavy, as if everything from my heart down had gone pure liquid and succumbed to gravity, landing with a splash at the lowest point. Between my legs. I leaned on the sink, off balance, throbbing where my legs met. When I pressed them together, the ache was satisfied and inflamed at the same time.

I heard him talking outside but couldn't make out the words. He seemed agitated. Probably needed to be left alone for now. A minute. Two. I could stay in the bathroom the entire five-minute break, and he'd be grateful.

That was all I needed.

I got my hand under my waistband, around the crotch of my elastic shorts, and unceremoniously rubbed my soaked pussy. Jesus, he could get his dick in me so easily. It would slide in. Stretch me wide. Pull my clit with the force of it. And the feral man with the sweat on his T-shirt would fuck me. He'd be on top. He'd hold me down and drive into me like an animal. Push my hips against the bed so his thick root would rub my clit.

When his imaginary hand went into my imaginary mouth, I lost my mind.

I was barely through my orgasm when a *crack* yanked me back to reality. Another one came right after, and my bathroom door was yanked off the hinges.

Carter stood on the other side, back in his suit, panting.

My hand was down my pants.

"Can you knock?" I pulled out my hand.

"You yelled."

I realized my right hand was slick with pussy. I hid it behind my back.

He laughed, but it wasn't humor. It was relief and realization. It was threatening, in a way, because it threatened pleasure.

"You made yourself come so hard you yelled." He came into the bathroom. I held my ground. "I made you come an hour ago, and you were quiet."

"We were outside. But anyway, you should knock."

Another step toward me. He was an inch away.

"What were you thinking about?"

I swallowed. Best to admit it, right?

"You."

"How? What was I doing?" Finally, he touched me, drawing his hand from my right shoulder to the elbow. "Was I fucking you?"

"Yes."

With gentle pressure he pulled my arm from behind my back.

"What position?"

"You were on top, but—" He raised my wet fingers to his lips, and I had to stop for a second to get control of another wave of arousal. "It wasn't like missionary."

"What was it like?"

He put one finger in his mouth.

"You were going very hard. So you held me down to keep me still so you could . . ." Two fingers went into his mouth, and he sucked them on the way out. It was so hot half my brain shut down. I had to stop talking.

"So I could? What?" His eyes closed when he kissed my palm.

"Pound me." I smirked a little, then averted my gaze. I didn't talk like that. "It was like you wanted to crawl inside me."

"I do," he said.

He lowered my hand and put it against his crotch. His cock stretched his pants, and when I pressed it, he sucked in air. I wanted it. My mouth watered for it. I'd never actually wanted to suck a man's dick before. I'd done it out of obligation.

"You gave me two," I said. "Technically."

He looked at the ceiling as if asking God for the resolution to the conflict. I made it as difficult as possible by rubbing his erection through his pants.

"You're too perfect," he murmured.

"Is that a bad thing?"

He moved my hand away and kissed the palm again before he spoke into it.

"I promise to get my cock deep inside you. I promise to hold you down when you come. Soon. I can't take much more of this."

"We have half an hour. We can lock the door."

Was I standing in the studio bathroom begging to suck his dick? What had come over me?

Past the busted door, in the studio, his phone beeped. He dropped my hand.

"You're in for the night?"

"Why?"

"Fabian's on the west side. If you want to go out, it's going to take him more than an hour to get here."

"Stay," I said. Stupidly. Impulsively.

"I have somewhere to be."

"Where?"

Before the word was out of my mouth, I realized he wasn't going to tell me. He was going to get so deep inside me he had to hold me down to do it, and he wasn't going to tell me where he was going with my erection?

Because yeah—that erection was mine.

"Just call one of us if you're going anywhere. Carlos will make sure you're accompanied."

"But you'll be *somewhere*?" I crossed my arms. Two minutes after an orgasm that was so strong I had to yell, and I was so sexually frustrated I couldn't hide my aggravation.

"Fabian will pick you up in the morning. I'll be in the studio tomorrow for Darlene. Then it's Saturday. Can we go out Saturday? A full date, with dinner, then the screw of a lifetime."

I should have been grateful that he was being such a gentleman. What woman didn't dream of a man willing to forgo his own immediate gratification for the sake of chivalry and safety?

"Sure," I said without agreeing to anything. Not in my mind. In my mind I was agreeing only to the date, not the spirit of the offer. I knew I was being dishonest, and I didn't care.

"I'll fix your door," he said as he crossed the threshold back into the studio.

"Don't worry about it." I smiled, but in my mind I was recalling the location of my keys and calculating the distance between the front door and the side driveway. "I'm getting in the shower. No peeking."

"Okay." He moved from the bathroom backward, hands up, smiling with the mouth that had just sucked my pussy off my fingers. He couldn't possibly kiss another woman with that mouth.

I reached for the shower knob, tinkling my fingers good-bye when water flowed.

He smiled and waved. Made the thumb-and-pinkie calling gesture.

I pulled my shirt up at the hem but slowly, so he could decide what to do. He left before he got an eyeful of tit.

When I heard the studio door shut, I pulled the strap back on, shut the shower, and ran to get my keys. Put on my clogs. Went outside. The door locked automatically behind me. I got in my car, pulling out before I'd finished buckling in, and tapped the wheel with impatience as the driveway gate slid open. My only hope was that he was going east on Olympic. If he was, he'd be stuck at the light long enough for me to catch him, and he wouldn't be going past the driveway where he'd see my open gate.

The black Audi was at the corner of my small street, waiting for a light that heavily favored Olympic Boulevard. If he wanted to make a right, he could have already done it. He wouldn't see me. I'd be stuck at a light for a second, but the light just east was poorly synchronized. I could catch up.

It worked out perfectly. His light went green. I pulled out in the camouflage of stopped cars. I caught up with him in three blocks. In rush hour, my Volvo looked like every other Volvo on the road.

"That's right, fucker. I got you. You can't keep secrets from me."

Left on Crenshaw. Right on Wilshire. Left on Lorraine.

Shit shit shit. He was stopping. In *this* neighborhood? The mayor's mansion was three blocks away. What were they paying the guy?

I ducked low and passed as he pulled up to a house that already had a crossover SUV in it. I parked at the end of the block.

Another car in the drive meant another adult in the house, and a crossover meant one thing and one thing only. Kids.

That fucking fucker.

For all his talk of security, his house didn't have a gate or a hedge in front. None of the houses did. It was getting dark, and I was still in my tight black shorts and clogs.

I scrolled through my phone. I needed someone to tell me I was being crazy. I couldn't call Darlene. She was probably busy. She was always busy. Simon should just be getting out of rehearsals. I could call him and tell him I figured out the steps to "Make Him Yours." Then I could blithely mention I was stalking my bodyguard.

Yeah.

No.

I should go home. I should put in a movie and just trust him. I should be a grown-up and ask him the way I asked Vince to lay off and expected him to just do it. Because being a grown-up had worked so well. Now I was the one living in a fortress because people were liars and couldn't be trusted.

Which reminded me. I was out of the house. On the street. By myself. At night.

To hell with it. I just wanted to know. I had a right to know. I didn't want to disturb or disrupt him. I just wanted to be sure I wasn't getting involved with a lying, cheating douchebag.

I walked down the block. The streetlights were old school, casting a warm, pleasant glow onto the tops of the old-growth trees. My clogs crunched against dropped leaves and pods. The houses I passed were set back. Wide porches. Big front windows. I felt perfectly comfortable and safe until I got to his house.

What are you doing?

"Just looking," I said to myself, believing it. I was just going to look, then I was going to head home and watch a movie.

There were high gates at the driveway. I couldn't get to the back of the house. I intended to look into the one side window accessible from the street. I'd have to be on the neighbor's property, and I didn't want to get caught, so I bent over and hustled to the house.

He has to have a security system.

I approached, waiting for an alarm to go off.

Nothing. No motion-sensor lights.

Maybe he didn't have it on when he was home.

Maybe it's not his house.

The side window looked lower from the street. When I got there, it was over my head.

Damn.

Quickly and with as much stealth as I'd ever done anything, I went around the front and up the steps to the porch. There were two mountain bikes against the brick rail. One was grown-up size; the other had wheels built for a kid. A boy, if I was guessing correctly. A third racing bike was pink. Grown-up size.

A deep rage built inside me. It came from the same place as the sexual arousal. It was base and instinctual. If it turned out he was a lying, cheating philanderer, none of it would matter anyway.

Crouching by the front window, I looked through.

No one. Lights on but not a person in sight.

There was a mantelpiece, and his life was on it.

Carter and a woman. He held her shoulders and kissed her forehead. Carter and a little boy. Carter and the woman and the boy. Boy and woman. Just boy.

His house.

His family.

Son of a fucking bitch.

A quick squeal and a bright light cut the air at the same time. The light turned blue-red-blue, and the sound of engines rose with it.

"Don't move!" More lights right on me. "Hands up! LAPD!"

CHAPTER 26

CARTER

No matter what anyone tells you, night-vision cameras aren't perfect. Not even close to halfway perfect. So when I went to the monitors to see what the system was beeping about, I didn't notice her clogs or the slimness of her frame. I just saw a black-clad person skulking around the house and up the porch.

I worked for famous people with crazy fans. Before that, I put people in jail. I made a very nice living and had things to steal. Mostly, and at the top of the list, I needed to protect Phin from my life without making him feel as if he lived in a prison. So the security system was invisible and thorough. It conformed to frustrating Historical Society guidelines. It had been silent for years.

When I saw the figure crawling around the house at dinnertime, my instinct was to protect first and ask questions later. I'd been a cop when Genevieve Tremaine and her estranged husband wound up dead. I took stalking very seriously. I told Phin and Mom to get upstairs *now*. When Phin asked questions, I practically threw him up the stairs by the back of his collar.

I scared the shit out of him.

My mother was more scared of me than the intruder.

Who wasn't an intruder.

Once the LAPD showed up, I went outside, where Emily had her hands up and the same sexy little black outfit she'd been in all afternoon. She was drowned in light, squinting, scared. Two uniforms had their guns on her. I stood away from it all, in a dark corner.

I felt a burning need to protect her as much as I'd felt the need to protect my family against her a minute before. An older cop came up the steps. I knew him.

"Fifty-one-fifty." He addressed me by my badge number.

Harry and I exchanged a quick handshake as one of the gun-wielding cops put his piece away and told her to turn around and put her hands on her head.

"I know her," I said.

"Got yourself a stalker?"

He seemed to think it was funny. Maybe it was. I didn't have much of a sense of humor about it.

"She's harmless," I said without thinking. One of the cops started patting Emily down, and my whole brain short-circuited. I jumped toward them.

"I'll do it," I said. The cop looked at Harry, who must have nodded. Emily should have recognized my voice, but she didn't turn around.

I got behind her.

"Hands on the wall," I said. "Above your head."

When she obeyed me, stretching her arms over her head and placing her hands flat on the siding, half my anger drained away. My dick woke up.

"Feet apart." I didn't wait for her to do it. Obedience was nice, but kicking her legs open was just a little more arousing.

"Carter." Her voice was an apology I'd accept later.

"No talking."

I frisked her, starting at her wrists, working down to her ribs. She wasn't hiding a damn thing under those strips of clothing except tits and curves and an ass shaped like two eggs in a carton. I took it slow, as if I didn't want to miss anything.

"I left you in your house. You were supposed to call me if you were leaving." I let my fingertips brush under her breasts, feeling the soft flesh yield underneath. "You put yourself in danger and ruined my dinner."

Belly, hips, thighs. I slowly ran my hands between her legs, because you never knew what a girl could hide between skin and Lycra.

I brushed her crotch quickly, then stood behind her.

"What did you think you were doing?"

"You said not to talk."

Harry and the other cops had gone to the lawn to wait. I waved them away and they waved back. Harry gave me a thumbs-up. I turned back and put my nose in Emily's hair. Behind me, doors slammed and tires crunched the driveway.

"This is a problem," I said. She smelled of fear and fresh sweat. "If I can't trust you, I can't work with you, and I certainly can't fuck you."

"I'm sorry."

I rested my hands on her hips. "Did you find out what you wanted to know?"

"Yes."

"Was it worth it?"

"Yes."

"Really?" I moved from her hips to the front of her thighs, to the triangle in between. She shuddered.

"How are you even touching me on your wife's porch?" She dropped her hands and spun on me. "That's sick."

"My what?"

She crossed her arms as if she were loading a weapon. "Don't bullshit me. Look behind you. Three bikes. One definitely adult female. The pictures on the mantel. You look really happy, Carter. Why would you do that to her? Why would you kiss me and touch me . . ." Her eyes went wide as if she realized something. "That's why you didn't let me make you come."

"Whoa, you are—"

Suddenly, I was on the defensive as Emily lifted an accusatory finger to my face.

"That's some kind of line for you and her, is it?" She jabbed my chest repeatedly. "Right? What normal man turns down a blow job? A *married*—"

I took her finger.

"I'm not married. Read my lips. Not. Married."

"Living with her?"

"No. The only woman I'm attached to is turning out to be a real psycho."

She jerked her finger away.

"I'm going to call Thor," I said. "If he's not around, I'll get someone to take you home."

"I can get to my car by myself, thank you. An explanation before you kick me out would be nice."

I got out my phone.

"I don't owe you one for peeking in my windows." I was getting more deeply entrenched in my position than I wanted to be, but her sense of entitlement rubbed up against my sense of safety. "I keep my personal life separate for a good reason."

Tap tap tap.

Phin knocked at the window. Mom stood behind him. They were both looking at the pretty lady on the porch.

I shooed them away, but Mom took that as a cue to open the door.

"Are you coming in for dinner?"

"Mom," I said, "go inside."

"She doesn't look dangerous at all!"

"Oh my God!" Emily exclaimed. "You're the one in the pictures. You look so young."

Her voice was thick with honesty. She wasn't flattering my mother, but Mom was flattered anyway. She put her hand to her chest and smiled.

"Please go inside," I said in a last-ditch effort to get control of the situation.

"Oh, stop," she said, holding her hand out to Emily. "We have plenty of food, even if it's a little cold." Emily was polite enough to hesitate, but my mother wasn't polite enough to know a damned social cue when she saw one. She took Emily by the elbow and led her inside. "Please," she said, "call me Brenda."

CHAPTER 27

EMILY

Let me count the ways this was awkward. I had been caught snooping by a security system that automatically called the LAPD. I was wearing sweaty dance clothes that were wet between the legs from a hot frisking that made me wish I had a weapon. Carter was mad at me for good reason, but I had no idea what his relationship with these people was so I had no idea what to say or not. And most important, my stomach growled loudly enough to wake the dead.

Carter's mother kept her hand on my elbow and led me through the living room, with a leather couch and mission-era coffee table, skirting a TV room with a flat-screen and old fabric couches, to the kitchen, where a nook was set up for dinner. She clapped her hands once, the rings on her fingers clicking together.

"You're not one of those vegans, are you?"

"No."

"Because I can work around that."

"I eat anything, actually."

"Phin!" Carter's mother called. The boy who had been looking out the window flopped in with the grace of the newly adolescent. He had freckles and big green eyes. "This is your father's stalker," she continued.

Phin put out his hand, and I shook it. "Nice to meet you. I'm kind of a stalker too."

"I'm not . . . Wait. What?"

I didn't like being called a stalker, but I'd earned the label. This kid, on the other hand, didn't look like much of a danger to anyone.

Carter spoke from the doorway. "That's not funny, Phinnaeus."

Phin reached for a plate, and his grandmother laid silverware on it. He put out the setting with clicks and clatters while Carter leaned on the doorjamb with his arms crossed.

I mouthed an apology.

He shrugged. I got the uncomfortable feeling that eating with his family gained me zero points. It may have earned me negative points, actually. I was fully and illegally encroaching. Despite the warm hospitality of his family, I was unwanted in that house.

Well, no doubt I'd earned the discomfort by ripping a page from the book of Epic Stupid. Best to just take my licks.

Mom pulled Carter into the room. Phin slid into the nook, Carter opposite him. Mom next to Phin, and apparently I was to sit next to Carter.

It was tight, to say the least.

"Grandma says the dining room table is too far away," Phin said as his grandmother dumped white rice onto his plate. "It's a pain to clean off."

"Call me Brenda."

Carter pointed his fork at the kid. "Clearing the table is your job."

"Not if he has homework. Do you like chicken, dear?"

"Please."

I sat as far to the edge as I could, but my arm was a quarter inch from Carter's. I could barely breathe without touching him. He had his own side for a reason. He took up most of the bench.

"So, what's with the getup?" Phin indicated my little shorts and crop top. "You come right from the gym?"

"No. From work."

"Got any pets?"

I opened my mouth to answer, but Carter interrupted.

"Don't answer any personal questions." Carter addressed me but stared pointedly at Phin. "The little hacker's looking for open doors. Ways to figure out your passwords."

Phin rolled his eyes. "I'm totally white hat, first of all."

I didn't want to interfere with this dinner and then close myself off, even if the little hacker was going to use every bit of intel to pry password clues out of me.

"The pet situation is in flux. I'm dressed like this because I'm a dancer and a choreographer."

"Cool. What kind of dance?"

"Contemporary. Jazz. Whatever we need. I mostly work with a pop star on her acts." I glanced at Carter to see if he wanted to add *who* we worked for or whether or not we worked together. He didn't add a word.

"When did you start?"

I'd worked with kids his age before, and they were usually more interested in talking about themselves than asking questions.

"I was a gymnast first. Then I injured my knee."

"Bummer. Was it bad?"

He shoveled rice and chicken into his mouth as if he hadn't eaten in days.

"Yeah. I tore my right meniscus, which—"

Phin dropped his fork and held up his hands. "No, no. The empathy. Ah . . ."

Carter broke in. "Phin asks about injuries, then gets empathetic pain."

"It's not pain," Phin said with a shudder. "It's like whatever body part you're talking about gets this weird feeling." He shuddered again and picked up his fork.

"Well." I smiled. "Medical school is out of the question."

Carter and his mother laughed.

"Speaking of school," Carter said, "how was it today?"

Phin told us about his day, from getting on the bus in the morning to an after-school White Hat Club meeting.

I felt Carter at my side, his shirt brushing against my bare arm when he moved his fork and knife across his chicken. I was painfully aware that I'd wronged him and that it wouldn't be forgotten. This dinner could be the last together. I'd blown it, for sure. He'd made a choice to conceal his family, but in the end he had nothing to hide.

Phin had his knee on the seat while he ate, then he put it down, seesawed his fork, twiddled with the hot-sauce container, snapped and tapped, interjected jokes, and pointed fingers when he agreed.

"You're cool for a stalker," he said.

"She's not a stalker." Carter had a dad voice that made even me sit up straighter.

"What is she?"

"I'm more of a lurker."

"Can I tell my friends we had a lurker over for dinner?" he asked Carter.

"No."

"Cleanup time," Brenda said. "Let's get the show on the road."

I picked up my plate, but Phin took it. "Me and Grandma clean up on Tuesday, Thursday, and Saturday. It's like a rule."

"The rule is *you* clean up," Carter interjected. "Your grandmother has a soft heart."

"I want it done this year, is all. And please, say Brenda. Not 'grandmother.'"

Phin rolled his eyes as he stacked the plates. While they were both at the dishwasher arguing about the best way to fill it, I turned to Carter and spoke softly.

"He's a great kid."

"Yeah."

"You're secretive because you want to protect him."

He touched his nose with his fingertip.

"And when I came here, I put that in jeopardy."

He touched my nose with his fingertip.

"I'm sorry."

He finished his water and put it down deliberately.

"Do you like tomatoes?"

"Sure."

"Come."

I glanced over at Brenda. She gave me the *shoo* sign.

I slid out of the booth, and Carter led me to the back door. He punched some numbers into a little panel by the door and joined me on the back deck. The yard was bigger than mine but not immense. A garage to the left. A soccer pitch to the right. A thick sycamore tree and a tire at the end of a rope. He led me deep into the shadows in the back of the yard.

"I can smell the garden," I said. He pulled me into him and kissed me in the dark. Caught off guard, I stiffened, but he persisted. I melted for him again. My muscles worked with his movement, going pliable against him. In the silence and passion of that kiss, he forgave me. Accepted me. Drew me inside his world.

When I opened my eyes, I'd adjusted to the light.

"Now I want to tell you everything," he whispered.

"I'll listen."

"You've got to be freezing." He ran his fingers over my bare arms, and they broke out in tingling bumps. "You're half-naked."

"I'm completely covered. And it's May."

"Speaking of the season, my mother grows these like nobody's business."

Against the fence stood a raised bed with lush tomato plants. Even in the dimming light, the colored dots of fruit were visible.

"Do you have a preference?" he asked, bending down and moving leaves away. "We have orange, yellow, plum, beefsteak I think. I don't know what the hell else she has back here."

He plucked a huge red and orange tomato from the vine. It was as big as his palm, and when I took it, my arm dropped. It had to weigh two pounds.

"This is going to last me a week."

"It's a gift so you don't get insulted when I walk you around the side."

"I'm not insulted."

"Phin needs routines. We try to disrupt them as little as possible."

"It's okay."

"If you go back in, he'll find a way to engage you, and he'll break his routine."

"I have my car key." I wiggled my little coil bracelet with the key on the end. "I can just go."

"Where's the car?"

"Down the block. I was trying to be stealthy."

He kissed me tenderly, letting his lips linger on mine.

"I'll walk you."

He laced his fingers in mine and took me around the side of the house, past hockey sticks and a folded goal and a skateboard.

"He's really into sports." I pointed to a basketball hoop on wheels.

"Not really. That was me trying to get him to play something. The only things he wants to do are code video games and make computer art."

He let me through the side gate, and we joined hands again at the sidewalk.

"Hey, Emily!" Phin called from the porch.

"Good night," I called back.

The kid ran down the steps and held up a little blue thumb drive. "I made this. It's fun."

He tossed it and I caught it.

"Thanks."

He suddenly looked timid, as if he'd stepped over a line.

"Size of my heart." Carter held up a fist.

Phin relaxed and held up his fist. "Size of mine." They bumped. He bounded up the steps and closed the door behind him.

"What was that?" I asked. "The fist thing?"

"It's a stupid way of measuring things that can't be measured."

I rolled the USB drive between two fingers.

"Love?"

"Yeah." He cleared his throat and looked at the sidewalk.

"Are you embarrassed to talk about it?"

He shrugged. "It's love. It's, you know, girlie and squishy. He and I eat bark. We're ultramen."

I laughed.

"Should I be afraid of this?" I held up the little USB drive before tucking it between my thumb and the tomato as we walked.

"Probably blow a hole right through your system."

"Can I ask about his mother?"

I didn't expect him to answer right away, but I didn't expect him to stay silent all the way back to the car. I unlocked it with a *chirp*, and he opened the driver's side door for me. I put the tomato and Phin's gift on the dash. He closed the door without saying good-bye.

Wow. I'd really screwed that up. I even asked if I could ask, yet . . .

He rapped his knuckle on the passenger window, and I let myself breathe in relief before I unlocked the doors.

He slid in. "You asked about his mother."

"You don't have to answer."

He started talking before I even finished.

"His mother was a fuckup. First-class. I shouldn't say that, you know? What happened to her wasn't her fault, and I should keep it civil. But that was how I felt, and I can't pretend otherwise. Some days I get really pissed off, but there's no point, because I love him. He's mine . . . my responsibility . . . and I'm not going to blame a dead woman for giving him to me. I should thank her."

He was so conflicted and raw that all my questions seemed trivial. Were they married? Were they even together? How did she die? And when?

"He seems like a great kid."

"He is. He's like her in a lot of ways."

"Did you love her?" The question came out before I thought about it, and I regretted it before it was even out of my mouth.

"Very much."

He'd loved a fuckup. I couldn't imagine the Carter I knew loving anything but clear-cut responsibility and accountability, but long ago, over lunch, he'd admitted to being a troublemaker. Maybe she belonged to that part of his life.

"I'm being a buzzkill." He took my hand and squeezed it. "I should be feeling you up right now."

"You can feel me up on our date if you still want."

"Saturday."

"Saturday."

"I should go back inside. I'm sorry I dumped all that on you."

"You can dump anytime."

The dome light went on when he opened the door. He didn't get out. He looked at our clasped hands and brushed my finger with his thumb.

"I don't know what it is about you. You made me dance. You stalked my house. I would have killed Vince over what he did to you. I haven't done that in a long time. Haven't talked about Phin's mother like that to anyone. I feel stupid, but at the same time . . . I'm kind of relieved."

"You're a basket of contradictions."

He smiled and kissed me, putting his hands on my face as if memorizing the shape.

"Promise me you'll go right home and lock the gate behind you."

"I promise."

"And call me when you're on your street."

"All right."

"I'm calling Fabian to lock you in."

He got out, and when he closed the door, he knocked on my window. I rolled it down.

"Fabian doesn't have to lock me in," I said.

"I know. But he's there already." He reached in and locked my door, then stepped back and pivoted his wrist in a circle, meaning "Roll up the window."

I did and he waved, watching me drive away.

CHAPTER 28

EMILY

I called him as I pulled up to my driveway.

"Is Fabian there?" he asked.

I waved to Fabian, who got out of his car and trotted across the street.

"Yeah."

"He's going to get you in the house and make sure it's clear."

He did. I set a bowl out for Grey while Fabian checked the shower stalls and closets, made sure the system functioned, and left. Carter stayed on the phone through my security check (tell him to check the studio), Phin's bedtime (brush your teeth, my God, kid), and a conversation with his mother about who was taking Phin to the bus stop in the morning. I brushed my teeth, peeled off my clothes, and crawled into bed naked.

"You're safe," he said.

"I'm safe."

"Everyone here is still awake or I'd ask you what you're wearing."

"Nothing. I'm wearing nothing."

"You're killing me."

"Good night, Carter."

"Good night, naked tiny dancer."

I hung up the phone with a laugh. Grey leaned on the glass door as if she was guarding me in partnership with Carter, Darlene, Fabian, and a top-notch security system.

As my mind relaxed and my breathing slowed, I prepared for the next day. My brain cemented the moves I'd decided on that afternoon with Carter. My mind was clear. I didn't interrupt myself with worry. I didn't wake up and wonder if the doors were locked. The day flicked past like a video on fast-forward.

I'd kissed.

I'd danced.

I'd been honest and vulnerable.

Gone to get answers.

Been forgiven.

Opened myself in every way.

Instead of putting myself to sleep with my missteps, I drifted off with the feeling of Carter's hand in mine.

Drifted off feeling what I hadn't felt in a long time.

I was all right.

I wasn't *going to be* all right.

I was fine *right now*, in that moment, all day today and again tomorrow.

I was who I was, and I was okay.

CHAPTER 29

CARTER

Phin had fallen asleep on his Kindle. I got it out from under him and wiped the drool off with my sleeve. He slept like a dead thing even on quiet days. His body was at 100 mph standing still.

I held up my fist.

"Size of my heart, kid," and touched his cheek with my knuckles.

One day his fist would be bigger than mine. I'd get old and small, and he'd be a man. Maybe he'd tell me my love was smaller because my fist was, but he'd be wrong. I'd always love him more.

I felt a twinge of guilt for bad-mouthing his mother to Emily. It wasn't respectful, but anything less than the truth felt like a betrayal. Or, at least if I couldn't tell the entire truth, I could tell her the truth of how I felt.

When I went back downstairs, Mom was in the kitchen wiping the counter.

"She seems nice," she said as I got a glass of water.

"She is."

"You seeing her again?"

"Saturday. Can you stay with Phin?"

She rinsed the sponge and wrung it out. "He's getting big enough to watch himself."

She wiped her hands with a towel. Her hands were strong and calloused. My mother had worked in a garment factory until my sister's career took off. Then she quit to manage the increasingly unmanageable.

"When he's fourteen."

"You said thirteen last year."

"Do you have something you need to be doing on Saturday? Or are you just breaking my balls?"

She let out a *pfft*. She wasn't scared of me or my outbursts. She reached up to a high display shelf and took down a Pyrex bowl. She got out her cigarettes and a lighter, then walked to the front porch as if she knew I'd follow.

Which I did. I wasn't a lapdog, but she was my mother.

I met her on the porch. She offered me a cigarette. I declined but lit hers. One a day might kill her, but if it did, I wasn't going to bust her ass about it. She'd been through enough.

"Here's the thing," she said, blowing out her first stream of smoke. "Sit down like you live here." She sat on the porch chair, and I sat on the rail. "The thing is this. You got this nice girl. What are you going to do with her?"

"Mom. Really?"

"Really. You going to do the usual? Go a few turns and never see her again?"

"How do you even know what I do?"

"I'm your mother. Just because you don't bring them home doesn't mean I don't have eyes and ears. The only reason she was here is because she followed you home." She took another drag and leaned her arm over a potted plant to flick the ashes.

"I don't know what I'm going to do. I'll let you know when I know. Or not, since you seem to know anyway."

She waved me off, sending the smoke in different directions.

"Phin's going to be a man soon, then it's you and me. Believe me, neither one of us wants that, so I'm going to get a place, and you can keep this big house to yourself. Or you can let a woman into your life. Unless you want to be celibate. You're not a priest, and you're not enough of a whore to keep this up."

"You know better than anyone why I keep this up."

"Yeah, I do. Believe me. If I'd known this secret would crush you, I never would have agreed to it."

"It's not crushing me. Give me a break."

She smothered the cigarette in the dirt and held the dead butt in her fingertips.

"I'll give you a break. Go have a life. When you go out with that girl on Saturday, let yourself fall a little in love. Just a little. See what happens." She got up and kissed me on the cheek. "It might not be so bad."

"I'll think about it."

"Good. Don't stay up too late."

She went inside. I lingered on the porch for a long time, wondering if that ship had already sailed. Odds were good I was already a little in love with Emily.

CHAPTER 30

EMILY

Fabian drove me to work the next morning, which was good. I got fifteen minutes of rest in the back seat and didn't have to find a parking spot. He didn't say anything to me until we were signing into Citizens Warehouse.

"You working Vegas?" he asked.

"Yeah, you?"

"Vegas, baby. Wouldn't miss it."

Vegas wasn't going to be fun, no matter how excited Fabian was. Preshows and first shows were a nightmare. No one knew where anything was. Big holes in the production became apparent too late. During the last preshow in San Diego, Darlene had a wardrobe malfunction at the crotch, and ten thousand people watched as the entire dance troupe formed a wall between her and them. The song went south, but thanks to the quick thinking of my dancers, the star's pride wasn't too badly damaged.

"Does the entire security team travel?"

"The top guys. Carlos. Me. Bart complains, but he goes. Not Carter. He's LA only. Hard limit, and man, Carlos ain't happy."

I tried not to smile, but it was impossible. He wasn't going on tour, and after the first couple of shows, neither was I. Good thing I was in the back seat, or Fabian might ask why I was so happy Carter was staying in Los Angeles for the length of the seven-month tour.

I entered the studio. At eight a.m., it already smelled of sweat and coffee.

"Simon!" I said to Darlene's lift partner. "I need to show you what I worked on yesterday."

Simon wiped a tiny spot of yogurt from the corner of his mouth.

"'Make Him Yours'?"

"Yeah, I think we can make it not suck."

"You're a magician."

"What are you saying about my songs?" Darlene interrupted. Her assistant was by her side, carrying bags. Carlos was right behind her with a wire in his ear and a bulge in his jacket.

"Not the song," I said.

"The song is perfect," Simon chimed in.

"The routine. Simon and I will go over it, and you can run it in a few hours."

Her assistant dropped the bag and went to the craft services table to get Darlene her coffee. Simon followed, and they giggled and dished together.

"You're announcing Vegas tonight?" I asked Darlene.

She nodded and blew on her coffee. "On *Entertainment Live!* Liam's set up this whole thing where I pick fans out of the line to win the best seats, then tickets go on sale."

"As if you just thought of it," I said.

"As if." She rolled her eyes. "You coming later?"

I often accompanied Darlene on her appearances. Just to keep myself occupied and keep her in the company of "someone real." I didn't feel like being the real girl.

"I'm skipping if it's all right."

"It's fine. Girl, I am not ready for this show. I'm not hitting the notes. I have cement feet."

"You always get nervous before a tour."

"I need to get laid."

Truth. But as she'd gotten more and more famous, getting laid got harder and harder.

"What about your manager? What's-his-face?" I tilted my chin toward a guy in a suit and shiny shoes talking to her publicist. It took me forever to figure out how their jobs were different.

"Liam?" She jerked her thumb at him as if she didn't care if he knew we were talking about him. Which she didn't. "I do not play that man's game."

"It'll relax you." I waggled my brow a little.

"Whatever. You look pretty relaxed yourself. You didn't come back after lunch." It was her turn to waggle her brow.

"We fed the cat."

"That a euphemism or something?"

I smiled. Maybe it was. "Or something."

"Whoa, girl. Really?"

"No, but yes. Anyway, I had dinner at his house."

Her eyes went wide, and I realized Carter was intense about his privacy. I had no idea what I could or couldn't say about his family, so I decided to hope Darlene didn't ask.

"Tell me everything."

So much for that. What was the most innocuous thing I could reveal?

"He has a nice house."

"Where?"

"Hancock Park."

Behind her, Liam hovered, jockeying for position in line for her attention. Darlene's day was about to begin.

"Are you serious? A whole house?"

"Yeah. So?"

"I know Carlos pays these boys nice money, but a house in Hancock Park? What street?"

I shrugged. I didn't know the circumstances around the house. For all I knew, it was his mother's, or a lucky rental, or the result of an inheritance. It wasn't my business any more than Darlene's. I didn't want to answer another question until I knew exactly what I was and wasn't allowed to say.

"I think Liam needs to talk to you," I said, indicating the handsome Englishman. He nodded slightly and muscled past.

"It's eleven fifteen in New York and . . ."

I backed up until I was out of earshot.

Hancock Park was a pretty big neighborhood, so I hadn't given away too much. I forgot about it soon after we started work.

I got the entire troupe on board with the new moves, and after a few tweaks, we had it ready for Darlene to do with Simon.

Carter showed up after lunch. I couldn't help but look for him. At one point, coming off a spin, I caught him looking at me while his boss was talking to him.

He didn't have business on his mind. His gaze was so intense and heated, I nearly fell over. It went on like that. His presence in the corner was a gravitational force. The world spun around us, but we pinned it with centripetal force until I felt as if everything spun but he and I were still points in the center. My body was aware of his attention and the spin around us, and my nipples got as hard as my underwear got damp.

Which was disorienting, to say the least.

"Five minutes!" I called, snapping up my towel and heading for the water station.

Simon met me there. "Good moves."

"Thank you."

"Too hard," Darlene said, stretching her arms. "I don't know who you think I am or where you come up with this shit."

"All in her head yesterday afternoon." Simon dropped a lemon peel in his water.

"I had help." I waved to Carter, who was looking at me again. He wasn't even my security personnel guy, but he watched me as if he were recording every move. "If he can do it, you guys can."

Simon's eyes went wide, and he looked Carter up and down. "That hunk of man can dance?"

"Well . . ." I didn't want to insult Carter, but I didn't want to put him in a position to have to prove himself either.

"Hey!" Darlene called out. "Mr. Hancock Park! You can dance?"

Carter had started toward us after the first "Hey," but at the mention of his neighborhood, the smile on his face disappeared into a thin, lipless line.

"I can't dance."

"He can lift."

"I've been told I can lift."

Our comic timing was perfect, but he wasn't looking at me. He was, in fact, avoiding my gaze as if I were Medusa.

I glanced at my watch. "Bathroom. Thirty seconds."

"See you back there," Simon said.

I trotted off to the back bathroom, hoping Carter would follow. I could clear the air with him and pee in forty seconds, get back to the floor, and make centripetal force with him the rest of the afternoon.

But no. He didn't follow me in, and when I was done, he wasn't waiting outside. He was exactly where he was supposed to be. In the studio, watching over his principal.

For the rest of the afternoon, I was distracted and leaden. I couldn't catch a rhythm. I was impatient with the front line, and my lungs didn't seem to have enough room for a full breath. The gravitational force was shattered, and I felt unfastened to the earth. It didn't feel free like flying. It didn't feel secure like doing lifts with him. It just felt as if my feet were off the floor because I was in the middle of tripping over it.

We broke for dinner. Everyone was staying late. We all had too much to learn in too little time. I didn't know how I was going to make it another few hours.

"Fabian," I said when I saw him come in, "I need to go home."

I knew I sounded mad. I *was* mad, but not at him. Not at the world. I didn't know if I was mad at myself or Carter or neither. I was mad because I felt insecure, and I hated feeling insecure. I'd worked too hard to kill self-doubt, and here I was resuscitating it.

"Let me get the car, then."

He left without asking another question, and good for him. Because I would have taken his face right off for poking in my business.

"Are you coming back?" Carter's voice came from behind me.

"Why?" I got my shoes on without looking at him.

"Because Carlos needs to know how to allocate staff. That's why."

"I'm going to feed the cat."

He walked away without responding, which was absolutely unacceptable.

"The cat you wanted," I snarled. He stopped. Good. The lines of his suit shoulders to the tight triangle of his waist stood straight and still, while his neck bent back and he looked at the ceiling.

"I can't have a cat," he said.

"Why not?"

He came toward me. Everyone was eating catered dinner, so we were alone in the little alcove to the door.

"None of your business."

"Phin's allergic?" I guessed, and from his expression, I knew I'd gotten it right.

"Did you tell her about him?"

"No."

"Are you sure?"

"I didn't mention your son. I said you lived in a house in Hancock Park. I did not give street name or occupants. I changed the subject. If you're mad, just say you're mad."

"This life your friend lives? It's insane. It's not normal. Did you know she has a fan group on Facebook that tracks her every move? Did you know a bunch of them tried to rent the upstairs floor so they could watch her? Do you know how many of them fantasize about killing her while they fuck her? I do. There are some sick people out there, and they know her security detail knows where she is before she's there. Don't you think one of them's crazy enough to find my son and use him to get to her?"

I swallowed hard. I swallowed the defensive reaction that would put him on the offense. I swallowed the denials that would keep me from hearing him. I swallowed an apology he wasn't ready for.

He continued at a low growl. "I've busted my ass to keep him separate. I've done everything to make sure he was the number-one priority. I'm not going to get distracted, and I don't need a leak right now."

"I'm not a leak."

"Yes. You are. You're a leak. You leak information, and when I'm with you, I leak self-control."

I didn't have anything else to swallow. My throat was full.

"That's on you." I kept my voice low but pointed. "If you don't want anyone to know you live in Hancock Park or Los Angeles or fucking planet Earth, then you need to tell me explicitly what you want hidden and why. This retroactive bullshit does not fly."

Fabian opened the door. "Ready?"

Carter set his mouth back into a tight line. "She's ready." He walked away with his jaw set against further discussion.

I went home to feed the fucking cat.

CHAPTER 31

CARTER

When Darlene announced my neighborhood, I wanted to hurl myself at her in slow motion and clamp my hand over her mouth. But it was too late, and I wasn't living in an action movie.

So I seethed like it was my job. I finished up my shift, watching Emily leave with Fabian, checking through the window to make sure she got in the car okay, as if that were my job too. Which it wasn't. Darlene was my job, and she was a lot tougher to watch than her choreographer.

At a West Hollywood restaurant, I stood outside the private room Darlene's manager had gotten for a late dinner. I was a spectacle in my stillness and seriousness. People looked at me in the crowded dining room, wondering who was on the other side of the door.

I watched them. They watched me.

When Officer Brian Muldoon brought my sorry seventeen-year-old ass to the boxing ring, they were watching me too. Older men of color, mostly. A few white dudes. I thought I was tough, but those guys? They could wring me out and hang me to dry.

The ring had cleared, and Brian announced that I'd made a choice to get in the ring or get arrested for assault. He didn't say I'd assaulted his son, he just said win or lose, I was going home. I'd made a choice.

The guys seemed amused, as if I wasn't the first screwed-up kid in the ring. The smell of tobacco from the open door cut through the sweat-heavy air.

Muldoon, still in full uniform, held up his bare fists and bounced. I was too good for technique. Too cool. I usually planted my feet and hammered whoever was in front of me.

His jab was light but well placed. I saw stars at the edge of my vision but recovered quickly. I caught a left in the cheek. More stars. A dull crack. I hadn't even gotten a punch in, but it wasn't like I was hurt either. I'd gotten hit plenty in my life.

Muldoon stopped bouncing and put down his hands.

"You gonna hit me?"

I thought about it. Imagined it. Knew I could do it. He was in his mid-thirties and heavy with a thick polyester uniform. If he was going to stand there with his defenses down, I could punch his clock pretty good. Probably get two quick shots in before he recovered or the guys pulled me off him.

"Well?" he said. "You gonna?"

I didn't know what the test was, but I knew I was going to fail it.

"Nah."

"Afraid?"

I shrugged, watching all the guys watch me.

"They ain't gonna snitch. It's okay. Come at me."

I could. I really could.

"Forget it. Hit me if you gotta. I'm good."

"Why not? You only hit kids?"

He was trying to goad me. I never hit anyone smaller than I was.

"You're too old. And that uniform's too ugly. I feel bad for your sorry ass."

Everyone laughed. I thought I was going to get the shit beaten out of me for sure, but Brian bent over and laughed. I just stood there like a knucklehead.

Brian held his hand out to shake and put the other on my shoulder.

"I knew you weren't one hundred percent shit. Now you can act like it."

———

Brian's son eventually became an actor. Soaps, mostly. Boxing fixed his attitude before he got his face smashed. I saw him sometimes, and his dad was still easy to find even twenty-plus years later.

McDerby's was a block away from the boxing club. Once we were of age, Brian took Devon and me there after we'd spent enough time pounding the heavy bag.

Emily had broken my trust that afternoon. She'd told a roomful of people where my family lived. I knew she didn't intend to hurt us, and I knew knowing my neighborhood wasn't a big deal, but Emily Barrett should know better than anyone how important security was. I needed to put it into perspective, and I knew I could get it at McDerby's.

When I sat next to Brian, he didn't look away from the TV. The *ping* and *beep* of arcade games came through the old soul tunes that were the only jukebox options.

Rick, the bartender, brought me a beer.

"Nice to see you," Brian said.

"Same."

He pointed his bottle at the TV. "Fucking Dodgers."

"No shit."

We drank in silence for a while. Brian had been exactly what I imagined a father would be. Strict. Tough as nails. Unforgiving.

Maybe I was everything he imagined a son would be. Or everything his son wasn't.

"How's your new detail?"

I'd been a private bodyguard for years since I left the force, but he still called it my "new detail."

"Busy."

"The kid?"

"Looks like his mother."

"Thank God for that."

Dash Wallace, the Dodgers shortstop, hit a home run to center field, and the ten guys sitting at the bar erupted in cheers.

"How's Devon?" I asked. "I think I saw him in a deodorant commercial."

"You did. National spot. Good money, that." Brian grew up in New York and spoke in a soupy code of nouns and adjectives. "Something on your mind?"

I tipped the bottle to the bottom edge and rolled it, making a line of condensation on the napkin.

"After Louise died," I said, rolling the bottle even after the moisture was gone, "you ever get involved with anyone else? A woman?"

"Thanks for clarifying." He smiled a little, letting the bottle rest on his lower lip before pouring beer past it.

"Fuck off. I just want to know how you handled it."

"Handled what?"

He and I could go on like this for hours, throwing half sentences around until we'd avoided saying anything. But I didn't have patience for that.

"There's this woman."

He looked away from the TV without moving his bottle, which stood erect in his hand like a green glass soldier. I hadn't mentioned a woman in years. This could really take all night, or I could make a stupid joke and get out of it.

"I'm not going to get all warm and fuzzy on you. But she's special. Can we leave it at that?"

"It's your show."

"But Phin. Bringing in someone else could fuck with that. She says the wrong thing to the wrong person . . . it could all go to shit, and there's a lot at stake."

"Jesus Christ, kid. No one told you to not get involved with a woman. Not me, at least."

"So why are you still single?"

He shrugged. He didn't want to talk about it. He never wanted to talk about it. He'd been on a gang task force and paid the ultimate price. Louise's death was a jailed gang leader's revenge.

My situation was different, but similar enough to draw a comparison.

"I'm single because." He made no move to add to the sentence.

"Because why?"

"Because I drink too much beer. Gave me a gut. Girls don't like it. You look good. Should get yourself laid sometime." He turned back to the TV, where a commercial advertised little blue pills.

I finished my beer convinced that I'd done right. Emily needed to go. Maybe when Phin was out of the house and Mom was gone, I'd get myself someone.

"Maybe I'll just get a gut instead."

"Suit yourself."

I would.

The inning ended poorly.

I was about to clap Brian on the back and thank him for nothing when the bartender changed the channel. *Entertainment Live!* was mid-show, and my employer sat in a chair on one side of a big screen. The anchor sat on the other side. On the screen between them, a camera panned over yelling, happy faces crowded together outside the studio.

"She's picking fans for a surprise show," the bartender said. "My girlfriend's there trying to get tickets. Crazy."

The shift schedule said Emily was with her. She was probably keeping out of the way of the cameras, but I watched. Seeing someone I knew on TV was strange. I'd never gotten used to seeing my sister on TV. Not when she was on her show or in an interview. I couldn't believe anyone besides a psychiatrist wanted to hear what she had to say.

"If she wins, are you going?" Brian asked.

"Hell no."

I saw someone I knew outside the building. Darlene pointed to him. Lucky winner. The tall, bony guy from Vince's driveway. I couldn't miss that Adam's apple. The MC on the Strip told him, and he hugged his girlfriend. The camera moved to the next potential winner.

"Come on, asshole," called a boozer from the end of the bar. "Put the game back on."

I watched for Vince. If he was there, he was close to Emily, and I had to call it in to security. The picture flipped to the game. I was never so disappointed to see Jack Youder at second base in my life.

I clapped Brian on the back.

"Later."

"Yeah."

I was almost out the door when he called my name. Half-in, half-out of the bar, I looked back at him.

"You don't want a gut."

I made a fist at him. He made a fist back.

I'd forgotten why I went to the bar. Forgotten what I'd asked and what he answered. My whole being was caught up in protecting Emily.

CHAPTER 32

EMILY

—Are you ok?—

The odd urgency of the text from Carter was undeniable, even in three words.

—Why?—

—Your ex is in the house—

What the . . . ? I shut off the movie I was watching. The most meaningless gesture I could have made and the last one I could manage before my body stopped obeying commands. My skin crawled and my muscles froze. Fabian had locked everything. I knew he had. He'd checked the whole house before catching up with Carlos at *Entertainment Live!* I was starting to wish I'd gone instead of sitting on the couch eating ice cream.

—Where?—

Was he watching me now? Would he take away the phone? Was I just waiting for a crack to the head? Would he hit me from behind or try and talk to me?

—*Don't know. Saw one of his friends outside. Get close to Carlos or Fabian right now*—

—*They're at EL*—

I waited for the three dots to appear, meaning he was typing. My ears were on high alert. My muscles were infused with adrenaline but motionless. I didn't hear a thing.

And no dots from Carter.

Two things happened at once.

Grey jumped on the couch, and the phone rang. I shrieked and dropped the phone on the floor.

Still sure Vince was in the house, I dove for the phone.

It was Carter. I scurried along the floor, putting my back against the wall, and picked up.

"Carter?" I whispered.

"Where are you?"

"My living room."

I heard a heavy breath from the other side. A car horn. Traffic. He was outside.

"What do I do?" I hissed.

"Nothing. You're fine. I'm sorry."

"What?"

"I saw one of his friends on TV lining up for—"

"Are you kidding me?" I was still speaking softly.

"I—"

"You just took years off my life." I'd spun from whispering in fear to yelling in anger with the torque of a backflip. "In the house. You said 'in the house,' right?"

"Yes, but—"

"Are you laughing?"

"I'm relieved you're all right."

"You're a son of a bitch, you know that?"

Grey, as if sensing everything was all right, jumped off the couch and into my lap.

"Maybe, but if I thought you were going to be at *EL!* with Darlene, he might think so too. So this wasn't a completely false alarm."

"Who was it? The friend you say you saw. Allegedly."

"Tall, skinny guy."

"Ichabod Crane. Aka Kyle Bedrosian. His girlfriend loves Darlene, okay? He had every bit of business being there. God, I can't stand you right now. You break up with me this afternoon, and now I get this call."

"I didn't . . ." A car door slammed, and the ambient noise around him disappeared. "I didn't break up with you."

"Because we were never a thing. That's why." I stood and traced the outline of the room in my bare feet, checking the locks and windows and closing the blinds. "Because you have this whole push-pull thing down to a science. You know, keep me interested but give me nothing? That. And I'm so sick of it. So sick."

"That's not what I was doing. I—"

"You nothing. Thank you though. Thank you for making me brave enough to start dating again."

"Wait a—"

"I have to go."

I hung up the phone and shut the ringer. The scare he'd put into me made me tired and grouchy. I was going to bed alone. Happily alone.

Grey followed me into the bedroom and purred at my feet. I picked her up. Her back went jelly and her legs stiffened, jutting out like pretzel sticks in taffy.

"What?"

She yawned. I brought her close and held her to my chest. She relaxed her legs, and her spine curved to fit against me.

I needed Carter to be more like a cat.

CHAPTER 33

CARTER

"Dad?"

I snapped out of a fantasy where Emily curled up against me and breathed into my chest more and more slowly, until she fell asleep in my arms. I'd gotten home in time for the last of dinner and studying. Phin was memorizing all the countries in Africa and struggled with the landlocked ones. "Are you watching?"

"Yeah." I leaned forward.

"Democratic Republic of Congo," he said, clicking an odd-shaped landmass on the computer. "It's different from the Republic of Congo." The map of Africa was completely blue. All right on the first try.

"Well," I replied, "you seem to have it down."

"Yeah." He shut the machine.

Upstairs, he got ready for bed, showering, running across the hall to the linen closet for the towel he forgot, probably leaving puddles all over the floor. Good chance he'd forgotten his underwear as well. He'd cross the hall in a towel, leave it on the floor, put his underwear on without really drying himself, and go to bed with wet hair. I'd hug him before he fell asleep, pick up the towel, hang it, and watch a little TV before bed.

Same as always.

Except I couldn't even keep my mind on African countries because I was anxious about Emily. I'd called Fabian, who assured me she was locked away like the crown jewels. I should have felt better about it. I should have been happy I'd nipped the leak about my neighborhood in the bud.

I dodged a pile of Legos and snapped Phin's damp towel up from the floor.

"Good night, kid," I said.

"Good night, Dad."

I put my fist up, but he didn't. He rolled onto his back and laced his hands behind his head. "Can I ask you a question?"

"Yes." I sat on the edge of the bed.

"How do you know if a girl likes you?"

I wasn't ready for this question. When all the other boys had started chasing after girls, Phin had declined to engage. He had female friends. He called them girl-spacebar-friends.

"You mean *like*?"

"Duh." His eye roll provided a great view of his frontal lobe.

"Well. She seems happy to see you. She's nice to you. She wants to know about you. Um . . ."

"What if she tells her friends you're not cute? Like she's not interested at all?"

"This." I waved my finger at him. "This is a very important thing to know. Friends are different for women than they are for men. Men want to hang out and do things, like play ball. Women are different."

"They don't do stuff together?"

"They do, but they also . . . kind of . . . they can get a little competitive."

"I thought we were competitive."

"Maybe. Look. Does she do all the other things? Is she happy to see you? All the rest?"

"Yeah. And today she—" He cut himself off.

"What?"

"She put her hand on my leg, and I, uh . . . I had a reaction." He made a passing gesture at his lower body. He covered his face with his hands.

"Ah. You know that's nor—"

"Yes, Dad! I know it's normal. Jeez."

"Jeez yourself. What's her name?"

He shrugged.

"Do you know her name?"

Another eye roll.

"I'll take that as a yes. Okay, ignore what her friends say. That's rule number one. Got it?"

He nodded. I held up my fist.

"There is no rule number two. Show me the size of your heart, D."

He made a fist. We bumped and I held him.

———

I thought I should take my own advice, then remembered that the stakes were higher. Then thought about Emily again, how warm she was, how she moved, how her face lit up when she came.

Darlene's slip about my neighborhood seemed like the pettiest concern I'd ever had.

Then the stakes. My son.

Then the stupidity of it all.

Then fear for Phin. And Emily.

I was watching ESPN. It sounded like the same generic shit they always said but with different names and teams. I couldn't focus.

Mom got home around eleven.

"How was your date?" I asked.

"I'm home, aren't I?"

"True." I bounced off the couch and kissed her on the cheek. "I'm going for a ride."

"A ride? Where?"

"I'll be back soon."

I left without explaining. I didn't have much of an explanation to give. I was in between thinking I could keep both Emily and my family safe the same way I always had. I didn't have to make any changes to my methods or my madness. Just check on Emily when I could and make sure everyone thought Phin was the son of an unmarried ex-cop. No more. No less.

Checking on Emily wouldn't take more than a second.

I drove over there, crawling down the dark street in my black car. I couldn't see much past the gate, but the light reflected on the bottoms of the leaves. I got out and walked over. I could hear the thrum of music from the studio. She was dancing.

I wanted to be in there with her. Watching. Feeling how she moved. Picking her up at the ribs when she asked. Putting my hands under her clothes.

"Down, boy," I muttered to my dick.

A scratching on the wooden fence sent me reaching for my holster, but it was the gray cat. She got to the top and balanced on the edge, walking to the property line from six feet above. When she was right over me, she realigned her feet and meowed as if to say, *Ready?*

She jumped into my arms.

"How's she doing?" I asked.

She purred. I ran my fingers over her fur.

A squawk came over the speaker.

"What are you doing?"

At the front gate, I turned to the nearest camera and pushed the button under the keypad.

"Visiting our cat."

Squawk. "My cat."

"Yeah. My cat."

Squawk. "Don't do the *Who's on First* routine with me."

The cat jumped out of my arms as if she were as annoyed as Emily. I pressed the button. "I came to apologize for scaring you."

That was a lie, but since I wasn't exactly sure why I was drawn to her, it was as good an explanation as any.

The front door opened, and she walked out in her bare feet. She hooked her fingers in the cast-iron gate's rails like a prisoner.

"Apology accepted."

"I'll see you tomorrow night."

"Carter . . ."

I put my hands on hers. We held the rails together.

"It'll be fun." I wanted to promise more, but I was trapped inside a cage of caution.

"I can't," she said.

I can't? What was that supposed to mean? An unreasonable, unwelcome, unbearable emotion stirred in my chest. It wasn't quite anger, but it was just as demanding, twice as fertile. It had the size of anger but not the heat. It directed itself inward, to the center of my confusion.

"Why not?" I kept my voice flat. If I betrayed a drop of this could-be-anger-but-isn't feeling, she'd run.

"You're not ready. I've done this before. I've tricked myself into thinking something was right when it wasn't. And if we were right, you'd trust me. You wouldn't get mad at me for saying something that I thought was harmless. You'd talk to me. But you won't, and I know I'm going to mess up again. It hurts too much when you get mad."

"I was wrong."

Wait. Was I wrong? I hadn't decided that, but it came out of my mouth. Maybe I was wrong.

"I shouldn't have said anything to Darlene, I agree. It was stupid."

"It's all right." I reached between the rails and ran my hand up her arm. Her eyelashes fluttered. "I overreacted."

169

"Yeah." Her answer was barely a breath. I waited for her to open the gate. She didn't.

"So," I said. "Tomorrow night?"

"I don't think so. I think we need time." She pulled her hands away. "Good night, Carter."

Where was the line between stalking and devotion? When could a woman be convinced? How could I show her I wanted her without scaring her?

She turned away from me.

If I let her go, took her word for it, I'd lose the moment and lose her. She walked to her door, and in three seconds she'd be behind it. I could cross the distance between us in five steps, twist the gate into iron junk, cross the air with sound, but not once she closed the door.

Desperation made a meal of common sense.

What was the difference between a stalker and a desperate man?

"I'm coming here tomorrow night." I didn't have a plan. I didn't even know what I was saying, but I kept on, even as she touched the front door. "I said I was taking you out on Saturday, and I'm taking you out, so you'd better be dressed and ready at eight or you're going to miss out."

She waved before she closed the door.

CHAPTER 34

EMILY

I had the day to myself. I cleaned the cat box, which wasn't too bad. I stretched, took calls about costumes. Made a tomato salad with Carter's gift.

I didn't think about eight o'clock at all. Nope. Didn't even worry half of a little bit. Except when I took out the bag of cat litter. I wondered if he'd be by the gate. And when the phone rang, I thought it might be him. And when I saw Grey, which was constantly, I thought of him then too.

But he didn't call to confirm or make sure. He didn't text. He didn't send flowers, which Vince had done once to get me back. It had worked, and I swore it would never work again.

Not that it mattered. No flowers came.

I plugged Phin's thumb drive into my laptop. Knowing what I knew about him, I shouldn't have. I'd chased Carter away, but I wanted a connection. No discipline in love. I was a danger to myself. Putting a prodigy hacker's flash drive into my laptop.

The screen exploded into a rainbow of flowers that burst and blossomed in a continuous, beautiful loop of color and light. If it killed my computer, at least it would die looking good, but it didn't die.

When he didn't text to confirm by 7:15, I figured he wasn't coming. I told him I wasn't going on a date with him, so he must have talked himself out of it. That would be wise. Very wise.

But if he did show up?

If he came after a day of not contacting me?

What would I do?

He wasn't coming, but if he did, I was going to be ready.

Aware that I made no sense at all, I showered because I was dirty, shaved because it was time, and dressed in something nice because sweatpants weren't good date wear. Garter and a soft pink dress? That was good for a date.

Not that there was going to be a date, of course.

But if he spent the entire day trusting that I'd get ready for him, without checking or bothering me, and if he still showed up not knowing if I was going to turn him away, that in itself was a commitment. That was a guy who respected me and wanted me at the same time. He was willing to come here and be hurt so that he could keep a promise.

Not that he was coming. As I put on my makeup, I was sure I was getting dressed up for nothing.

But if he *did* come, I'd underestimated him. He wasn't Vince at all.

The front gate buzzed at eight on the dot.

Holy crap.

I went to the closed-circuit monitor with the panel underneath. He stood at my front gate in a suit, holding flowers.

Was I being stupid?

Was I just falling for a different kind of crazy behavior? I'd told him no, but I'd put on a dress. I'd convinced myself he wasn't coming and gotten disappointed about it.

Do you like him?

I liked him. A lot.

Do you trust him?

That couldn't be answered so easily.

"Carter?" I said through the intercom. He looked at the camera. "I said there was no date tonight."

He leaned into the keypad panel. "I know." He let the button go, then pressed it again. "You can't blame a guy for trying."

Could I?

He stuck the flowers between the gate's rails and stepped back. Waved at the camera.

He was really going.

I spoke sharply into the panel so he'd hear me.

"Wait!"

CHAPTER 35

CARTER

She came out in heels and a light-pink dress, fully made up with her hair in a twist and a matching purse. One side of my brain wanted to grill her about when she knew she was coming on the date and how long she'd intended to keep me kissing the intercom.

The other side of my brain wanted to take out those hairpins and watch her blonde hair fall over her naked shoulders.

"Hi." She unlocked the gate. "Let me bring these in."

She swung the heavy gate open and pulled out the flowers. I took them and held my other hand out to her.

"Bring them in later." I put them on the ground just inside her property. "If you go in, I'm going to follow you, and if we're alone in the house, we won't make our reservation."

"Where are we going?"

"Downtown."

She pulled the gate closed. I let her in the car and went around to the driver's side. I barely had my seat belt on when I smelled her perfume. I usually saw her at work, where she smelled like sweat and lemongrass. I thought that was hot. This perfume with the pink dress was a whole new level of sexy.

"We going to go?" she asked.

"You look amazing."

"Thank you." She touched her hair as if I'd told her it was out of place. If she kept doing that, it was going to be more than out of place. It was going to be tangled in my fist.

I got us onto Olympic and headed east. It was a straight shot to our destination.

"Thank you for coming out," I said, because there was nothing else to say. Gratitude was all I felt. It was in the way of any other conversation starter.

"I had nothing better to do," she said with her head high in fake arrogance. When I stopped at a light, she was smiling at me.

"Good. I figured we'd check out the *Three Stooges* marathon at the Rogue Theater."

"Divine. Then a boxing match, perhaps?"

"Actually, you're making me really nervous about what I have planned, so stop joking around."

"Okay, no joking. How is life? Are you going to move, since Darlene announced your neighborhood?"

"Nah. I'm going to pretend it never happened." That wasn't a real strategy, but I didn't have much of a choice. "But I'd appreciate it if you kept away from specifics when you talk about me to all your girlfriends."

I turned down Factory Place and into a parking lot.

"I can do that."

"Thank you." I stopped the car and put it in park.

"If you tell me why."

Her fingers hooked around the top of her purse, and she held her head high. I twisted to face her as much as I could, getting an elbow on the steering wheel and draping my other arm over the seat.

"When?"

"When, what?"

"When do you want me to share everything that's important to me?"

175

Her head tilted slightly and her eyelids scrunched. She was thinking. "Sometime. Not today. But not never."

"Deal."

I got out of the car before I spilled everything just to get it out of the way. I was going to have her. I had no doubt about that, but I didn't need to go off half-cocked just because my dick was working my brain's control panel.

I walked her across the lot.

"Are we going there?" She pointed up a flight of corrugated iron steps to the Los Angeles Gun Club.

"Yeah." I put my arm on her shoulder and stroked her skin. "I booked half an hour. It's fun, and this way you'll know how to hold a fake gun."

"I don't carry that anymore. You scared me out of the habit."

"Good."

I opened the door.

CHAPTER 36

EMILY

The ear protectors muffled the pops and cracks around me. The visor was so clean and light I barely knew it was over my eyes. The gun was pink, which I didn't think was possible, but it was the club's most popular rental. I liked it because it wasn't as scary as the others.

All I felt was Carter's body behind me. His right foot pushing mine into place. His arms around mine, meeting at the focal point of our joined hands. His hips just an inch away, too far for me to feel for his arousal.

I had earmuffs on, so he tapped my shoulder when he wanted me to squeeze the trigger. My arms bent with the recoil, and I smelled a more intense Carter smell—gunpowder. The bullet missed the black and white paper target by a mile.

Carter moved the muff away from my ear.

"You keep flinching when you shoot. Don't turn your head."

"I can't help it."

"Pretend it's Vince, and if you turn your head, he might come at you."

He slid the earpiece back on, pressed his body against me, and squeezed my hands. I squinted until I could see Vince's goatee, his leering smile, smell his sense of entitlement.

I shot, missing the bull's-eye. But I didn't turn my head, and I didn't flinch.

I pushed my mufflers off my head. "I did it!"

"Got him in the shoulder," Carter said. "He's at least on the floor screaming while you dial 911."

"I can't believe I didn't do this before." I gave him the weapon, and he chambered the next bullet. "I'm going to put a hole in his head this time."

"Whoa, girl."

He held the gun away even though I was eager to go again. I'd spent so much time feeling like a sitting duck, waiting for my security to be breached. For the day to come when Vince finally killed or raped me. Taking that power back made my skin tingle. I wanted to jump up and down. Carter's eyes went a little wide.

"I've never seen you like this," he said.

"Like what? Give me the gun." I clenched and unclenched my grabby little hands.

"Happy."

A bell rang twice. The pops and cracks of the other shooters stopped.

"Time's up," Carter said. I sulked. "We'll come back."

"Promise?"

"Promise. You'll be a sharpshooter in no time."

———

I lost my mind in the car. As soon as he closed his door, I was on him, hiking my skirt up so I could straddle him on the driver's side, pushing down on his cock. We kissed and sucked, yanked at clothing, reaching for skin. I undid his belt, clawing at everything between me and his dick.

"Wait," he breathed.

"Hell no."

"The first time we fuck isn't going to be in my car."

"No, it's not. I owe you. I'm going to suck your cock, and I'm going to swallow every drop."

The surprise on his face was unmistakable.

"You dirty-mouthed little girl."

"Wash it out with your cum."

He took my cheeks in his hands and squeezed until my lips slackened and opened.

"When you take it, you take it all." He bit my bottom lip and pulled, letting his teeth scrape and release. "Every inch. Mouth only."

He let my face go. I was wet and throbbing, but I could wait.

I got off him and put both my knees on the passenger seat. I reached for his dick like a starving woman. It was long and thick, with a darker head. A drop of fluid ran down the back, and I licked it off. It was salty and warm, and I kissed him with it still on my tongue.

"Filthy." He groaned. "You're filthy, and I like it."

I reached over and pulled the lever on the side of his seat until he was at a comfortable recline. Pulling up his shirt, I ran my fingernails over his abs and up his cock, then held it steady as I lowered my head onto it, sliding my tongue against him slowly, pushing down my tongue so he could enter my throat without stopping.

"Oh my God," he whispered when I got his massive dick all the way down. Not a small feat. It had been a while, and I had to scold back the gag reflex. When I pulled up slowly again as if I were in complete control, I sucked on the head and popped off.

"That okay?" I looked up at him. He reached for the hem of my dress and pulled it up, exposing my panties to the window.

"Next session's over in twenty minutes. So unless you want everyone in the club to see us, you better keep going."

Twenty minutes?

Easy.

He slid his hand under my panties and stroked my ass. I took him again, faster and faster, breathing in between thrusts, pushing my nose against his belly. He fisted my hair and paced me, thrusting into my mouth with hot gasps.

"Coming," he grunted. Two thrusts later, he came down my throat with a long, sultry murmur, sticky and bitter, warm with life. That groan, that orgasm, that loss of control, was the sexiest thing I'd ever seen.

I put his underwear over his still-slick penis and kissed his cheek. He rerouted his face to kiss me on the lips.

"Thank you."

"Can we skip dinner? We can eat at my house."

"What do you have?"

"I have a little Meow Mix left." I pulled my skirt down and sat facing front.

"I love Meow Mix."

He started the car, and we went back to my place.

CHAPTER 37

EMILY

No amount of hot passion could keep Carter from checking the windows and doors. I got down to my fancy underwear, and seeing Grey at the back window, I went out to feed her. I was crouched in front of the cat in my lingerie, petting her as she ate.

"Does the food get more nutritious if you pet her while she eats?"

He stood in the doorway in his suit, and I was dumbstruck for a clever answer. His beautiful body was covered and yet revealed by the slope of his shoulders and the folds of his tie. I was the one in the sexy lingerie. He was just wearing a suit. Same difference.

I stood and stepped into the room. He brushed by me and snapped the door closed.

"Sorry, Grey," he said from behind me. Then he whispered in my ear, "Don't move."

"Okay." My voice cracked.

Carter kneeled behind me and unhooked my stockings, then pulled my panties down slowly, running the rough lace and his soft fingers over my skin. I felt his breath on my bottom, then his lips. When he got my panties to my ankles, I stepped out of them.

"Bed," he said, swatting my bottom. I squeaked and turned on him, but he was on his knees, smiling up at me. "Go, or I'll spank you again."

I backed up until my thighs hit the mattress. I sat.

He stood over me and got undressed. Threw his jacket on the chair. Unstrapped his shoulder holster and put the gun on the night table. Then tie. Belt. Cuffs. Front placket. Shirt off. Undershirt off, hiding his face for a split second so I could drink in the perfection of his body, the dark hair on his chest. He watched me lean back onto my elbows as he took off his pants, and his cock came out like the threat of a clubbing.

I kept my knees pressed together, because there was something I liked, and it wasn't fun to ask for it.

He put his hands on my knees and yanked my legs open.

That was the thing. A rush of sensation flooded my body. I would have done anything for him after that point. I went slack, and he pushed my knees up and out, exposing my pussy to him.

He put his middle and ring fingers into his mouth, drew them out, and laid them against my wet skin. Up to my clit, which was hard and aching, down to where his fingers slid inside me to the base.

"I'm going to lick you, but don't come."

"Okay."

"No matter how hard I suck your clit."

"Yes."

He left his fingers inside and bent over, keeping his eyes on mine. When his tongue flicked the tip of my clit, I nearly came. When he ran his lips along it. When he sucked gently and pulled his fingers out, only to jam them in deeper.

"Yes," I said, which was only the start of a series of affirmations.

I dug my fingers into his hair while his free hand held my legs apart. He sucked and licked, watching me, fucking me with his fingers. I grunted syllables like an animal, then he took his hand out. I squeaked for the second time.

"Hush." He slid a condom out of his wallet with his teeth while his hand worked me.

"You're making me crazy."

"Good." He put the condom on and kneeled between my legs, sliding his cock along me, landing at my entrance like a threat. "You ready?"

"Yes. Please." I was barely coherent. He pushed forward, stretching me open gradually until he was all the way inside. His body pushed on my clit.

"I wanted this from the minute I saw you," he said, pulling out then driving back again. I clawed his chest, unable to respond. "Get inside you." He pushed my bra out of the way and stroked my nipple with his thumb. "Take your body. Can you feel me?" He drove in hard, and I cried out. "Can you feel how much I want you?"

I could feel it. Every inch of it, but I wasn't verbal. He drove against me slowly, then quickly, as if reading my body for what it wanted, then providing it.

"I . . ." He ripped through me, and I couldn't finish. "Oh God."

He got on his elbows and put his nose to mine, swaying his hips in a new rhythm.

"You ready?" he asked.

"Yes."

"Me too."

Faster. Harder. Stretching until it hurt, until I couldn't bear it another second, I clenched my fists and gave in to the pleasure of his cock. He let loose inside me with the same low groan I'd heard in the car.

That groan was my gift. I gave it to him. It was for me and no one else. I touched his face at the end of it as if grabbing his orgasm and putting it away for safekeeping.

We wrapped our bodies around each other for the night, and I felt safe. Maybe the feeling was fake. Maybe I was fooling myself. But his kisses were warm, and his body fit to mine as if they were made for each other. If there was ever a world-class security system, Carter Kincaid was it.

CHAPTER 38

EMILY

I woke to the sound of purring. Grey was just above my head, pushing her paws into my pillow. There was something nice about the attention but something uncomfortable about its intensity. I reached for Carter and found his warm body right there. He rolled over to face me.

"Good morning."

"How did the cat get in?"

"She was at the door. Really persistent. And loud. You didn't hear her?"

"Nope. Slept like a baby."

"Babies don't sleep like you slept." He ran his fingertip along the ridge of my nose.

"Did Phin sleep well when he was a baby?"

His flash of uneasiness lasted a split second, but it couldn't be denied.

"Sorry. Was I not supposed to ask?"

"It's fine. I'm just not used to it. What do you want for breakfast?"

I sat up and rubbed my eyes. "I don't know what I have in the fridge."

"You shower first, and I'll see what I can scare up."

He kissed my cheek and got his naked body out of the bed.

My God. What had he created? What had he given me? Had the flawless man standing over me just given me that perfect body the night before? He was lean and rippled, his proportions even more golden without clothing. At half-mast, his dick was thicker than any other I'd seen fully erect. I was sore from him but not sore enough.

"Don't look at me like that," he said as he put his pants on.

"Why not?"

"Because I'll take you again."

I dropped the sheet, exposing my breasts.

"That would be terrible," I said, putting my hands behind me so my back curved and my chest jutted forward.

He arched over me, hands leaning on the mattress on either side of my hips, and kissed each of my cheeks.

"I have to take Phin somewhere. So I have to get home and make sure he's awake, because my mother sleeps in."

He wasn't specific about where he was taking his son, and I tried not to be insulted. The protective layer he'd put around the boy would either flake off for me or it wouldn't. It wasn't for me to say, even if it hurt.

"I think I have yogurt in the fridge. Fruit. Granola in the pantry."

He pushed back on his hands to stand, then swooped his undershirt off the floor. I said good-bye to the sight of his body as he wrestled into it. When his head popped out of the neck, his hair was messed up, and his expression was loose and unselfconscious. He smiled at me, and it was gone.

"Coffee or tea?" he asked.

"Coffee."

"Great." He kissed my cheek and took off for the kitchen. I sighed. Too good. All of him. His body. The way we'd fucked the first time and made love the second. I stretched the sleep out of my muscles, extending my fingers to the headboard and pointing my toes.

Grey was on the night table. She'd pushed aside a picture of me and my parents in Disneyland and wedged herself between a stack of hardcovers and Carter's gun.

She looked at me with stoic green eyes. They said, *This? You know you want to take a look at this.*

I took the holster off the night table, the shoulder straps dragging behind. I unsnapped it with some effort. The metal fastener had obviously been built for a man's strength, or to make sure he was positive he wanted to take out his gun.

I expected a wooden handle and silver metal. I thought his gun would be Old West, but it was black and modern. It looked like a worn and well-loved toy. A little screw in the grip had a chip in the black paint. It smelled like Carter. Gunpowder and hot metal. Fifth of July.

How long had he had it? Since he was in the LAPD? How much of his life had that gun seen?

"Emily?" he said from the door.

It was too late to put the gun down. I felt as if I'd been caught peeking at his diary.

"Sorry." I held it out for him. He took it and snapped the flap closed.

"How do you take your coffee?"

"Black, two sugars."

He kissed me quickly and looped his arms through the holster.

"Go shower or the coffee's going to be cold."

CHAPTER 39

EMILY

He stayed at my house when our work schedules dovetailed with Phin and Brenda's. He and Fabian quietly worked out scheduling with Carlos so that when Carter was around, Fabian wasn't. I was still Fabian's principal. Even though Carter insisted he was useless as my bodyguard as long as we were sleeping together, doubling up seemed ridiculous as well as uncomfortable.

"Are you in trouble?" I asked one morning after he hung up with Fabian. "For sleeping with a client?"

"Only a little."

I didn't want to hear that, but I needed to.

"What does 'a little' mean?" I bent over to get my heel into my shoe.

"It means he fired me—"

"What?" I almost fell over.

He caught me and pulled me up, holding me steady until my foot slipped into my sneaker. Was I supposed to give him up so he could work? Was that the ethical thing to do? I wouldn't. Couldn't.

"I talked him off a ledge," he said.

"How?"

"I told him how incredible you are." He shrugged as if it was nothing and my incredibleness was a blue sky or wet rain.

"Why would that make a difference?"

"It means you're not a fling. We should go or we're going to be late."

Over the next two weeks, I figured if I was going to be trapped in a cage, I could do a lot worse than Carter Kincaid. My life wasn't my own, but I didn't want for sexual satisfaction. He took care of my every need, held me close, talked and laughed with me in the night, tickled me, stroked me, sighed in my ear. He watched me as if he wanted to eat me alive, which seemed possible because I *was* alive. I didn't realize how lonely I'd been until Carter found me.

The birds sang their improvisational jazz of notes, and the morning sun cut through the slit in the curtains. I reached for his pillow and buried my face in it. It smelled like a certain midsummer morning. Me on my bike telling Mommy I wanted to go to Darlene's. She sent a cab for my friend instead, and we played on the block (no farther—do *not* cross the street by yourself) picking up dud bottle rockets that had flown over the roofs the night before. It was the memory of the fifth of July, when the air smelled of crackling fire and unexpected treasures, the scent of endless possibilities and Carter Kincaid.

When I got to the kitchen, he was laying out eggs, toast, and yogurt with the granola from the pantry. He held my chair out for me, then sat across the little breakfast table.

"Sunday morning suits you." He flipped the Tapatío against the heel of his hand and unscrewed the cap. He liked his eggs spicy, so I'd stocked up on hot sauce.

"What does that mean?"

"Saying you look fucking gorgeous seems like I'm exaggerating—even if it's true."

I pressed the side of my fork into my egg. The yolk was wet, with a fold of gooiness in the center, but not enough to create a flow onto the whites.

"Perfect," I said. "Again. I wish you'd let me watch you make them."

"Then you'd know my secret." He slid his fork into his mouth, and the gesture seemed so fluid and masculine I could barely swallow.

"I might just turn one of the cameras on you one of these mornings."

"Good luck with that. What do you have planned for today?"

"Why?"

"I just spoke to Carlos. Fabian's with Darlene. He's got someone else to work with. So I'm going to coordinate with you."

He was all business. I loved how seriously he took his job.

"Okay, first of all, does Fabian ever take a day off?"

"Nope. The thing is, I have something to do with Phin."

"Well, I'm not going anywhere today."

He looked at me suspiciously. "Nothing?"

"Really. Go do your thing with Phin. If I want to go grocery shopping or something, I'll do it when you get back. Or I'll get delivery. Whatever."

"I should be back by four."

"That's a long day." I blurted it out before I thought it through. I sounded judgmental and, worse, I sounded like I was trying to get information out of him. "Sorry."

He shook his head and waved away the apology.

"It's a robotics tournament. I'll be in a gym all day cheering for a robot to pick up a ball."

"A big robot?"

"No. It's on a table. They program the robots to push things and pick them up. It's . . . We get all wound up like it's a football game."

"Without the concussions."

He smiled over the rim of his cup, and for a moment I imagined us eating breakfast on any given morning, preparing for our day. Phin would chatter at us, and Brenda would insist I call her Brenda. I'd be sore from the previous night, and he'd make eyes at me across the table.

I imagined a life with people around me. People who loved me. Noise. Talking. Plans and preparations around each other. A life that buzzed with love.

I didn't picture it as unsafe. I didn't feel the lockdown. Didn't make sure the imaginary doors were locked. The safety didn't come from dead bolts, alarms, and closed-circuit monitors. The safety came from family.

CHAPTER 40

CARTER

Phin was in an unusually pensive mood, which suited me fine. I felt really good but didn't want to tell him it was because I'd spent the night with Emily. I ran over everything I wanted to do with her body as we cruised over the 101. When my dick got hard, I thought about all the places I wanted to take her, all the ways I could make her laugh. I wished I could dance, because I would have shared that with her. But maybe I could pick her up again. Help her out with my ham hands and clunky feet. And once she'd had a ton of safety training, I'd get her her own pink Glock, and we'd hit targets together.

We were exiting the freeway when Phin shut the radio.

"Dad."

"Yeah?"

"I got a D on my Africa project."

"I know. That was two weeks ago."

"So I need an A on the family tree project if I want a B on my report card."

"Okay."

"There's a ton more stuff on your side and nothing on my mother's side but a bunch of names."

Crap. My happy buzz was shot down like a slow-flying clay pigeon. "That's all I got, kid."

"What if I made it up? I could get pictures off the internet. I could add some places and a little anecdote or whatever. Who would know?"

I'd know. That's who would know. I'd know that he lied because I'd have to tell lies. I'd know the man who was raising him had shown him the wrong way to live his life, and I couldn't live with it.

"Make it as good as you can. They can't dock you for having one parent."

He twisted his lips into a puzzle-solving sulk. Something was cooking in his head, and it smelled like trouble.

CHAPTER 41

EMILY

I did everything there was to do in the house and ate lunch in the shade of my tree. I fed Grey some scraps, read a few chapters of a book, but realized I was bored by noon.

Darlene was at church. That was her Sunday thing, and it was absolutely nonnegotiable. Sunday was for worship. We didn't go out, and I didn't call her until dinnertime. I respected that, but I felt different this Sunday than any other. My night with Carter had supercharged me. I felt expansive, bursting with potential. As if I'd gotten great height on the jump but couldn't fold into a somersault.

I figured I'd work on something. Some new steps. Whatever. I'd tire myself out, at the very least.

Then Simon called.

"Hey," I said into the phone while I picked up my plate.

"Girl, I have nothing in my closet for Vegas."

"You're supposed to keep dance clothes in the drawer."

"Don't make me laugh; you'll crack my foundation," he said with faux seriousness.

"Did you see the schedule? There's no time to do anything but work and sleep. I wouldn't worry about it."

"Vegas doesn't sleep. And besides, I'm going the night before."

"You better not be tired—"

"Stop it already. You're hurting my ears."

"Do not party the night before. Do. Not."

"I'll be fine. I have electrolytes. A Boy Scout is always prepared."

"You were a Boy Scout?"

"Of course. But I left. The uniforms sagged with the pins and badges."

"I can't imagine it."

Simon sighed with frustration. "I'll just go to Nordstrom myself."

I scraped my dish and put it in the dishwasher next to the ones Carter and I had used for breakfast.

"I can't."

"Why not?"

"Because Darlene . . ." I stopped myself. Was this about Darlene's paranoia? No. It was about the fact that her paranoia was justified. "Because it's not safe for me to be out without a bodyguard right now."

Simon let out a long groan. "Who's going to tell me when I don't look fabulous?"

"You always look fabulous."

"I do not, and you know it. That's why you have to come."

"I can't go without—"

He gasped so hard I clapped my mouth shut.

"Emily!"

"What?"

"I'll be your bodyguard!"

"Simon. Really?"

"You've seen me naked. I am all muscle, and you know it."

"But—"

"I'll come pick you up and chauffeur you around like a queen! Royal treatment. If anyone even speaks to you, I'll slap them."

I leaned on the counter. The house was so empty and quiet. I wanted crowds and noise.

"I need to be back by seven." Carter and I had made no plans to do anything, and I assumed he'd want to be with Phin, but I felt like a teen sneaking out the bedroom window. I had to get back in time or I'd get grounded.

"Yes!" He clapped, and I smiled. If my presence could make another person happy, so be it. There were worse ways to live.

CHAPTER 42

EMILY

We went to the Grove. Simon looked fabulous in everything. I had to pick a few reasons to be unenthusiastic in order to maintain my credibility. A washed-out olive color. Baggy pants that didn't accentuate his dancer's ass. A necklace that was simply too feminine.

He had a bunch of bags, and I had none when I tarried a little too long in front of the La Perla store. This was a mistake. Simon was too intuitive to let that slide.

"Excuse me?" he said, leaning on one hip.

"I like the color."

The mannequin wore a lavender baby doll with a deep purple lace bra and panties underneath.

"Just the color?"

"It's unusual." I pressed forward. The Nike shop was ten steps away, and I needed socks. "Maybe they have something in that color." I didn't hear Simon answer. "Or do you think it's ugly?"

I looked for him, but he was gone.

"Simon?"

He poked his head out of the La Perla store, waved, and went back in. I stood in the doorway. The store was mood-lit, filled with wordless, sensual music, and Simon was holding up a purple lace bra with nipple flaps.

"Are you kidding?" I asked.

"If you don't try it on, I will. And I'm going to post it on Twitter and tag you."

Vince would see. He'd freak out. Was it normal that my first thought was that I wasn't safe if I was tagged on Twitter?

No. It wasn't.

"I'll try on this one." I picked up one without nipple flaps.

In the dressing room, I looked like a different woman. I ran my hand over the curve in my hips the way he would and felt my nipples tighten. When I fastened the garter, I imagined Carter unfastening it, brushing his hands inside my thighs, kissing the place where the fabric met the skin.

Those lips.

Inside my thighs.

On the curves over the bra.

I swallowed hard. Turned to look at my back.

The panties played on the curve of my bottom, and the lines of the garter elongated my body. I ran a finger under a strap.

He'd do that. He'd get his fingers under there and grab it.

"Em!" Simon's voice came from the other side of the door with a jarring knock.

"Yeah?"

"Let me see."

"Hell no!" I unsnapped the bra.

"Don't be embarrassed!"

"I'm not. I'm buying it." I unhooked the garter and slipped out of the stockings.

"You like it?" He seemed very excited, and so was I. Not only did I love it, I was pretty sure Carter would too.

When I got back to the house, the 8 button on my driveway keypad was a little sticky, and it wasn't as loud and beepy as the others. When I pulled in, the gate clacked behind me, and when I stopped in front of the garage, the motion-sensor light went on just like it was supposed to. I switched my La Perla bag from my right hand to my left so I could put my code in to unlock the door.

But the light over the side door didn't work. Grey leaped up onto the back of a chair and watched me from the window.

I was sure I'd left her outside.

She tapped the window with her paw as if trying to tell me something very important in cat language. I peered in the window. The house seemed dark and empty.

Grey arched her back, raising her hackles at me. Her mouth opened in what I knew was a hiss.

CHAPTER 43

CARTER

"The bus? You're on the bus?" I repeated Emily's words, then my own.

We were mostly done with dinner. Phin had gloated over a second-place finish for a solid hour and a half, while Mom kept looking at the clock as if that would keep her from being late for her date. I usually didn't answer the phone when we were sitting at the table, but I checked the screen on the pretense of clearing the dishes, and it was Emily.

"It seemed like the safest thing to do under the circumstances."

The first thing she'd told me when I answered was that she was fine, but she thought Vince could be in the house.

"If I got in the car, he could jump out, and I'm just faster on my feet. But then he could chase me down the block, so I got on the bus."

"Where are you now?" I stared into the sink, which was stacked with lunch's dishes because Mom never emptied the damned dishwasher.

"I don't want him to hurt Grey."

"Where are you?"

"Fairfax and Olympic."

"You took the bus *west*?"

"That's the side of the street I was on."

I heard the bus's bells ding from the phone. She was only getting farther away.

"Get off," I said. "There's a coffee shop on the corner. Wait for me."

"Can someone go check on the cat?"

I sighed. The cat was my fault.

"Yes. I'll have someone check on the cat."

"Thank you." Her voice softened with real gratitude, and inside, past all my disruption and aggravation, in the space where I held the things that gave me peace—Phin, Mom, my responsibilities at home—I felt a deep whir of gladness.

I was serving her, and it made me happy.

I hung up the phone.

"Ma, can you stay here for another hour?"

She had her fingers wrapped around the condiment bottles, ready to put them away.

"An hour? No. I have fifteen minutes."

"I need to do something."

"It's a third date."

Mom didn't have many third dates. Most of the guys she dated got cut loose after date two. Even Phin seemed impressed.

"Wow, Gram. Good going."

"She doesn't need encouragement from the peanut gallery."

"As a matter of fact, I could use some."

I took the dishes away. "Just go late."

"I could have him meet me here." Her offer was meant to be rejected, so I fell right into it.

"No!" I put the dishes on the counter with a clatter that almost broke them. "Phin, put your shoes on. You're coming with me."

"But the family tree—"

"Just do it!"

His body went boneless, and he dragged his feet out the door.

"What's the problem?" Mom slapped the condiments on the shelf.

"He needs to do what I tell him the first time."

"No, I mean he's thirteen. You can leave him in the house for an hour."

"No."

"What's he going to do? Sneak in an extra hour of video games?"

"It's not him."

"What's the worst that can happen?"

"Ask his mother."

I snarled with a finger pointed and a shoulders-forward posture. I regretted it all immediately. I regretted my tone, threatening her with the worst, forcing her to remember something she didn't want to, pulling out the trump card to end an argument. All of it.

She left before I could apologize, stomping upstairs for a date I figured I'd already gone a long way toward ruining.

Phin was at the front door, poking at his phone with his neck bent at the same angles as his friends. They huddled in groups with their heads down like they were praying.

"Put that thing down." I snapped up my keys.

CHAPTER 44

EMILY

I sat down with my tea and took out my phone. I considered texting Darlene and telling her what happened, but she'd be either mad or worried. Simon wouldn't want to talk about anything serious, and I didn't want to avoid the topic either.

"Emily?"

I looked up from my phone. It was Peter of the crowbarred nose. He held a big cup of something in either hand. He'd changed his glasses to the rimless kind and kept his facial hair in a nice scruff. I remembered his crooked smile and his long neck. His affable sense of humor and general inoffensiveness.

I'd been looking for that in a guy, because it was the exact opposite of what I'd just run away from. Those traits made him a perfect victim too.

"Hey, Peter. How are you?"

He shrugged. "Good!"

A girl about my height with a pink pixie cut and a nose ring sidled up to him, looping her hand in his elbow. She had a One Eyed Jack tattooed on her neck and more tattoos peeking from under her sleeves.

"Hey. I'm Roxie."

"I'm Emily." I held out my hand, and we shook.

"*The* Emily?" An eyelid lowered a notch.

What had he said? Was she going to punch me in the face or just make rude comments?

"Yes." Peter handed her the coffee in his right hand. I felt as if I'd walked into the room in the middle of a conversation about me. "And it wasn't her fault. So—"

"Did you get rid of that creep yet?" Roxie asked.

I sighed. "Yes, but he's tenacious."

"Bummer. Nice bag." She indicated my La Perla bag and winked. I didn't know where she was coming from or what she wanted, but I was exhausted already. "I hear you're a dancer?"

"Choreogr—"

"Me too!" Now I knew what she wanted. Hollywood was a magnet for entertainers of all stripes, and though struggling actors and musicians were most commonly encountered, dancers came to make it too.

"You ever start singing again?" Peter asked. Had he even known about that? Hadn't I been too bruised to tell him I loved to sing? Maybe not. Maybe at the first sign of comfort it had burst out of me.

"No." I waved and uttered a nervous laugh. I was ashamed. He'd gotten his nose broken, tried to stay with me in spite of it, and when I stopped returning his calls, he'd moved on. My feet had remained stuck in wet cement, and every month that went by, it got harder to move. "I'm glad . . ." I stopped, reworded. He didn't need to know I was happy he moved on. "Your nose healed perfectly."

"I tell that story all the time."

"That's how he got the job at Paramount." Roxie gleamed. "Charmed them all with his busted nose story."

My phone dinged and vibrated on the table.

"Excuse me." I picked it up. Darlene. "I have to take this."

"Nice seeing you." Peter took Roxie's hand and she swung it, waved to me, and whirled out as if Fairfax Avenue were a suburb of heaven.

"Are you all right?" she asked before I'd uttered a syllable of greeting.

"I'm fine. I was going to tell you, but . . ."

"But you were afraid I'd go crazy?" I couldn't hear anything in the background on her side. She wasn't out, but she couldn't be in or there would be music playing.

"Something like that. I called Carter. He's picking me up."

"How do you think I found out, dork?" She didn't sound angry or worried for a change. "You're in good hands."

"What about you?"

"I'm in good hands too. I sent Bart to your house. If there's nothing left in the fridge, you can send him the grocery bill."

The La Perla bag was at my feet. I'd been worried Vince would catch me and see it. I was afraid he'd know I was going to wear lingerie for another man and it would make him mad.

"I'm tired of living like this."

"I know, sister."

"Sometimes I think I should just rip all the cameras off the house. Let him come. Just deal with it."

"No, no . . ."

"I'm not living. Not really."

"No, you're not. But you gotta hang tight."

There was no parking in front of the coffee shop, so when I saw the black Audi pull to a stop in the red zone, I gathered my things.

"Carter's here."

"Call me tomorrow."

I was about to hang up but stopped.

"Darlene?"

"Yeah?"

Putting my back against the door, I burst into the noise and hum of Fairfax at night.

"Thank you for everything."

"Get out of here, crazy." She hung up.

Phin got out of the passenger side.

"Hey," I said.

"Hi." He opened the back door with a wave, looking sullen.

"Phin!" Carter leaned across the center console. "What do you do when a lady gets in the car?"

"I don't know, Dad! Why don't *you* do it?"

Despite the protest, Phin stood by the front door and offered me his hand like a gentleman. I took it, trying to make his job easier. I slid into the front, and Phin closed the door behind me.

He got into the back, exuding palpable hormonal rage.

Carter pulled away from the curb.

"The reason I didn't do it—" Carter started, but Phin interrupted. "It's fine."

Phin's "fine" was anything but.

"Is because I didn't want to get out into traffic. And you need practice. It needs to be a habit."

"Whatever."

Carter glanced at his son in the rearview, then at me.

"Sorry," Phin grumbled in my direction.

"Can I tell you guys something? Since you're not going to talk to each other?"

"Sure." Phin kept his hands in his lap and his eyes out the window. Carter nodded.

"My parents were 'enlightened.' They're both lawyers. Busy lawyers and really ambitious people. They thought really hard about parenting before they did it. They read books about how to do it right. I had organic food until I left the house. I don't think I had a toxin in my body. I had all the best developmental toys. They didn't buy me any pink clothes or princess stuff until I begged, because they didn't want to perpetuate the myth of weak femininity."

I checked Phin to see if he was paying attention, and he was. Carter was driving and typically impossible to read.

"But otherwise, I ran the show. I decided what I wanted to eat. I decided when I wanted to go to bed. They didn't want to impose their will on me or make me do anything that was even a little unpleasant. Everything I did was perfect and special. And if you think they're weird, it wasn't just them. It was everyone in my school and all my friends."

"Yeah," Phin objected. "That's how it is for everyone but me."

"Kid . . ." Carter started to speak, but I squeezed his thigh hard.

"Except Darlene," I said. "She had strict parents. She wasn't in my school, but I became her friend because when I stayed at her house, it was like I could breathe. They had rules, and I knew what I had to do to get it right. Really right. Not fake right. Not like . . . *everything you do is special and precious.* I had to work at it. My parents complained about Darlene's parents all the time, but I craved *their* approval."

I turned fully to Phin, because if I was going to butt my ass in, I was going to completely butt in.

"My point is, everything in my life since then is me looking for order and sense and discipline. I've made a lot of bad choices because of it. And I love my parents, but I wish they were more like your dad. I bet a lot of bad stuff wouldn't have happened if I'd had internal discipline and went out looking for freedom in life. But it was the opposite."

I sat straight and folded my hands around my bag.

"I'm sorry. That was probably out of line. I don't know you guys that well, but that was my experience, and I'm sticking to it."

Carter turned north on Olympic in silence. I had no idea if I'd done more damage than good. Parenting was so personal, and I had zero experience with it.

Carter reached for my hand and squeezed it right before he pulled into his driveway.

I didn't realize I thought I'd upset him until the moment I realized I hadn't, and my relief was as surprising as it was welcome.

CHAPTER 45

CARTER

I called Bart as soon as we got back to my house. I'd left Phin with his homework and Emily in the kitchen making coffee.

"The house is clear now," Bart said. "But she was right. He was here. Her bedsheets are shredded."

"I don't want her to see that."

"We can change them when LAPD leaves."

"How did he get in?"

"He tried busting the keypad then climbed the fence. His mug's on the recorder. I think he ate a hard-boiled egg. There're shells on the counter. Unless she left them."

"Yeah, no." Emily wasn't a slob. "Can you hang out there until I get back to you?"

"Sure."

Letting a woman into my life was a problem I was figuring out slowly but surely, but now that everyone was in the same house, my house, I had an intractable problem. I never wanted to choose between my son and a woman. That possibility was always the fear. Now, here I was in the exact situation I was trying to avoid.

"Thanks, Bart."

I couldn't bring her back to her house with a broken security system and an active stalker. I couldn't stay with her. I couldn't bring Phin.

She stood at the sink, filling the teapot. I could see the shape of her shoulder blades through her shirt, and her ass was a perfect heart shape in her sweatpants. I got right behind her and put a hand on each cheek. I couldn't help it. They fit over them perfectly. She was so tiny and tight.

"Carter," she whispered sharply, "Phin's right upstairs."

I slid my hands around her waist. "What do you have in that bag?"

She turned, the full teapot between us. I pressed her against the counter.

"You'll see."

"When?"

"I don't even know where I'm sleeping tonight."

I pushed off the counter. Yeah, there was that.

"Bart checked out your house. It's secure for now, but he was there."

She turned to the stove. In the split second I could see her face, I saw it fall into a kind of resigned despair. She put the teapot on the burner and set the flame.

"I'm tired." She spoke to herself, the teapot, the universe. I put my hands on her shoulders, but she shrank under my touch. "I don't know how to live like this."

"I'd offer to beat the hell out of him."

"Didn't you already do that?"

"Yeah. He's stubborn."

It's one thing to feel like you're restrained from doing what you want to do to protect someone. It's another thing entirely to have done that thing and seen it fail. Having gone to the ultimate solution first, I now had to backtrack to the things that always seemed like ineffective first steps.

"I'm out of ideas." She adjusted the teapot a quarter turn.

"We can get LAPD in to investigate breaking and entering. At least we can get the order of protection renewed."

She sighed and looked at the ceiling. "Sure." She turned and looked at the floor as if she couldn't meet my eyes.

Suddenly, like a flash flood in my heart, I rebelled against her compliance. I fought her sighs and shrugs. I hated her exhaustion and her forbearance. No. Just no. She wasn't meant to live like this. She was meant to dance and laugh. She was built to be loved, not to be so emotionally beaten she forgot how to care.

"Emily."

"Yeah."

"Look at me."

She wasn't crying. Her eyes were as dry as my mouth. As if she'd borne so much and this was just another day where the rug got pulled out from under her. I held up my hands. It wasn't to hold her back or calm her down but to put the brakes on the unstoppable flow of my impulsive words.

It didn't work.

"Nothing is going to happen to you as long as I can stand on these two feet. As long as I can breathe, you're safe. You are under my protection. Let me say it again so you understand what it means when I say that. There's Phin, and there's you. You are my business. Your safety and . . . no, not just your safety. Your happiness, your comfort, your well-being . . . I'm taking the responsibility for those things off your plate. It's all on me."

She bit her lip between her teeth and looked down at the floor again. I tipped her chin so she had to look at me.

"You are under my protection."

"I can't do that to you." What was dry was now wet. Her mouth got sticky when it moved, and her eyes filled. "You have enough." She flipped her hand toward the door, and I knew she was talking about Phin. "I know why you didn't want to get involved. You can't take your eyes off him, and that's the right way. He should be your first priority."

"I can do both."

She shook her head, and I let her chin go. She brought her knuckles to her mouth as if she could grasp her sobs and throw them away.

"I don't know, Carter. It's too much. I hate being a burden. And don't say I'm not. Nothing you say is going to make that go away."

"Listen. Can you listen?"

"Sure."

"I can get you an emergency restraining order."

She pointed her left toe perpendicular to the floor. The arch of her foot curved at an extreme angle I wanted my lips to experience.

"And I guess I stay here?"

"You get to watch Phin."

"Good. I like him."

"I don't want you to worry about anything."

"I am worried. Mostly, I'm worried that you and I are supposed to be getting to know each other, and instead I'm your job."

"I love my job."

It was too soon to say anything like that, but it was true.

I kissed her before she could object or confirm, and she pushed against me. Her fingers ran through the hair on the back of my neck, and I dug my hands under the back of her shirt.

"Uh, hey?" We separated at the words and found Phin poking his head in. "I'm getting on the internet to research. Go on with whatever you were doing."

"Wait," I said as he was trying to get away. "I have to go somewhere. Emily's going to hang out with you."

"Okay." His cartoonish effort to look nonchalant made him seem completely disrupted. He ran off.

"He's a little . . ." I drifted off.

"Normal?"

"Just a little."

"Go, please. If you still need to go, just go."

I kissed her one more time and left.

CHAPTER 46

EMILY

I peeked in on Phin. He sat in front of a huge screen filled with alphabet soup, if the alphabet included all the characters in the corners of the keyboard.

Going back to the kitchen in silence, I wondered what Carter was doing in my house. There had been no way of talking him out of going back to my place.

It was never going to be over. Vince was tenacious and bored. If he had any romantic prospects, he wasn't following up. I didn't believe no woman could match me. I believed I was his muscle memory. I was his automatic fixation when he felt bad or good or bored or needy. Or maybe he obsessed over me in the in-between times.

I didn't know. I'd never know.

Could I leave? Could I just walk away? Slip into anonymity? I'd thought about it so many times and in so many ways. Everything from going back to Chicago to live near my parents to driving until I stopped in the Middle of Somewhere, USA.

My imagination never got far. Dancing for a living was a privilege given to very few, and I loved it. I was honored to do what I wanted, to live the dream of so many. Darlene was a huge part of that success, and she lived in Hollywood because that was where her business was.

My dream was coming at a price. As long as I was in Los Angeles, I was going to be a target, and as long as I was a target, I would never be free. Would never be able to have a relationship and, by extension, a husband and children.

I tried not to think about that. I usually drowned out that sorrow in dance or music. I could go to a party with Darlene or work until my feet turned to leather.

"Hey." Phin poked his head in the kitchen doorway. I was cradling a cup of tea like a handful of shiny coins.

"Hey."

He bopped in, opened the fridge, and spent way too long deciding to take out a carton of milk. He just stood there with the milk as the fridge door closed. He was an open book. Didn't have a sneaky bone in his body. I knew exactly what he was thinking.

"I know I'm not your dad, but I'm a snitch. You should use a glass."

He flopped to the cabinet as if his limbs were loosely attached. He had freckles and angular features. I could see a touch of Carter in him and another, less robust person. He poured the milk into a short glass, letting a splash land on the counter when he tipped the carton back up.

Without cleaning up or putting the carton away, he slugged the milk, ending with an *ahh*.

"Liquid gold." He poured another cup and put the carton away.

"What are you doing up there?" I handed him the kitchen rag. He looked at it, then back at me. I pointed to the splash of milk on the counter.

"I have a family tree project I need to get an A on." He took the rag.

"Ah. Sounds like fun."

He wiped the counter without cleaning up all the milk. I couldn't have done such a bad job of it if I tried.

"It's not when your father *and* your grandmother are telling you a bullshit story about your mother."

I took the rag and wiped up the spill properly. Was he allowed to say *bullshit?* Seemed unlikely.

"I doubt that."

"Yeah, well, the name they gave me isn't on any of the birth certificate records at city hall."

"Maybe she wasn't born in LA."

"Dad said she was."

"Are you supposed to be looking in the public record or taking your father's word for it?" I ran my fingers along the edges of the wet cloth.

He shrugged and went for the door. He seemed so dejected. As if he'd hit a roadblock, asked for help, and no one came to his aid.

Before he turned the corner, I spoke up. "You should look at your own birth certificate."

"Good idea," he called back, not slowing down a bit. Carter texted me just as I was folding up the dishrag.

—*How are you doing?*—

Did I want to bring up the conversation with Phin? No. I couldn't. His mother's family history wasn't my business.

—*Your son just drank half a gallon of milk. Pick up more on the way home*—

—*Wow. This relationship devolved really quickly*—

I laughed.

—*I better think quick*—

(. . .)

213

—I can't wait to see the contents of that La Perla bag on the floor—

—Appropriately sexy—

—Great—
—I'll pick up milk—

—How is my house?—

—Intact. We're going to make it safe again. Promise—

Something thumped upstairs. I pocketed the phone and went up. "Phin? You all right?"

"Yeah."

The stairwell was lined with photos. I stopped at Carter's police academy portrait. What a sexy bastard. The rest were the same three people I'd seen on the mantel: Phin, Dad, Grandma. Was Mom ever in the picture?

"I'm coming up to check on you."

"End of the hall."

I passed Carter's room and tried not to linger. I wanted to see if his pillow smelled of gunpowder, check his closet for ephemera and memories. Was that a little fifth of July coming out of the room? I stopped and took a deep breath.

"Hey," Phin said from down the hall.

"What happened?" I tore myself away from the plaid bedspread and rich russet woods. "I heard a thump."

"Fell off the ball." He indicated his room, where a huge blue yoga ball sat in front of a desk with a large-screen computer. "It happens. I'm a little clumsy."

On the screen, a set of windows was open, and inside one of the windows, text scrolled and scrolled. It didn't look like a family tree. He saw me looking and shifted in front of it.

"Whatcha doing?" I stepped forward to see the screen. I had no interest in exposing misbehavior. I was just curious.

"Running a script. It's nothing."

"Wow." I peered over his shoulder. "That looks really cool."

He brightened, then shrugged dismissively. "Just a little something."

"What's it do?"

He was so expressive with his face and body I could almost read volumes from the shape of his mouth and the way he waved his hands. His body and face contorted to say, *I shouldn't tell you, but I really want to.*

"Is it anything to do with the present on the thumb drive? I loved that."

He brightened again. This kid was jumping out of his skin.

"I'll tell you, but just tell me you know what a white hat is?"

"A white hat? It's a white hat."

"No. A white hat is a hacker who hacks for good and never steals or anything."

"Okay. And you're a white hat?"

"Totally." He tapped his head as if touching an imaginary white hat and let me pass into the room. It was covered in Legos, books, shoe boxes full of pieces of things, a soldering iron I hoped was off.

"Where's the bed?"

He rolled an office chair to me.

"No screens in the bedroom. So this is like, whatever, my work space. Okay so, I developed this to do my project and, remember, white hat." He touched his forehead again, absently as if it were automatic.

He rolled the ball back to the desk and sat on it, bouncing while I sat in the chair. The characters rolled fast inside the little window.

"What's all this?"

"This is the script running, so this is how it works. I went to the LA County Registrar and found out what their email naming convention is: first initial last name @LACR. Easy. Then I found out what department has access to birth records and then found out who's in that department. From there I can rebuild email addresses and put them with names. So then I have this other script . . ." He opened another window. "It checks social media for those people's birthdays, addresses past and present, pet names, hobbies—"

"Whoa."

"White hat." Head touch. "So then I developed this script that takes all that and creates possible passwords, then I just run an easy-peasy brute-force attack, which, oh look! Bang."

Before I could object or ask him if his dad knew what he was doing, he was on the search page for employees of the LA County Registrar, tapping keys lightning fast.

"So then it's just putting in the password, doing a search for my name, and here we are, my birth certificate, which is the *only* thing I'm here to see, white hat, since Dad says he can't find it."

The screen showed a scanned birth certificate with the seal of the state of California, county of Los Angeles.

"Huh," Phin said. "That's . . . weird."

I looked closely with him. "What?"

"That's not Dad."

He pointed to a section on the certificate.

FATHER: George Owen Whitman.

The name rang a bell, but I couldn't place it.

"You should really talk to your father."

Phin moved his finger across the screen.

MOTHER: Genevieve Tremaine Kincaid.

"Wait. Her last name is right, but . . ." He ran his finger over the baby's name. "Could someone have my same name and birthday?"

"Obviously. I think—"

I thought a lot of things. Genevieve Tremaine Kincaid had a first and middle name too specific to be ignored.

Phin bounced up and went to his closet. The sliding door was already open, revealing the disaster inside. He jumped for a box on the top shelf.

"There's an SSN associated with the birth certificate, so if I could just see mine." He managed to grab the hanging corner of a folder, and the whole top shelf tumbled down. Undaunted, he picked up the box and opened it, letting the top fall. He took out a little wallet and picked out his Social Security card. He put it between his teeth while he got back on the big blue yoga ball.

His body language said he was very sure he was only checking the obvious before moving on.

"Huh," he said, then whipped around to me. "Sometimes with ADHD I don't pay attention to details and I miss things, so can you check this?" He tapped the screen where the associated SSN was and handed me the card.

I checked. They were the same.

"You really should talk to your dad about this."

"Sure."

New window.

Google.

Genevieve Tremaine Kincaid.

Nothing much. But he scrolled down, and results with Kincaid below it appeared.

The screen flooded with images of a beautiful woman who, now that I could see them side by side, looked as much like Phin as Carter did. Same coloring. Same nose. Same almond-shaped eyes. Her full, real last name must have been known and not known at the same time. You'd find it if you looked it up, but eleven years later, who was looking?

Phin clicked on one picture of her where she was smiling, sweet and approachable. Above the picture was a bold headline with the word *murdered* in it.

"If this is my mother . . ."

"You should talk to your father."

I think he heard me the third time, but I couldn't be sure. He didn't make a move when the stairs creaked.

Carter, still in his coat, carrying a milk carton–shaped shopping bag, turned from the stairs into the hall. From the end, he could see the computer screen.

I waved. When he saw what his son was looking at, he dropped the bag.

"Phin?" I said softly.

I was barely finished with the last syllable when Carter leaped into the room, stepping on Legos and open notebooks, crushing a shoe box, reaching behind a chair and snapping the switch on the power strip.

The room went dark.

"Go to bed."

"I haven't finished my project."

"A D isn't going to kill you. Go to bed."

"Who is Genevieve Kincaid? Is she my mother?"

"Go to bed!"

"I want to know!"

"I want a minute of peace and I want you to clean this room, but we don't always get what we want. Now go to bed!"

Phin stormed into the hall, grabbed one of the doorknobs while still moving forward, opened the door with the force of the torque, spun, and—

"Don't you slam that—"

—slammed the door so hard the walls shook.

Carter went to the hall, paused in front of his son's door. I wanted to tell him not to go in, but this was bigger than I was, bigger than whatever Carter and I had developed in the short time we'd known each other. He passed the door, picked up the milk, and went downstairs.

I wanted to go home. Whatever was going on, this family needed space. I felt like an intruder in something deeply pivotal and personal.

I hustled down the stairs and found Carter in the kitchen, opening the carton of milk.

"I can stay at Darlene's."

"Yeah. I don't think so." He slugged right from the container and wiped his mouth with his sleeve. I sat on the edge of the nook.

"I can stay in a hotel?"

He put the milk away and stuck his head in the refrigerator.

"I'm not trying to speak ill of the dead or anything, but his mother was a fucking pain in my ass." He came up with plastic packages, kicked the door shut, and dumped cold cuts on the nook. "From the time we were kids."

Plates. Knives. Napkins. Little cutting board. All on the nook. He stood at the end of it. Had she been a childhood sweetheart? Had they married, shared a name, lived happily until she cheated on him with George Owen Whitman?

I stayed silent. He was deep in thought as he put two pieces of bread on each of two plates.

"She dropped her clothes all over the house. She always left the front closet door open. Always. When Dad got on her about it, she blamed me, and I had to get up and close it." He held a yellow jar. "Mustard?"

"Yes."

He spread Dijon on each stack of bread.

"I was home in the house alone from the time I was seven because *she* had to go to auditions and *she* had to be on set. That was why Dad left. Mom was more interested in Genny's career than anything in this family." He cracked open a package of turkey. "My sister was smart, but it messed with her head. I was screwed up, but she was worse. Way worse." He let a slice of meat hover over the second sandwich.

"Turkey's fine."

He dropped it onto the bread, piling it deli-style. I hadn't put together what was going on, but it wasn't water under the bridge for him. Whatever had happened had blocked up the river and drowned the valley. I didn't want to sate a curiosity; I wanted to know what he needed from me.

"You're judging me," he said.

"I still don't know what you're talking about."

"Lettuce and tomato?"

"Whatever you're having is fine."

He sliced the tomato. "My sister and her ex were slaughtered like animals. She made me crazy, but she didn't deserve it. Nobody deserves that. Her son"—he jerked the knife upward, where Phin was sulking in his room—"saw the whole thing."

I put my hand over my mouth when it clicked into place.

"Oh my God. I'm so sorry."

"He was four and a half. He doesn't remember it. Sometimes with ADHD, memories don't stick, but no one knows if he forgot because his brain's made of Teflon or because the experience was traumatic. I don't want to find out. I never wanted him to see the crime-scene photos, but they're all over the internet. I never wanted him to know who his mother was because he'd find them and remember. We took Genevieve's money and fought the press to keep his name buried. I got into security so I could be more flexible and take care of him. We bought this house under a new name and made up stories he could tell himself until he had distant memories of a pretty lady." He sliced the two sandwiches into rectangular halves. "She was beautiful, my sister. Really beautiful."

"I didn't know." I took his hand. He was shaking. "I would have stopped him, but looking for his birth certificate . . . it didn't seem like a big deal."

"It's not your job to protect him." He pushed a plate to me and sat across the nook. "It's mine. *Was* mine. Now he knows I lied." He looked me in the eyes as if he expected to find an answer there. "How am I supposed to protect him now?"

I didn't know what to say. I didn't even know how to keep a cat safe. I couldn't tell him what to do or offer a word of advice, but he needed me. I was here, and he needed me.

I went to his side of the nook, put my knee on the bench, and took his face in my hands. This strong, stable man looked about ready to break. My heart twisted. I shouldn't have been in the house when this went down, but there I was, and maybe it was for the best.

"Can you talk to him?" I asked.

"No."

"Really?"

He coiled his fingers around my wrists and pulled them off his face.

"I'm glad you're here."

I started to object, but he kissed my wrists, then my lips. He wrapped his arms around me, and we held each other until another thump came from upstairs.

CHAPTER 47

CARTER

He was under his bed, and really, who could blame him? I'd be under my bed too. I shut the door behind me and sat on the floor. It was cleaner in here than his workroom, but I still had to move a couple of books and a wool cap out of the way.

"Hey. How are you under there?"

"I don't want to talk about it." His disembodied voice came clearly from under the bed. He'd pushed art supplies and a box of clothes he'd outgrown from under it.

"Okay."

"The only way I'm getting an A on this project is if I make stuff up. So either I can go all in and say my mother is Diana Prince from Amazonia and she was sculpted from clay by Queen Hippolyta, or I can go with plausible deniability."

"Is that the same as lying?"

"We talked about verisimilitude in humanities."

"I have no idea what that means."

"It means truthy. Like truthiness. Just that. A truthy tree. I just need an A, and that means I just need truthiness and for you to sign it."

It sounded a lot like lying, but I'd put him in a terrible spot. There was no way he could digest what he'd just learned and get an A on his family tree project at the same time.

Not that it mattered. What I observed as a cop is that people who experience trauma will get stuck on what they were doing right before the event. A woman attacked on the way to the grocery store will worry about how the attack is keeping her fridge empty.

"Here's what you need to do. Keep the project the way it is. It's mostly true anyway. Or it's the truth as you've known it."

He didn't say anything for a long time. I lay on the floor with my cheek to the rug. He was facing me, the light from his watch shining on his tear-streaked face. He looked like a toddler again with smooth skin and rounded features, crying over a cookie or a missed nap. When I first took him in, I thought he'd always be that small, that easy to guard. I never planned for the inevitable. Mom told me it would happen. My nephew would get older and wiser, the march of information would pass, and he'd see what I'd hidden from him.

"I can't figure it out. She had the name Kincaid before you were married? Or together? Is that a coincidence? And who was that George guy?"

"Genevieve was my sister. George was your biological father."

I never doubted my decision to wipe his first years clean until he looked at me from under the bed with his cheek squished against the floor and an Obi-Wan Kenobi above his head. I wanted to say I was sorry, but I wasn't. Not really. I was uncomfortable and sympathetic, but given the choice, I would have done the same thing. I just would have done it better.

"I wanted to protect you."

"From what?"

It was a good question. The only question. But the answer would hurt him the most. If I told him he'd been there and I didn't want him to remember, would that trigger the memories?

I took three seconds to think about it, but Phin didn't have time for that. He went right to the next thing.

"Is the guy coming? The one who . . . did it?"

"No. He killed himself."

"Does he have any kids? Is his mom mad? I don't want them to find us."

"Phin . . ."

"I'm scared."

"You don't have to be."

"I don't care about the project. I don't want to hand it in tomorrow. What if someone sees through it? What if they know? They'll come and find us. Grandma's here too, and if someone kills her, then, oh . . ."

He broke down into a fugue of panic.

I reached for him. His eyes were huge, just like his mother's.

"The man who killed your mother had a nice family. They don't want to hurt you. They feel very sorry about what he did. You are safe."

"Then why did you want to protect me? From what?"

"Did anything you saw jog a memory?" I didn't want to ask because I was afraid of the answer, but if he remembered, he'd need help coping.

"No."

He was telling the truth. I knew him at least that well.

"I'm protecting you from your memories. There were things . . ." How far was I going to go? Was I going to tell him everything? "I don't want you to remember the day you lost your mother."

"But maybe I want to remember her."

"You saw some pictures on the computer. Did you recognize her?"

"She's on the show with the purple house."

"I have a box of things from her. We can talk, and you can see if you remember the good things."

"What's in it?"

I hadn't looked at it since the day Phin called me Dad and I didn't correct him. A month after the murder of his biological parents, he'd struggled to figure it out by placing the mantle of "father" on me, and I took it. His father hadn't been around much, and I'd played that role as long as he could remember.

"Some pictures. A bracelet. An Emmy."

"She won an Emmy?"

"Yeah. Her residual checks pay for your school."

That held no meaning for him. I was trying to show him how she was still in his life, taking care of him, but I'd already tried to wipe her clean. Bringing her back would take more effort.

"So you're really my uncle?"

The term felt like a slap in the face. I'd been thinking of him as my son for so long, I'd forgotten he wasn't. More than forgotten. This wasn't a slip of the mind; it was a change of heart. Uncles were nice, but the term didn't fit me and Phin.

"The minute you came into my life, you were mine. I want you to know that. When you were a baby, your dad walked away from your mom. I changed your diapers and kissed your feet, same as any father. When your mother and father died, you became mine. I've never thought of you as anything less than my son. So I don't care how the blood flows. You're everything I ever wanted in a little boy, and now that you're almost a man, I'm as proud of you as any father. That's the end of it. You're my son. I won't take anything less."

He still fit under the bed, and his eyes were as big and green as a child's, but he was becoming a man. The wonder drained out of him every day. No matter what his hormones did, he was almost grown. I couldn't tell him what to think.

"If you don't want to call me Dad anymore, I understand. But you can't call me Uncle Carter."

His nod was horizontal against the carpet.

"Maybe you can do what Grandma thinks everyone should do. Call me by my first name."

The hurt of my own words cut deep. My mother wanted to deny her age. I was giving Phin the option of denying my relationship with him. It was his choice, and he had the power to wound me.

He untucked his hand and held his fist out to me. I bumped it, then laid my hand over his. He closed his eyes. I thought he was thinking, but his back rose and fell slowly. He'd fallen asleep, as he often did when he was overwhelmed.

I got up and went downstairs. Emily was asleep on the couch. I put a blanket over her, tucking it around the edges, making sure it covered her beat-up dancer's toes.

I was sure everything was ruined. Whatever she and I had almost been to each other, it was over. Who would want to be with me? A man who lied to a child. Stole him away from his mother's memory. Bad enough I needed Phin's forgiveness. What would she think of my life and lies?

With Phin coming to know the truth and Emily sleeping on my sofa, I knew my life had taken a hard pivot. I wished I knew which direction it had turned.

CHAPTER 48

EMILY

Talking.

Banging.

Hissing pipes in the walls and whooshing traffic just outside the window.

The *click* of the stove before the gas came through the burner and the clatter of plates.

Aching back and chilly feet.

Mouth like a slab of yuck had settled between tongue and palate.

I usually woke to silence or the first threads of my radio alarm. Light through the drapes in the warmer months.

I never woke to the sounds of other people. I stayed still on the couch, shifting only to ease my back, and listened to Phin mumble, Carter bark orders, Brenda in the bathroom upstairs, running the plumbing.

Moving would have disrupted it. Opening my eyes would have shattered my dream-state appreciation of the irregular beat of activity. I didn't want to observe it. I wanted my ears and body to be filled with it.

Half-in, half-out of consciousness, I didn't have the self-awareness to ask why I enjoyed the presence of other people so much. Why I felt comfortable instead of awkward. I just lived in it like another ingredient in a nourishing soup.

The hard *click* of an open door woke me fully.

"Shh," Carter whispered. "You'll wake her."

"I'm up," I said, opening my eyes. Phin stood at the front door with a huge pack, and behind him, his dad stood, preshower, in jeans and a light jacket. I remembered what I'd learned about him last night, but seeing them together, all I saw was a resemblance.

"Sorry," Phin said, cringing.

"You're going to school?" In half sleep, I had no filter.

"He insisted," Carter said defensively, as if he would have kept him home after the night before and needed me to know what a gentle dad he could be.

"Have a good day, then."

"I'm dropping him at the bus stop." Carter looked at his watch. "Five minutes."

Phin opened the screen door, stopped himself, and addressed me. "Sorry about last night."

"Why?" I rubbed the gunk out of my right eye.

"That was a little intense." Phin rolled his eyes at himself, making light of what he'd been through.

"But I learned how to hack the LA County Registrar or whatever," I said. "Totally worth it."

He laughed, agreed, and walked out with his dad. Uncle. Both.

I watched them through the window. Carter looked back at me as he got into the car, as if he knew I was there. I waved. He winked.

Brenda padded down the stairs in yoga pants and a tank top. She was a beautiful woman with her hair up in a twist and no makeup. That must have been where Genevieve got it.

"I was hoping you were the lump on the couch I saw last night. Did he make coffee?"

"I don't know. What time is it?"

228

"Six thirty." She disappeared into the kitchen, and I threw myself off the couch, untangling my legs from the blanket as if it were attacking me.

I folded it, laid it on the back of the couch, and went into the kitchen. Brenda put a cup in my hand before I had a chance to tell her I was calling a cab so I could make it to work by eight.

"Thank you for being here," Brenda said. "Last night was a big deal."

"I felt like an intruder."

She shook her head. "Trust me. You were a nice buffer. I knew the shit was going to hit the fan someday. I figured I'd be the one with the stained shirt."

"Do you think he'll be all right? Phin, I mean."

"I do." She picked up the pint of half-and-half and gave it a shake to see how much was in there. "He's got more advantages than most kids but enough disadvantages to screw him." She dropped half-and-half into her coffee. "My daughter had everything. Didn't do her much good."

"I'm sorry about what happened to her."

"Yeah. So was half of Hollywood. What a circus. I lost a child. A piece of my heart. And they turned it into a spectacle." She shook her head slowly and sipped her coffee. "Thank God for Carter. He's going to be the one to get Phin through."

As if summoned by his name, the front door opened and Carter called out, "Emily? You still here?"

"In the kitchen!"

He appeared like a white knight, unshaven, unshowered, ready to do battle for the people he loved. He exuded manliness and safety, like a king swearing to protect the realm.

It was a beautiful thing and yet, troubling. I didn't know where my place was in his kingdom, or if I wanted a place in it at all.

"Call time is eight," I said. "Are you on the schedule today?"

"Yeah. We gotta roll." He took my cup, placed it on the counter, kissed his mother on the cheek, and guided me to the door.

"I don't know about you, but I have to shower," I said as he opened the car door for me.

"You can at your place." He closed the door at the end of his sentence.

"We're never going to make it," I protested when he got in.

"Never say never."

He backed out onto the street before I could object. I had plenty to say. Traffic. My house was in the opposite direction. Traffic. I hadn't put my day bag together. And also . . . LA basin traffic.

But none of it mattered. By the first left onto 4th Street, Carter was a man on a mission. Five miles over the speed limit, changing lanes safely but frequently, intuiting where the traffic was and whipping turns to avoid it, he had me at my front door in six minutes. The car was barely at a complete stop when he got out and opened my door.

The emergency restraining order was taped to my front gate.

I rushed through the gate, then into my house. Carter closed the door behind him and slipped my bag off my shoulders.

"I can—"

He planted a kiss on my lips, opening my mouth with his tongue, which tasted of minty toothpaste. I pushed him away.

"I haven't brushed my teeth."

He didn't say a word, just pulled my shirt over my head and threw it to the side. His eyes blazed with intention. He looked like a man with a job to do and a hot desire to get it done. His hands curved around my rib cage and caught the edge of my bra, pulling it over my head. My nipples were stone hard for him, and he looked at them for no more than a second before getting under my waistband and pulling down, underpants and all.

I gasped. "Carter. Wait."

"Shower. Now."

Right.

Shower.

I stepped out of my pants legs and into my bedroom, passing the kitchen where Grey sat by her empty bowl.

"Give me a minute," I said as I made my way to the bathroom, turning on the water. I stood half-in, half-out of the shower with my hand under the stream, waiting for it to heat up. I didn't think we were going to get to work on time, but I could play along.

The water had just turned hot when Carter entered, naked, all hard muscle and taut skin. He was magnificent. A full-color statue of David, walking into the bathroom, shutting the door even as he moved in my direction with his hands out, pushing me onto the wet tiles and planting his mouth on mine for the second time.

I tried to speak but couldn't work around his tongue, and his touch sucked all the air out of me. My body said what my mouth couldn't, pushing into him, seeking his erection. I lifted a leg, and he put it at his waist so I could meet him, and the second his hardness touched my softness, an electrical buzz vibrated the length of my spine and stung my throat into a groan.

Yeah. We were going to be late.

He ran his mouth over my cheek and down my neck.

"Say you still want me," he said.

"I'm naked in the shower with you."

"After last night. What do I have to do to prove myself?"

"Nothing, I—"

"Just tell me."

"Carter. You did your best for him. You did what you thought was right." I dug my nails into his skin as if that would wake him up, but his eyelids only fluttered half-closed, the dark lashes stuck together, water dripping off them onto his cheeks like tears. "You did what *was* right."

"I can't bear that I found you at the same time as this happened. You weren't supposed to come in the middle of a storm. You were supposed to walk into my life when all the storms were gone."

"What good would that be?"

I reached down between us and found his erection. "Let's get this ready."

We got the condom on. He leaned into me, sucking air through his teeth when the head went in. I wrapped both legs around him, and he put his hands on my ass to hold me up.

He kissed me once, then drove deep into me. We stayed joined for a second, still and silent, letting the water hit us, and slowly he rotated his hips, forcing pleasure out of me. He had me with my shoulders against the wall, up in his strong arms, moving my tiny frame however he wanted.

I let go in his arms, giving him control over our motions, and every stroke brought me closer. He bit his bottom lip, holding back.

I touched my clit, which was all I needed to explode around him. I arched and wiggled with pleasure, but he held me tight. When he came, he held me more firmly, three feet off the floor and as safe as I'd ever been.

CHAPTER 49

EMILY

I left Grey enough food for two meals. I had no idea if that would work, but I didn't have an extra minute to think about it. We barely made it to work on time. A minor miracle that was the result of Carter's uncanny ability to make the right turns on the right streets at the right speed. He had to slow down at the turn-in. A line of paparazzi waited behind sawhorses at the parking lot entrance. Carlos waved us through. I slid down my seat so they wouldn't photograph me. I was no one. A nonentity. But my picture in a public place could set off Vince.

"They found us," I said.

"They always do." He pulled into the lot and into a spot, kissing me quickly when the car was in park.

"Do you think Phin's going to be all right?" I asked. "At school?"

"I hope so. But the staff members are like hawks over there. If the kid has a bad day, they notice."

"Do you think you'll work Vegas after this?" I said hopefully and, I admit, selfishly. "The showers in the Bellagio are really nice, but maybe next time."

"I don't know. Let me see."

He squeezed my hand, and I didn't feel so alone. Carter and I each had problems, and together we could solve them.

We went into the building. He disappeared into the corners to watch everything.

I kicked off my shoes, dropped my bag, and peeled off my hoodie, jumping into the dance studio where everyone waited in their lines, chatting.

"All right!" I held up my arms and shook my hands. It took a few seconds for everyone to quiet down. Darlene came in at a leisurely pace and stood behind me. "We have five days until the show! Are you ready?"

Murmurs. A distinct lack of enthusiasm.

"If you guys could see what you've done from up here, you'd know you were ready as surely as I do. We're going to run it through today and in costume tomorrow. By then, I promise you'll be raring to go. Got it?"

Some claps.

Darlene called from behind me. "Bitches! Are you serious? You are the best team I have ever, and I mean *ever*, worked with. This right here is going to be the only ticket in town. We're going to be bigger than Michael Jackson. Bigger than Beyoncé. Right now, Jesus Christ himself is clearing a seat at his right hand. They're going to talk about this show with their grandchildren, and those kids are going to be in awe. Who hears me?"

She held up her arm, pointing to the sky.

"I hear you!" I shouted, holding up my finger.

"Who hears me?"

"I hear you!" Simon pointed.

"Who the fuck hears me?"

She had to ask only twice more before the entire troupe was shouting and pointing at the ceiling.

"Let's run this bitch through!" Darlene clapped, and we got to work.

Because my knee wouldn't tolerate daily shows, I wasn't going to be onstage. I was the watcher. The checker. The improver. It was my job to make sure everyone was where he or she belonged and send everyone out into the world prepared.

By lunch, I was sure they were more than prepared. They were ready to kill it.

Carlos found me in the lunch line. "This says you're staying at the Bellagio." He pointed to his clipboard.

"Yes?"

"Everyone else is at the MGM."

"I always stay separate. It's safer." Word inevitably got out about where the dancers, musicians, and staff stayed. If I wanted Vince to find me, I'd stay with them. Carlos had never questioned it before. I didn't know what was supposed to be different this time.

"You're a principal this time. I need to book a room for one of my guys."

Hopefully, one of his guys was going to be staying in my bed, but I couldn't say that.

"Keep me at the Bellagio, but move my room if you have to," I said. "Sorry I didn't let you know."

He gave me half a salute and marked something on his clipboard before moving to the next problem.

I had lunch with my team and didn't notice Carter was missing until the afternoon break. He wasn't in his usual corner, in the hall, or hanging around Bart and Fabian.

"Fabe?"

"Yeah?"

"Have you seen Carter?"

"Dude. He just quit."

I tried not to look stunned. Acting surprised was only going to make me look like an outsider. I must have failed, because Fabian put his hands up as if to say, *It wasn't my fault, so don't look at me.*

"I have no clue," he added. "I'll ask him after the shift."

"Thanks."

"Maybe he got a better offer."

"Yeah. Probably."

With a minute left in break, I reached into the bottom of my gym bag for the phone. I was worried about him. The previous night had been harder than either Phin or Carter had admitted.

I found a text from him sitting in my notifications.

—Phin needed me—

CHAPTER 50

CARTER

I was not like any of the other parents at Phin's school. I expected more than they did. I had rules and clear boundaries. I didn't pretend Phin was my friend, and I didn't call him "buddy." I didn't lose too much sleep over the emotional bumps and twists of the early teens.

Until I got a call the morning after Phin found out who his mother was.

They said he was crying uncontrollably and refusing to talk about the reason for the tears.

I felt guilty for sending him to school, and that was only the most recent of a long list of things I could have done better. I didn't know when it would be too much. When the list would get so long it would strangle him. I'd burdened myself with lies, and now he was burdened with the truth.

When I got to the office, it was worse than I'd been told. Cora, the assistant head of the school, looked up from her desk, pressed her lips together, and handed me a box of tissues. Phin was on the couch, curled into a fetal position, facing the backrest. His shoulders shook.

Cora spoke softly and clearly. "He found out something about his mother, apparently? He was presenting his project and said it was all a lie."

I sat on the edge of the couch and stroked his hair.

"What was a lie?" she asked in a flat voice.

"Specifically," I said, "the project and his life."

Phin's eyes were closed, and his skin was clammy and wet with tears. When I touched him, he didn't react.

She stood up. "Let's let him rest."

We went onto a bank of couches outside her office. I was sure he was getting kicked out. The hippy-dippy school actually had very strict rules about lying and keeping your shit together. Without cooperation, the whole system fell apart.

Phin's project was a lie, and who knew what crazy thing he'd said when presenting it? I'd seen kids get kicked out for less.

Maybe a more structured education was what he needed anyway. Except he loved his school, and taking him out would hurt and disrupt him. As Cora indicated one of the sofas, I decided I was more concerned about Phin's stability than what he'd said to the class.

"He had a rough night," I said as I sat, "but he wanted to come today and hand in the project, which I know was supposed to be based on fact. We understand his grade will reflect that it's not."

"We're not concerned with his grade."

"He might . . ." I couldn't finish. He might fail. He might not be in the rest of the week or month. He might need more attention than you think. "I can't guarantee he'll finish the semester."

"Mr. Kincaid, is there something on your mind?"

"He loves it here."

"And we love having him. We're not in the business of kicking kids out when they're having a hard time. What happened today was normal under the circumstances."

"What happened? What did he say?"

"That his mother was Genevieve Tremaine, and his dad is his uncle."

I rubbed my eyes hard enough to see stars. "He didn't know," I said from behind my hands. I took them away so I could look at her. "I didn't want him to. But now he does, and he's not good at secrets."

"We're trying to make sure the class is discreet. We've spoken to them about it."

It all came to me. Cora exuded calm and competence, but asking anyone to keep such a juicy story secret was a waste of time. I was out of my mind thinking he could stay at the same school. There was no way that was going to turn out well.

"They're in seventh grade." I didn't have to do more than state the simple fact. She nodded. They'd tell their parents, who included a TV executive, a studio lawyer, and an actor in $100 million tentpole movies. Who all knew who else. The murder would be rehashed in the *Hollywood Reporter* in forty-eight hours or less. It would filter to the internet sites, where Phin would see it even if I threw the router in the trash where it belonged.

"I've spent the past eleven years protecting him from what happened to his mother. You don't have to like how I did it, but that was my motivation. Now there's no way to keep him from it."

"He was going to find out eventually," she said. "The community here can help him deal with it, but I don't think we can pretend it didn't happen."

"It's one thing for him to know. I didn't want the world to know."

She nodded, hands folded in front of her. I didn't know if she was judging me or how difficult it was to hide it. Fortunately, I didn't care what she thought of me. I cared only about my son.

My nephew. Whatever. My responsibility.

I stood and held out my hand. "Thank you for speaking with me. I'm going to take him home."

"Let us know how it's going."

I went back into her office. Phin hadn't moved. I picked him up. He was so skinny I could carry him as if he were a baby again, one arm behind his knees and another at his shoulders. He started crying when I moved him. His face was beet red and swollen. I backed through the school doors to get into the parking lot. The security guard stood up when I came through. His name was Marco, and he and Phin always exchanged a few words of greeting when he passed.

"He all right?"

"Yeah." I held him closer. I didn't want anyone to see how upset he was. I didn't want him to have to explain tomorrow or ever. I still wanted to protect him. "I can't sign out with—"

"It's okay, it's okay. No worries."

"Thanks."

Phin's cries echoed on the concrete walls and floor. I got to the car. The keys were in my pocket. I'd have to put him down to get them.

What was I supposed to do? I couldn't let him out of my arms to put him into the back seat of the car. To drive where? For what reason? I stood at the side of my car and realized I couldn't let him go, period. Even if he'd stand on his own two feet, I couldn't let him go.

Right after Genevieve had been killed, he'd been fine. He was just hanging at Uncle Carter's house for a week. His young brain just rolled with it until he realized his mother wasn't coming back; then he cracked like an egg and everything came out. He cried for two days. He wouldn't be quieted with food, water, or utter exhaustion. The doctor gave him a sedative, which, thanks to the undiagnosed ADHD, made it worse. The only thing I could do was pick him up and carry him. He turned it down to low sobs as long as he was close to me and I was moving.

At the end of day two, he'd collapsed into sleep mid-sob. When he woke up eighteen hours later, he called me Daddy. And that had been that.

He was thirteen years old and eighty pounds when he found out what happened to his mother. But I carried him nonetheless. When I stopped to take a rest, he cried harder, so I kept moving. I carried him around the corner, down Olympic, back down some random street with a lot of trees. He'd always loved looking up into the trees. Loved digging in dirt and chasing birds. Had I exposed him to enough nature? Had I taken him camping? Skiing? Had we eaten outside enough? Looked at the stars and talked about God? Or had I just demanded perfection?

The lies were over now. As he sobbed in my aching arms and I walked up and down and around the neighborhood, I knew it was over. The secrecy I'd enforced. The security I'd demanded. The Plexiglas shell I'd put over him was gone. He wasn't my son. He'd never been my son, and he knew it. He probably hated me. He had to.

I deserved it. All of it. But I carried him because I didn't know how to stop.

CHAPTER 51

CARTER

When Phin had stopped crying, I stopped carrying him. My elbows were locked in position and my shoulders ached, but he'd stopped crying.

In the hours I carried him around tree-lined streets of the west side, I'd run through everything I'd done to protect him over the years, and I decided my one big mistake was keeping him in Los Angeles. I'd been trying to reduce disruption in his life. A new house. New neighborhood. New people caring for him. It seemed like quite enough.

The second mistake had been less clear. I hadn't given him a more truthful narrative to believe. I'd kept the lies very broad and simple so I wouldn't contradict myself. I told him about his mother, minus the acting, which he could look up, and minus the fact that she was my sister. I told him I'd loved her, which was true, but left out the murder. I didn't want him to have the inclination to try and remember what he'd seen, and I didn't want the shock of it to blindside him. His toddler's tears those first days when his mother was gone were so strong, so gut-wrenching, that I never wanted him to experience that again. And when he'd called me "Daddy," I hadn't wanted to deny him the truth he'd created to comfort himself.

Mistake number two was going with it and letting him determine his new reality. I should have based what I'd done in truth.

You wanted to be his father.

I did. I'd taken care of him since he was born and his real father split like Road Runner in a cartoon cloud. I'd slipped into a role, spending more time at my celebrity sister's Hollywood Hills mansion with the nannies than I did with my own friends.

Mistake after mistake. Now the lies were dropping like a distracted juggler's pins.

When he had his second crying fit, at thirteen, he did the same thing when it was done. He fell asleep in my arms.

I'd let my guard down because of Emily.

I'd gone to her house to take care of her, leaving him alone to work on his family tree. If I hadn't done that, if I'd been giving him 100 percent of my attention like always, he wouldn't have hacked the LA County Registrar. He wouldn't have hacked anything while I was in the house. I could have helped him with that project so he wouldn't have felt the need to break into a government database. The whole thing wouldn't have happened.

That regret sat heavy in my gut, and it was absolute bullshit.

I had nothing to regret. I'd done my best. The truth was going to come out at some point. I couldn't lie to the kid forever. I knew that. But I couldn't beat myself up with it.

"Do you want to turn a light on?"

Mom stood in the doorway as I sat in the dark of Phin's bedroom. He was under the covers in a fetal position, body rising as his lungs filled. No other movement came from him.

"No."

"Do you want to eat something? I can stay here and watch."

"I'm fine."

"Carter."

"Leave me alone."

"He's going to be fine."

"Yes, he is." I was more determined than ever to make sure of it.

"You should—"

"Not now."

She left, closing the door behind her. I was formulating a plan in the dark. I didn't like it. I wasn't going to enjoy it. It meant that the days of happiness I'd had with Emily were going to be nice memories and no more.

The sadness about losing her was woven into the darkness, and it was shot through with a stabbing regret. She'd woken me up to the possibility that I could love. My feelings for her had been the first bottle rocket on the Fourth of July, and it had been shot out of the sky before it could light up.

Well, good. If I'd gotten more deeply entrenched with her, it would be harder to leave. I would have had to talk to her about it. Asked permission. Included her. Broken up with her. Broken both our hearts.

But it hadn't gone on that long. It'd hurt for a little while, then go away once Phin was settled. If I thought really hard, I could remember her rib cage under my fingers, remember how it felt to lift her, remember the grace of her body and feel the remnants of hard work on her feet. I'd never kissed the curves of the arches or rubbed the roughness of the heels. Her feet told stories I'd never know. The absence was a true regret.

But I couldn't think about that.

I had to think about Phin.

He was first.

CHAPTER 52

EMILY

—Are you all right?—

I'd replied to Carter's text, but I didn't hear back. I didn't get a text that night or the next day. Carlos wouldn't tell me anything, and none of the other security guys seemed to know. Darlene was physically accessible, but her body was twisted so tightly around the upcoming tour that asking her to track down her ex-bodyguard was unfair. But I was leaving for Vegas, and I didn't know if he and Phin were all right.

I looked up Genevieve Tremaine's name and, in three seconds, found enough gruesome descriptions of the scene that I had to skim the accounts. Digging into more local and less celebrity-driven outlets, I found out about what Carter had gone through when it happened. He'd worked to have crime-scene photos sealed. Phin's name had been public knowledge. Along with Apple, Pilot Inspektor, and Moon Unit, Phinnaeus was a running metaphor for everything that was wrong with celebrity naming conventions. Carter had requested anything that had to do with the child be sealed. He put all his sister's money in trust for the boy and whisked him away without taking him far. He did not do interviews or talk to the media. He and his mother issued a public statement declaring that Genevieve's son was off-limits and that any attempts to photograph him would be followed up with the full force of the best legal team millions in residual checks could buy.

Public opinion was on Carter's side, and in less than twelve months, stories about Genevieve Tremaine's death fell off the radar.

I respected what Carter had done for Phin, but who had been there for him? Who had been there for him when his sister died? When all the years taking care of a child who wasn't his got to be too much?

His last text weighed on me.

—Phin needed me—

Things could be bad or they could be worse, and as the hours and days went on, a tension built in my chest. Phin needed Carter, but who did Carter need? And if it were me, would he ever ask for me? The walls he'd built around his family were so strong and high, he might not even know how to get through them to ask for help.

—Are you all right?—

I stared at my text from two days before. Was it adequate? Was it clear? Did it look as if I was soft-shoeing around doing something? If I sent something else, was I bothering him? Stalking him?

When Vince hit me that first and last time, I minimized it to Darlene. I told her it wasn't a big deal because I didn't want to upset her. She had enough on her plate. My compulsion had been normal, but her reaction had woken me from invisibility. Her intervention had saved me from who-knew-how-much trouble and pain.

Carter wasn't a victim of abuse, but he was as much a victim of circumstance as I was. Was I doing him a disservice by letting him build a higher wall?

I was behind my own wall. Bart and Fabian were always present, and I found out what it was like to have security that didn't take up any of my attention. Their job was to be invisible, and they were. I had my cameras and my security system. I'd felt trapped before, but only because I'd thought I should get out and do some vague thing.

Now the wall was between Carter and me, and it was really pissing me off.

Fabian's station was a chair on the front steps. He walked the perimeter of the property every fifteen minutes, or twenty-two minutes, or whatever, so no one would pick up a schedule. I found him checking the locks on the studio.

"I need to take a drive."

"Now?"

"Now." I didn't think to make up a story about grocery shopping.

"Where?" He took out his phone. He'd have to log it in with Carlos.

"I'll tell you where to turn."

He raised an eyebrow. He had nice eyebrows over brown eyes and thick black lashes. Very handsome, yet nothing stirred in me.

Where was I going at six o'clock on a Wednesday evening? I ran the map through my head. East. Left. Right. Park.

"I'm going to church. I'm nervous about the show, and I need to go to Saint James Church, but you need to take the route I say."

"Why? I mean, look. It doesn't matter to me. But I'm just curious."

"Superstition."

"I like you, but you're weird."

"I like you too. Can we go?"

We locked up and drove east on Olympic. I was more nervous than I had business being. I didn't know what to hope for. If Carter was home with his family, finding the comfort of old routines, the lights would be on and they'd be finishing dinner. He'd want that for Phin. He'd built his life around making sure the kid knew where he'd be from day to day and establishing sequences and schedules. So the lights would be on.

Unless everything had gone to hell. Phin finding out about his mother's death and his real relationship to his father could have broken the kid. He was thirteen, with all the eye-rolling insolence one would expect, but he was also a complex kid. He'd sent me a gift because he wanted me to like him, and it had been bursting bubbles and blooms, not wars and swords. He had a sensitive side he wasn't afraid to show. He was curious and perceptive.

The revelations could have done real damage. My heart went out to him. I knew Carter would do whatever he could to protect his nephew/son, but who was going to be there for Carter? He'd already been through hell with his sister. Securing Phin had taken so much energy, he probably hadn't taken a minute to himself. And now it was all coming back.

He'd need someone, and if he let me, I was going to be there for him.

"Left on Lorraine." I leaned over the front seat. Fabian insisted I sit in the back because it was procedure, but I was jumping out of my skin. "Hard right onto Wilshire and left onto Irving."

I'd have to guide him back to Wilshire to get to the church, but I had a few more crazy turns planned just for kicks.

When he turned onto Lorraine, I pretended I wasn't looking onto the right side of the street, but at the last minute I did. It was just after dinnertime. I expected to see the car in the lot and the lights on.

Instead of lights and life, the windows were dark, and in front of Carter's beautiful Craftsman sat a **FOR SALE** sign.

My heart wrung itself into a ball and lodged in my throat.

CHAPTER 53

CARTER

I took him to his favorite strip-mall Thai place. It had a Buddhist shrine in the front with bowls of fresh fruit and flowers and faded photos of specialty dishes that curled at the edges. We couldn't pronounce the name of it, and most of the menu was in Thai, but we had things we ordered every time. I wanted something . . . anything to be the way it was before he knew I wasn't his father.

Over the past twenty-four hours, Phin had started waking up. He ate a little. Went to the bathroom. He spoke in a full sentence while looking at the Thai menu, which was a relief, except that I had to answer his question.

"Where are we going?"

"After dinner?"

"When you sell the house."

"I was thinking Northern California. There's a lot of tech up there."

"Is Grandma coming with us?"

"She's getting her own place here."

"Can I stay with her?"

The waiter came to take our order before I could react as strongly as I felt.

"I'll have the chicken basil and a Thai iced tea, and he'll have a pad Thai with—"

"I want the crying tiger." Phin folded up his menu.

"That's very spicy," the waiter said.

"Make it mild," I interjected.

"I'll take it spicy." Phin picked up my menu and gave both to the waiter. "And a Thai iced tea too."

The waiter bowed and left.

"There's caffeine in that tea. You'll be up all night."

"I've been sleeping for two days, Da—"

He cut himself off before finishing the word. I folded my hands on the table and tapped my thumbs together. He pressed his chopsticks in the paper napkin until they made crescent-shaped dents.

"I don't know what to call you."

"What do you want to call me?" It wasn't like me to give him that kind of power in the relationship. I made the rules. I was the parent. But without the armor of my lies, I didn't know how to maintain my authority.

"Jerk." He said it matter-of-factly, without reprimand or venom, but I was filled with a blood-saturated rage and snapped his chopsticks away.

"Do not dare," I growled.

He wouldn't look at me. Without chopsticks, he used his fingernails to emboss crescents in the napkin.

"Fine." He pushed the napkin toward me, and I picked it up. Even as I was about to make a scene in a Thai restaurant, I loathed how I was behaving. My anger was disgusting to me but undeniable.

A waitress passed by with a tray of lemongrass and basil, and I was reminded of Emily. Her life in a fortress. Her beautiful smile. Her vulnerability with a red *X* on her chest. Everything came to me in a flood, and I saw myself and my anger through her eyes. How would she react to my behavior?

"I'm sorry." I took his forearm across the table. I wanted it to be a stabilizing force between us. I wanted to transmit my love for him with a squeeze to the arm. "This is hard."

"I don't want to go," he said. "Please don't make me go."

"Everyone's going to be talking about it."

"I don't care."

"You will."

"Maybe. But if we run away, I'm going to make all new friends, and what am I going to tell them? At least everyone here knows me and I only have to explain, like, half of it. Or none, maybe. And I'll be the center of attention for a little while, but it's going to go away. No one gets attention for that long. When Glen Crouch and Frida Langston got divorced, everyone felt sorry for Indigo for, like, a week. Ten days, tops. Then it was like, whatever. No one cared."

I'd decided a long time ago that Phin wouldn't run the show. Major decisions about his life would go to the adults in the room. Yet he'd brought something to my attention. As I started to let the idea of staying enter my mind, I saw where my resistance was coming from.

"You always said not to worry what other people think." He was stuffing more words into ten minutes than he had in the last two days. "And here you are worrying what other people think."

"It's not about what other people think." Untrue. When did I become such a liar? I was the one who didn't want to make explanations for what I'd done. If we stayed, things were going to change, and his school, his friends, the people in my life, would all want to know why I'd made this boy's life a lie. "It's about . . ."

. . . *protecting you.*

It wasn't. Protection was my default. My core motivation. Without it, why did I do anything?

What is it about, Carter Kincaid?

What are you running from?

251

Phin continued as if he didn't need to hear the rest of the sentence because he knew damn well what it was about. It had been about protecting him, up until it wasn't. Now it was about protecting me.

"And what about that girl you like?" Phin continued like a used-car salesman trying to close on a clunker. "Emily? She seemed really nice. You're just going to leave her behind?"

"Stay out of my love life, kid."

"You seemed really happy. I never saw you hold hands with anyone."

"Hey now . . ."

"I'm just saying. Look. Here's the thing. I'm really mad at you. Like, really mad. But I want you to be happy anyway."

"So you want to stay for my own good?"

"Well, partly. I guess? I don't know." He looked lost. He was thirteen. What else was I going to dump on him?

Our food came. I handed him back his chopsticks and napkin.

"I'm a jerk," I mumbled.

"Yeah."

"You may never forgive me." I waited for word of his forgiveness but didn't get any. He shrugged and poked at the chili-crusted beef, letting me continue. "I only ever wanted to take care of you. I know that's not an excuse. But whatever you decide to call me, Uncle or Dad or Carter . . . I want you to know something really important."

"I know you love me." Phin kept his eyes glued to the plate and put a piece of meat between his teeth and chewed.

"Yes, but no. I want you to know that I loved being your father. It was everything I hoped. Raising you into the young man you are? It's the best thing I've done. And if it ends before I want it to, I'm okay with that. You calling me 'Dad' made me proud every day. I didn't give up a thing that was worth more than being your father. And Phin. Just so you know. You can call me Uncle Jerk to my face or behind my back. I'll always think of you as my son."

252

He was bowed over his food, so I couldn't see his face. A tear dropped to his plate, and I thought I was going to have to carry him out on another crying jag.

"Phin?"

He grabbed his glass of Thai iced tea and downed half of it. His face was red and slick with tears and sweat.

"Kid," I said, "they call it crying tiger for a reason."

He coughed and took another piece of meat. "I got this."

He chewed and swallowed. I'd had crying tiger from this restaurant, and it was authentic in ways one had to suffer through to appreciate. "You might start hallucinating."

"Maybe it'll trigger puberty." He choked on his words, and I laughed. The waiter, as if seeing the white kid deal with a fire in his face, brought a bowl of iced cucumbers and cabbage.

I ripped off a cooling cabbage leaf and handed it to him. He stuffed it in his mouth and sucked, chewed, swallowed, and went for more crying tiger.

"I have an idea," he said before he ate the next flamethrower.

"We switch plates? I went through puberty already."

"Better. You go to Vegas." He ripped off a cabbage leaf and put it on his plate. "While you're not here, I'll explain to all my friends what happened. This way, you don't have to, like, be embarrassed, and they'll tell their parents whatever they want." He used chopsticks to put a few pieces of meat into the cabbage leaf.

"I don't think so."

He rolled the meat up in the leaf. Clever. I was as proud of the way his brain worked as if he were my own. "By the time you get back," he said, "it'll all be over."

He ate the rolled-up crying tiger, and I watched him chew.

Go to Vegas. See Emily. Share a bed. Start something with her. Something real. Something happy. Something completely distracting that could leave Phin exposed without me.

253

"I have reasons I don't travel. One: I'm not leaving you."

"You could take me."

"I can't watch you when I'm working. Next time."

"Really?" His face lit up from excitement or chili. Possibly both.

"Really. And two, I hate hotels. And airplanes. And long drives."

He took a big bite of his rolled-up meat and chewed. He handled it all right. Just a little wetness in the corner of his eyes.

"You gotta live a little, Dad."

He sucked down a third of his iced tea without mentioning that he'd called me Dad.

CHAPTER 54

EMILY

I didn't know how to worry about someone. I'd known only how to read worry in other people's faces, and that worry usually had to do with me.

After seeing the **FOR SALE** sign on Carter's house, I had to cover with Fabian, so I continued the way I'd said we were going. I sent him left, then right to St. James.

In the air outside an open door to a gym, I heard Darlene's voice singing. She sounded like unconditional love. I knew she had the gift of making every person who heard her feel as if she were singing just for him or her. I hadn't understood the truth of that until "This One Time" played in an elementary school gym.

"Stop."

He pulled over by a school attached to the church. The gym had an adult aerobics class happening. I pretended I needed to attend and left Fabian to watch the door. I sneaked into the line, but after a few moves I went to the back of the room and sat on the floor with my back to the wall.

I clutched my phone.

I didn't know whom to call. The music pumped and throbbed with high-energy optimism. I'd never felt so distant from anything.

The dance moves. The tempo. Someone else's enthusiasm. I knew how it felt, but I didn't know how to feel it.

Darlene was days from starting a tour. She obsessed over every single detail and had no room for anything personal. I couldn't call her. She was incapable of giving me her attention.

Simon flipped everything off as drama and went for fake cheer. I didn't need cheering up; I needed release, and not through dance. I'd tried that. Moving my body made me feel better, but I didn't want to feel better. I wanted to feel *right*, and all I felt was wrong. I must have done something wrong. Maybe it was my past. Maybe it was me. Maybe Carter knew I loved him and he got scared. Maybe it had nothing to do with me at all, but I was nothing to him. Not worth a call or a check-in to say, "Hey, I'm moving. It's been fun."

I watched the ladies dance to Darlene's music. I could do this. If they could do it, I could.

All I had to do was get up and let the dance take me away. Dance was a reset button. An end to the loop of self-loathing. This wasn't my church and it wasn't my class. I wasn't dressed for aerobics, but I got in the line and danced like no one was watching.

———

I went back home sweaty and mentally clear. Fabian locked me in my tower and went home to his life. I packed for Vegas, going through the motions of folding, rolling, sorting. I had expensive leather luggage in a cheerful pink. My parents had bought it for me when I went to college. It was wonderful, high-quality, high-end, and hateful. The color was like a slap in the face, and the monograms were a reminder that I was the same girl I'd always been.

Traffic went by outside, and I listened for a car to stop by my house. Listened for footsteps. For the difference between a cracked twig underfoot and the clicking of the wind. My attention stretched to the edges of the property. My muscles itched to move, but I couldn't dance the bags packed. I had to live with this insecurity.

Dancing made me feel safe. Dancing and Carter.

Grey jumped on the bed, tucked her feet under her, and wiggled herself comfortable in my duffel bag. I shooed her off, so she settled into the pile of underwear I'd set out.

"Crap," I said. "I can't leave you alone here."

She closed her eyes slowly and opened them with deliberation.

"I have a cat-killing ex-boyfriend, and who's going to feed you?"

She yawned. It was my problem. I'd agreed to take care of her. Somehow.

"Carter," I said. "He found you. He can help with you."

I scooped her up before she could run away.

CHAPTER 55

EMILY

I wasn't supposed to leave the tower after lockup. That was the rule, and I was starting to hate the rules. I was starting to think the rules that kept me safe kept me from living. Until Carter made me feel safe, I hadn't felt out of danger.

If I could see him for half a second, maybe I'd feel less vulnerable.

I could have texted him. I could have called. I could have sent a message through a mutual friend. I could have taken a later flight and spent the morning finding a pet babysitting place. I didn't know what I thought I was doing. His house had been dark the last time I'd passed it, and the **FOR SALE** sign meant he could have left already.

But something inside me had shifted. I had to do something. Take a risk. Move forward.

Grey hadn't been cooperative, but I got her by the back of the neck and put her in the car. She curled up in the back seat as if nothing I could ever do would be a big deal to her. There was nothing she couldn't get over. I admired that. It would be stupid to think I could emulate her equanimity, but I respected it.

I turned onto Lorraine. Earlier in the evening, when I'd passed with Fabian, Carter's lights had been off. Not this time. This time the windows glowed with homey light. I parked in front.

The first time I'd been to his house, I was peeking in on his life.

The second time, I'd used his home as a haven.

This time, I didn't know what I'd come for besides the cat, but I'd come for more. I knew that. Poor Grey was just an excuse.

When I opened the back door, she slipped out before I could grab her and ran up to Carter's porch. She looked at me from the top step and meowed as I walked up the front path.

I was just going to pass Grey over and ask politely if he'd like me to get the supplies out of the trunk. We'd promise to have a clean handoff when I was back from Vegas. I'd ask if he'd mind watching her when I traveled. He'd say he'd love to watch her. Phin could take an antihistamine. We'd be the most reasonable feline custodians in Los Angeles.

Grey accompanied me to the door and walked figure eights between my legs as I rang the bell.

Brenda might answer. That would be a bummer. She was great, but I didn't want to see her. I wanted Carter, and as the seconds passed, the feeling of expectation expanded in my chest until I thought my ribs would fracture.

Rustling behind the door. A *click* and a *tap*. A *whoosh* as it opened.

It was him with two-day scruff and a T-shirt that had been new at the turn of the millennium. His feet were bare under the cuffs of his jeans and as perfect as anything I'd ever seen. My chest deflated as I breathed. He looked fine. Just fine. Exactly as I expected, his features and shape clicking into place. When he said my name, the sound of his voice was like the last of a thousand-piece puzzle.

"Emily?"

"Carter, I . . ."

"Crap!" Grey had run into the house and lodged herself on the couch. Carter went after her, but she dodged, running into the kitchen.

Carter ran for her, and with a quarter turn, a pointed finger, and two words, he broke my heart.

"Stay here."

Stay here? I couldn't come in the house? Did I have some kind of disease? I could hear a small commotion and voices.

I walked in, through the living room, cutting around the dining room.

"No. I said no. Two letters. N. O." Carter's voice came from the kitchen.

Phin replied. "I read this article where if you want to get over an allergy, you have to expose your—"

He sneezed midsentence. I peered around the wall into the kitchen. Phin had Grey in his arms.

"I'm not moving a cat."

"I. Don't. Want. To. Move." Phin's eyes were on fire.

Grey saw me and jumped out of Phin's arms. Carter's gaze followed the cat to me where I stood in the dining room.

"I told you to stay there."

"I'm not a delivery person," I said. "You wanted me to keep the cat, but I have to go to Vegas, so you need to watch her."

"Yes!" Phin shouted.

Carter and I were locked in a heated stare. This wasn't going the way I'd hoped. This was going full shitstorm.

"Phin," Carter said without moving his eyes from me, "go upstairs. Please."

He hopped to it, and I couldn't have explained his enthusiasm until Carter's eyes flicked away from me. Phin had scooped up the cat as he headed for the stairs.

"No!"

The kid ignored him and took the steps two at a time.

Carter went for the stairs, stopped himself, turned to me, pointed as if he wanted to say something, then balled his hands into fists. He was frozen in the chaos. I wanted to hug him and slap him, in that order.

"I have the supplies in the trunk," I said. "I'll be back on Monday."

I stormed out. I didn't think he'd follow me, and with his bare feet, I didn't hear him behind me until I was on the sidewalk, clicking the button on my key. The lights flashed and the car chirped. The trunk made a satisfying *pop*.

"You don't get it," he said, and I spun to face him. "We're not the cat's mommy and daddy."

"What are we?"

"I don't know."

"You don't know?" I went at him, and he had to step back or get run over. "You had your dick in me. You don't get to ignore my texts and move away. You don't get to say you don't know."

"I have other things on my mind. You knew that better than anyone. But you make it worse. You come over here by yourself. Where's Fabian? You ducked him, didn't you? And why? Because you want me to worry about you too. Good job. Now I have to get you home and lock you in or I won't be able to sleep."

I slapped the trunk open because, fuck him. I didn't want him to worry about me; I wanted him to love me. I didn't know if he knew the difference, but I sure did.

"Look." He indicated the contents of my trunk. Cat stuff and pink luggage. "You're packed. You were going to leave for Vegas without security at all."

"This is not even about me."

"The hell it—"

"It's about your sister." I moved my makeup kit out of the way as if it were personally offensive and yanked up the bag of cat food. "You were a cop when she was killed. You didn't protect her. Now you're overcompensating. Which—"

"Don't psychoanalyze me."

"—is understandable. It's actually kind of admirable. But then is then and now is now." I threw the cat food on the grassy strip at the curb. "The kid wants a cat. Send him to an allergist, and give him a cat. But you're all about refusal, aren't you? You're like a one-man *no*. Nope, can't travel." I flung the cat box at him. He caught it. "Nope, can't bring you home." The food bowl. "Nope, can't be with you even though I love you, and don't deny it. You love me." I dropped the plastic bag of clean cat litter at his perfect feet. I couldn't believe I'd said that. I was either clearer than I'd thought, braver than I'd thought, or fucked in the head.

I put my hand on the lid of the trunk. There was nothing in there but my cheerful pink luggage. I slammed it closed. "I understand the problem," I continued when he neither confirmed nor denied he loved me. "What happened was awful and traumatizing for you and Phin both. But you've painted yourself into a corner, and you can't get out of it because you don't want to get your shoes dirty. So you act like a jerk."

"I am not a jerk."

"Jerk." I chirped the doors unlocked. Two steps, and I reached for the door. Lightning fast in his bare feet, he got between me and the handle.

"You're not going home alone."

"You're leaving Phin here? I don't think so. Not until he's twenty."

I reached around him, and he bent to speak softly. I could smell the gunpowder on his body, all buzzing fireworks and things that exploded.

"I was going to call you and tell you."

"When?"

He stood up straight. "When I thought I could look you in the eye."

The funny thing was, he was looking me right in the eye, but his arms were crossed and his knees were locked. He was telling me about his vulnerability in a defensive position.

"You don't let someone stew and feel like shit and wonder what she did wrong because you're ashamed to talk to her. That's on you. I like you. I don't . . ." A sob hitched. I was so mad, so upside down, so hurt I could barely think. "I don't like you. You're a jerk. Nobody likes a jerk.

But I feel . . ." I tried to talk myself out of continuing by swallowing a bunch of gunk that had lodged in my throat. "I thought I loved you."

"Emily—"

"Shut up. I love you."

He kissed me in response, running his full lips across mine and back, until my mouth came alive for him. He didn't flick his tongue against mine to arouse me, even though the taste of it was pure sex. He spoke without words, leading me into him just enough to crack my resolve. I could fall into those cracks, back into the shell. I could be safe in him and a mouth that quieted me.

My hands pressed against his chest, feeling how firm and stable he was, how real and strong, then I pushed him away.

"I want more." I let my hands slide down, appreciating every hard curve under his shirt.

"How much more?"

I opened the car door. The dome light went on and the dashboard beeped.

"Just more."

I got into the car. He stretched across the distance between the door and the chassis.

"You have to come back for the cat."

"Take care of her."

"I'll take care of her as if she were you."

He stood straight and let me close the door.

CHAPTER 56

CARTER

Phin was allowed on his phone only until seven o'clock at night. Then it was to be on the charging shelf by the breakfast nook, facedown. If I happened to stroll into the kitchen after seven, I'd often find him at the nook, reading a magazine upside down. If I picked up his phone, it wouldn't be sleeping or locked, because he'd put it down in a hurry when he heard me coming.

After I watched Emily's car turn the corner, and after I decided to let her go without following, I picked up the cat's eating and shitting provisions and went to the house. Phin was on the couch, petting the cat. The rug was wrinkled, and the blanket was off the chair by the front window as if he'd hurried back to the couch when he saw me walking back.

He sneezed.

"How's your mouth?" I asked. The crying tiger had a heat that lingered for hours. He'd eaten all of it like a warrior.

"Better." He sneezed again.

I dropped the cat supplies by the door.

"Do you want some antihistamine?"

"I'll get it."

He dashed for the kitchen. By the time I got there, he was standing on a chair, reaching for the medicine shelf. I plucked the box out of his hand.

"What did you see? Out front?"

"Nothing." He swung the chair back to the corner.

"What kind of nothing?" I asked, pushing a pink pill through the foil.

"The kissing kind of nothing." He held out his hand, and I dropped the pill in it. He swallowed without water, a disconcerting habit he'd begun when he started taking daily medication.

"Ah."

"You know," he said, wiggling his shoulders as if he was nervous about saying what he was about to say but was resigned to the fact that he was going to say it, "you really should go after her."

"You don't do that when a woman leaves. You respect her."

"Not in a stalkery way. More in a . . . kind of . . . 'Hey, I like you and don't go away mad' kind of way."

"You got that from the kissing kind of nothing?"

"Might have heard a little of it too."

"I can't leave you here alone."

"No, Dad. Really. You need to go and get her."

He'd called me Dad again. Was it a choice or force of habit?

"Don't you have homework?"

"No. I don't. Okay, but really. I'm old enough to be home alone until Gram gets back. Seriously."

"Not yet." I walked out, but he followed.

"When? When are you going to stop?" His voice seemed older, surer, deeper. But when I turned around, he was a little boy again. "I know, okay? I know about Mom and who she was. And I lived. And I'm going to live a long time thinking about it, but dude . . . just asking . . . When are *you* going to live?"

Did he just call me dude?

"Phin." I intended for my tone to be threatening, but there was too much pleading in it.

"She's nice. All I'm saying. She's nice, and you like her."

When he looked away, it wasn't out of submission or humility. I knew him that well. It was because he didn't want me to see sadness.

"What happened with that girl?" I asked.

Shrug. "Summer. Her name's Summer. Not as nice."

"What happened?"

This was what worried me, in addition to everything else. His friends would backstab him over his mother. They'd invent nicknames and taunt him. They'd exchange knowing looks over a situation they knew nothing about.

"I heard her talking to her friends about how much money Gary Singh had . . . He doesn't have a lot . . . or maybe he does, but he doesn't dress like it or act like it, and his dad drives a Toyota. Which she was making fun of, which . . . It made me not like her so much anymore."

More shrugging.

"Good call." I walked up a few stairs before he called up.

"Are you going to get her?"

I didn't answer him; I just kept walking to my room.

I couldn't go chasing after the woman I loved looking like a bum.

CHAPTER 57

EMILY

I drove home with his taste on my lips, my heart beating in the rhythm of that kiss. The cadence of it changed me. I drew breath re-creating it. I didn't have words for what had changed, just a feeling of transformation between Carter and me that altered the patterns of how I fit into the world.

He didn't know what he'd done. He didn't know what he wanted any more than I did. His life had been spun around, and he was just starting to get his feet under him. Expecting him to commit to anything but cat-sitting was unfair.

The streets were so familiar, yet the route was so new that I missed my turn, overshooting my block by a quarter mile or more. I came around and pulled into the driveway, opening my window so I could reach the keypad.

The number 8 stuck a little before it clicked. Could have been left over from the other night. Could be new trouble.

I sighed as the gate clattered open. The sigh was acceptance of a course of action I'd kept locked in a cage. It was the key to freedom. A breath strong enough to turn the tumbler so the animal could escape.

I parked the car calmly. Popped the trunk. Got my Louisville Slugger. Closed the trunk just as the driveway gate snapped shut.

It took me four steps to get to the side door instead of six. I checked behind me, slapped the screen door open, and put in my code. The house was dark, and I left it that way, taking big but careful steps from room to room as quietly as possible.

No one was there. I knew it from the first few seconds, but I checked every corner with the bat ready to swing. Then I turned on the lights.

I went to the little closet with the bank of monitors and fast-forwarded through the previous hour, from the time I left to the current minute. The bat was still slung over my shoulder as I watched. Everything had been quiet. Not a bug or a bird.

Vince had just been to the house two nights before. He was still a threat.

But I couldn't live like this anymore. I was sick to death of it. I hadn't done anything wrong, and here I was being punished for a humiliation I hadn't earned.

All of it, every second of shame for something that wasn't my fault, every moment I'd wasted checking codes and locks, every quickened heartbeat, was inside that bank of closed-circuit monitors.

I lifted the bat off my shoulder. I could have just slid the length down my palm and put it away, but I didn't. I lifted it higher and brought it down on my surveillance system. It scuffed the frame. Instead of feeling lucky to get a good swipe in without doing damage, I got frustrated. The frustration translated into rage, and the rage brought the bat into the leftmost screen from the side. The glass shattered into a web.

"That's how you do it." I sounded really sure of myself. I must be right.

I swung again at the next screen and the next, until all four were shattered and broken. I hit the black box with the hard drive, but the wooden bat did no discernible damage. Didn't matter. I had a job to do, and I wasn't going to let a steel casing slow me down.

Slapping the side door open, I went into the side yard. The camera's light went on with the movement and shifted toward me. I swung the bat, hitting it hard enough for it to pivot a few degrees. The light stayed on. It would stay on through a nuclear holocaust.

I hit the arm that attached it to the house. Nothing. Again. Nothing. I swung until the stucco under the metal plate it was screwed into started to crack. My arms ached. My lungs burned. The sound of clanging metal, thumping wood, and grunting filled my ears, but I hit it until it came loose, dangling from the wall by umbilical wires, the light still on.

I wasn't interested in hitting my house, so I went to the next camera, and the next. When I'd gotten all the cameras down, I went for the intercom at the front gate, smashing it with every bit of strength.

Then the bat broke. The end spun off and hit a parked Chevy, leaving me clutching a splintered stump too light to beat a chicken breast.

I hadn't realized my hands hurt. The tender new blisters on my palms had broken into sticky white fluid. My wrists were shot through with pain, my elbows ached, and my cheeks were wet with tears I didn't remember shedding.

I threw the rest of the bat over the fence and stormed back to the house.

The switch for the security system was in the little closet. I stepped over the busted monitors, put in my code, and just shut off the entire thing.

Relief—true relief—is like a drug. It flooded my system, pushing out stale worry and low-level panic. I smiled in a sort of disbelief, putting my hand over my mouth, sliding down the wall until I was crouched in the hallway, laughing. I rolled until I was lying on my back, arms spread, so happy, so liberated, so unencumbered that I couldn't feel the wood under me, swearing I was floating inches above the floor.

CHAPTER 58

CARTER

Once I thought about putting on clean clothes, I had to think about showering. I'd lost my opportunity to chase her down the street anyway, so I was going to have to be more deliberate. She was probably home already, stewing about what an asshole I was.

I let the water run over me, thinking . . . could I do this?

Could I let Phin be alone for a few hours? Could we stay in Los Angeles and deal with the blowback over his mother? Could I commit myself to Emily and Phin? Didn't people do it all the time? Didn't men care for large families every damn day? What made me so special that I couldn't?

"You're wearing a suit?" Phin said when I came downstairs. He was petting the cat without sniffling or sneezing.

"Grandma will be back in an hour. You should go to bed."

"Yeah."

"Look, kid. Here's the deal—"

He put his hands over his ears. "La-la-la-go-get-her-la-la-la."

I could have argued with him about how important bedtime was, but he was a big boy, and he was right. I had to catch Emily.

CHAPTER 59

EMILY

The differences between Darlene's life and mine were most visible in the drive up to her house. The trees got older, the streets quieter, the traffic lighter.

Darlene and I used to dream, and when we dreamed, we dreamed big. We'd get in my car, drive through the richest neighborhoods in Los Angeles, and choose our houses. I'd take the one on the left with the circular drive, and she'd take the one on the right with the rose garden and the fountain. We'd argue over imagined bowling alleys in basements and the sizes and shapes of pools we couldn't see.

But always, we were equals. We were going to make it together, buy two huge houses, and tear out the fences between them.

In the end, I bought a tiny place in Mid-City, and she got a three-story Tudor at the top of Van Ness. It didn't matter at the time. We didn't make comparisons. I'd traded my dreams for a chance to be something to someone. Maybe if the someone had been less of an asshole, the choice wouldn't have been so obviously wrong.

In the end, I got my house. I just needed a place with high walls and a security system.

Darlene's gate opened before I'd even stopped the car all the way. The lady of the house stood by her front door in her pajamas. She looked too small and too young for the structure behind her, as if she were sleeping over a rich friend's place.

"Come here." She bounded down the front steps in her bare feet and threw her arms around me before I was even out of the car. "Are you all right?"

All I'd told her was that I'd smashed my security system to bits, and could I come over?

"I'm fine." I tried to pull away, but she wouldn't let me. "Really, I just got fed up. But I don't even have locks on the doors. So—"

"We'll take care of it." She didn't loosen up her hug.

"I'll take care of it."

"I want you to be safe."

"I will be. But Darlene, I have to take some risks."

She let me go. "Try Rollerblading without wrist guards."

"Not always that. I know what you mean, but it's not always breaking bones and imminent danger. Sometimes . . ." I took a breath.

"What is it, crazypants?"

"Carter can't be with me, but then he can, and then I can't be with him, and it's like neither one of us will just shut up and let it be what it is. I want to be free, and he won't let me because I won't let me. It's about Vince, but then it's not. At some point, it starts being about habits you pick up that keep you in a constant state of dread. The cameras remind me I'm supposed to be afraid. Then my house reminds me. Then my job is my job because I gave everything up to be afraid. Now the man I love is just a reminder that I'm scared."

I'd said it. More than I'd wanted to. It was one thing to tell Carter. He was the object of my love. Telling Darlene made it very real.

"I want to be reminded of not being worried." I took my best friend's hands in mine. "When we came here, do you remember? The drive over? No money. No contacts."

We regarded each other in the front yard, half an arm's length away. Her hair was a wreck, and she didn't have a stitch of makeup on. For a moment, I could imagine her next to me, driving to Los Angeles, singing the entire way. We'd had all the hope in the world. All the forward movement two talented young women could muster.

"Risky." Her voice was lathered in suggestion. "It was damn risky."

"It felt so good to just get in the car and go. I haven't felt that good in forever."

"Yeah. Me neither." She nodded slowly, as if savoring the movement. "I wish we could do it again."

Darlene and I had agreed on a lot of things in the previous years, but we hadn't had a meeting of the minds until we stood in her front drive with no one else around. The space was finally big enough to fit our friendship, and I knew we were thinking the same thing.

"We should," she said.

"How quick can you pack?"

"Everything's on the way to the plane. I can buy the rest." She hopped up the steps to the front door. She disappeared inside. I was sure one of the security guys was going to come out and blow the lid off our plan. I got in the car. A few seconds later, Darlene came out in her pajamas and slippers, carrying a Prada bag. She closed the door behind her and skipped to the passenger side of my undistinguished little car.

"I love you," she said when she got in.

"I love you too." I put the car into drive. "Viva Las Vegas."

We sang it all the way to the freeway.

273

CHAPTER 60

CARTER

I don't panic. When there's danger or something isn't right, I get calm, which is why I'm a bodyguard in the first place.

What I saw when I pulled up to Emily's house had the makings of a panic. Busted cameras. Banged-up front and side keypads. Half a Louisville Slugger on the curb.

Her car wasn't in the driveway. Had she left already? Had she been taken away?

—*Are you all right?*—

I texted her before I did anything, and I was rewarded.

(. . .)

Maybe, in spite of everything I thought of myself, I had been panicking, because when the three dots appeared, I stopped adding to my mental list of protective measures.

—She's fine—
—She's driving. This is Darlene—
—She says why?—

Why? Was she kidding me? Her house was open to the world, her security system was busted, and she was nowhere to be found. Why was I asking?

—Because her security system is all over the street—

A black BMW parked in a dark spot down Citrus Street, too far for me to see the plate.

—She says she got sick of it—

So she'd been the one to trash it. I could live with that, and I couldn't blame her for getting sick of it.

—Is it connected to LAPD? Because they should be here if it broke—

—She says yes—

—Where are you?—

I got behind a tree, dropping into the shadow, and turned the light down on my phone.

—She says not to tell you. IDK why. I think it's spite—

A car door slapped closed. A man's voice came closer, but the ambient noise from Olympic and the distance kept me from understanding what he was saying. I leaned around the tree. It was him, talking on the phone and sticking to the shadowed side of the street. With a backward baseball cap and elastic nylon shorts, Vince had come to win his woman looking as if he were meeting his buddies for a kegger.

—Tell her I deserve it. And keep her away from her house tonight—

I put the phone away when he got close. He seemed as surprised by the busted security system as I'd been, standing back and looking at the camera dangling from a wire.

"Oh man," he muttered with real distress. "Oh shit no. No, no fucking no." He punched numbers randomly, stepped back, walked around the corner toward Olympic with his neck craning as if he were tall enough to see over the hedges.

I followed him around Olympic. Cars whizzed by too fast to see anything amiss, even when he went to the driveway gate and pulled it open. Disabling the security system had probably unlocked it.

He didn't open it all the way. Just enough to slip through. He closed it behind him, which meant I couldn't follow him without announcing myself.

I took out my phone. I had to make sure she wasn't in there. I had a message from her.

—I don't need you to tell me what to do. I am a grown woman and I can determine where I should and shouldn't be. I'm with my friend and we're having a good time—

Vince is in your house.

I typed it but couldn't send it. She'd be afraid, and I was tired of seeing her afraid. And she deserved an answer that wouldn't drag her away from feeling like a grown woman.

Torn between getting to Vince and talking to Emily, I had the choice made for me. I could hear Vince on the other side of the hedge, talking on the phone.

"Dude, I don't fucking know. Oh man, this is so bad."

He sounded truly worried—caught between whining and growling. Pacing back and forth like a caged animal while above me, the gate rattled.

"If I call the cops, I have to tell them why I'm here, and she's got that fucking paperwork . . . Don't . . . Dude, no . . . Because I don't like cops, that's why. And they'll blame me instead of that new guy."

His voice drifted in and out of range as he paced. He was invading her space, violating her privacy even if she wasn't there. But I'd already smashed his face, and nothing had been accomplished. He'd barely slowed down.

"Yeah . . . Kyle found out he's one of the bodyguards."

I froze. How much more did they know?

"Sure. He probably did this shit . . . ," he continued. "Right . . . she's getting deeper and deeper with Darlene. Like that time she was up there and everyone was looking at her. Dude, I saved her from that, okay? She never appreciated it . . . Right . . . No one wants to be with someone everyone else is looking at. I don't even know, man. Don't even know. It's like, not attractive, yo."

I smiled to myself. I had no business being amused. Vince was on Emily's property, and I was on the other side of the fence. But one aspect of Vince's motivations became crystal clear. He didn't want anyone looking at what he thought was his. He was turned off by it. That was why he didn't want her onstage.

The way to get rid of him for good was inside that realization somewhere.

"And now, this?" he said. "*This?* It's like, it's all trashed. Fucking shit!" He yelled as if the broken security system was a personal affront.

Unsnapping the holster at my side and slipping out my Glock, I swung open the driveway gate. It clattered, and Vince turned to me at the sound. He put his hands up in front of him as I advanced, aiming at his head because it was scarier than aiming at his chest.

"Dude."

"Drop the phone."

He reached back and put it on the table, snapping his hands back up.

"Sit." I tipped the gun to a little ledge between the path and the big tree.

He navigated to it with his hands still out, acting as if he were the one calming me down. Maybe he was. I was the guy with the gun, after all. Stepping into the light, he still had yellow bruising around his left eye. Weeks had passed. I must have done a number on him, yet here he was, persistent, stupid, possibly in the only kind of love he understood.

"I was just passing by," he said.

"Sure."

"Did you see this shit?" He pointed to each busted camera.

"She's all right."

"You break it, asshole? She piss you off?"

I wasn't sure if he was brave or reckless, but if he called me an asshole to get a rise out of me, he had the wrong guy.

"She's not here. And you know you're not supposed to be. That restraining order's real, and it's not toothless like the last one."

He couldn't keep still. He kept pointing to the cameras. As if bursting, he cried, "The keypad! Did you see it?"

"Vincent—"

If you stopped and listened, you could always hear police sirens in Los Angeles. So when the whine came from far away, Vince wasn't affected.

"No, no, this is not good. I need to talk to her."

"She's doing her own thing," I said. "She's not even the same person she was a month ago. So you can keep stepping on your own dick. Your stupid plays keep me employed. But even if you got her back, you wouldn't like what you got."

The sirens got closer. How long had it been since she left my house? Forty minutes? Ten to get here. Ten to trash the place. With a twenty-minute response time, she could be dead.

"You don't know what you're talking about. This is not about you. It's about *us*. Me and her."

"Don't come and check the block again. Don't come in here even if there's a neon sign with your name on it. And I swear, if anything happens to that cat, I'm going to skin you."

"I didn't kill Socks." He stood up with his finger out. "That was my cat too."

The sirens came down Olympic and stopped at the driveway. Vince's face went blue then red then blue again.

"Stay there," I said, holding the gun on him. I was engulfed in chaos seconds later.

"Freeze!"

Shit. I took my finger off the trigger and held up my gun, getting to my knees.

"Occupant has a restraining order against—" I had the wind knocked out of me when I was pushed down. I let them disarm me. In those few seconds, Vince took off. I didn't see where he went because I was wrestled to the ground and cuffed.

CHAPTER 61

CARTER

They let me go once they saw I was ex-LAPD, I was licensed, and I was working as the occupant's bodyguard. The worst part about it was that they'd focused so much on the guy holding the gun that they'd lost Vince.

Having heard some of what he said, I put together a plan to get rid of him on the short drive home. She'd avoided singing so he wouldn't get angry with her. She'd given up ever appearing in front of people. But what if doing exactly that turned him off? What if it disgusted him so much he lost interest?

It wasn't violent or earth-shattering, but if it turned him off to Emily, that was enough.

By the time I pulled into my driveway, I knew I had to get to Vegas to talk to her.

When I peeked into Phin's room, he was in bed. He thrust his hand under his pillow as if he were hiding something. I went in.

"Good night, Phinnaeus."

"Good night."

I reached under his pillow and found the hard edges of his phone.

"Thanks. I'm done anyway," he said as I shut it off.

I kissed his cheek and gave his ear a loving tug.

"Can I see my mother's stuff?" he said just before I got out the door.

"It's late."

"I promise I'll get up tomorrow."

I didn't have time for Genny's box. I had to get to Vegas to talk to Emily and Darlene. I had to make sure Mom was going to be home with Phin, and I had to get in a few hours of sleep before I got in the car for a long drive.

But I wasn't going to be able to sleep. I could skip that and show Phin his mother's stuff. I hadn't looked in that box in years, and for the first time in a while, I wanted to.

"Meet me in the living room," I said.

Phin shot out of bed as if he'd been sleeping on a catapult.

I got the cardboard box out of the back of my closet. It was lighter than I remembered. Or maybe I was stronger.

He met me in the living room in the plaid robe I'd gotten him for his birthday. He'd insisted on a robe with a hood, which was nearly impossible to find.

I sat on the other side of the couch and put the box between us. Phin grabbed at it, ready to rip it open as if it were Christmas morning. I was suddenly afraid he'd dive in and the memory of the night his parents were killed would flood back.

"Hang on." I put my hands over his. "One thing at a time. Okay?"

"Okay." He folded his hands together and pressed them between his knees, but he was bouncing on the cushions in the least restrained way possible.

I opened the box.

Jesus. It smelled like my sister. Lavender everywhere. She'd loved lavender.

"First thing." I took out a picture of Genny and George holding baby Phinnaeus. "I've told you this as your father. Now I'm telling you as your uncle. You were the most beautiful baby I ever saw."

Phin held the frame in both his hands and stared at the picture. It had been taken in Mom's apartment in Torrance with dozens of paparazzi outside. To the tabloids they had been "Georgevieve" and "G2," but to me, and in the picture, they were normal, attractive people so happy about their baby.

"I look like my dad."

"You have his chin."

"Was he nice?"

"He was all right. Busy."

The front door clicked and opened. My mother's lipstick was gone, and her hair was a little out of place. Once she closed the screen door, the car parked in front of the house left.

"Oh," she said, closing the door behind her. "You're looking at Genny's box!" She whipped off her bag and sat cross-legged in front of us. She took the picture from her grandson. "Phin, you were the most beautiful baby. Carter, honey, is the wedding album in there?"

I fished around for it. Mom sighed. She'd looked at it more than I had since that day.

The album was covered on the bottom. I couldn't grab it. I handed Phin the Emmy to get it out of my way.

"Cool." He checked its weight by gently bouncing it. "Really cool."

"Your mother was a special woman," Mom said. "She had more talent in her little finger than the rest of them did, all put together."

I stopped myself from adding that she was also a disorganized, undisciplined, forgetful pain in the ass.

I got out the album. It was Italian leather, decorated with Japanese ribbons and put together by a Downtown artist. So much work for nothing. I handed it to Phin, who held it closed, frozen in space.

"What's wrong, sweetheart?" Mom asked.

"I just . . ." He pressed his lips together in a rare thoughtful moment. "What if I don't feel anything?" Putting it on his lap, he ran his fingers over a ribbon. "What if I don't recognize them?"

"The doctors told me, a long time ago, that you might never remember them."

"I'll feel bad though."

"Do you want to wait? You can digest this stuff a little at a time."

Looking in the middle distance, he thought about it. He had a lot to take in, and I didn't know if he could handle it. I wasn't sure if he could regulate his emotions enough to understand everything that was happening to him. Mom and I exchanged a glance, then I put my focus back on Phin.

"You all right, kid?"

"Yeah." He snapped out of it. "Hey. Can I keep these in my room?" He held up the picture and the Emmy. "I can look at the rest later."

"Good idea."

I closed up the box. Phin faced me with his knees on the couch and held out his arms.

"Incoming!" He landed on me in a hug. We hadn't played that game in years. I held him tight. "Can I still call you Dad?" he asked into my shoulder.

"Yes," I said. "Yes, you can."

He hugged the mementos to his chest and stood up.

"I'm going to bed."

"Me too." I stood. "I'm leaving in a few hours for Vegas."

"The Sexy B-word preshow?" Phin asked, eyes wide. Darlene wasn't his genre, but apparently excitement over the tour crossed middle school lines.

"How did you find that out?" I snapped. He wasn't supposed to know who I worked for.

"I don't know. Common sense?" Phin looked genuinely incredulous. "Whatever. Okay. Just, you're a security guy, and a bunch of my friends are going to Vegas for it."

I was going to drill down to details, but he was thirteen and he had a brain. That was how he knew.

"That's exciting." Mom leaned on the couch to get up. Her bones cracked.

"Yes. It's a dream come true," I said flatly, then pointed to Phin. "Go on. Bed."

He grabbed the Emmy and the picture and hopped up the stairs, getting distracted by a photo that had been on the stairwell wall for years.

"Is this Mom here?" He pointed to the left side of the picture, where his mother was under the white mat.

"Yes," I said.

"Not cool."

He ran up.

"We're going to have to remount a few of those," Mom said.

"About time." I picked up the box and shook it, making the Girl Scout medals and drama awards dance.

"Are you relieved?" she asked.

"Yes and no. I'm still worried he'll remember."

"We'll take care of it if he does. I'm going to bed."

When the water pipes stopped hissing, I knew Phin's shower was over. I tried to give him five minutes to get dressed but lasted only three before I went upstairs. I was worried about him. I wanted to know what he was thinking and how he felt.

"Did you get clean?" I asked as I tucked him in. His hair was a spiky wet mess.

"Yes. Sheesh."

Phin had put the Emmy and the photo next to his bed.

"I won't be here when you get up, but you call me if you need me, all right?"

"Uh-huh." His eyes fluttered.

"And Grandma's staying around, so if you need her, you call her."

He stuck his hand out from under the covers, reaching for the night table.

"Can I have the thing?" As if he was too sleepy to form the word *Emmy*, he pointed to it and made a grabby motion, missing by an inch.

I gave him the statue. He put it next to his chest, under the covers.

"Good night," I said, shutting the light.

He groaned a response and was asleep before I even got out the door.

I tried to rest after that, but I just lay in bed for an hour and a half, waiting to get up.

I gave up, made coffee, packed a few things, and got in the car. I was on the 15 heading north in no time.

CHAPTER 62

EMILY

Darlene and I made it to Vegas by midnight because she had no respect for speed limits. We got to her MGM suite earlier than planned. We had plenty of time to stay up watching movies and laughing like giddy schoolgirls.

I didn't get to the Bellagio until two a.m.

Vegas really didn't sleep. The lobby was crowded, and as we walked through the casino to the elevators, I had a feeling of peace and well-being in the middle of a storm of noise and activity.

The suite was on the twenty-fifth floor and had a gorgeous view on two sides, but I was too tired to appreciate it.

My bags sat by the door. Each one had a little envelope tied to it. The room number and a welcome note from the concierge were inside. It was good to stay in a nice hotel. Good to be welcomed. I was high on exhaustion and goodwill.

But wait. I was missing a bag. One of my monogrammed pink leather bags. The smaller one with the makeup. Crap.

I called downstairs. My movements were slow and deliberate, as if my body wasn't taking anything for granted.

My phone dinged. Darlene.

—Thank you for that. I almost feel normal again—

—Wrong. You are always special—

—Whatever. Good night. See u tomorrow—

—Tomorrow—

The phone lit up again when I finished brushing my teeth. Carter. I smiled but was concerned because of the hour. He should be in bed. Everyone outside the city of Las Vegas should be in bed.

—Are you up?—

I was about to text back when there was a knock at the door. Was he here? My heart jumped. To be so tired and fall asleep in his arms like a rock on a soft, sandy beach would be the perfect end to the day.

We wouldn't need to apologize to each other.

We wouldn't need to talk.

We would just obey our bodies and hearts.

I looked in the peephole. Flowers. He'd brought flowers again.

I swung the door open with a big smile on my face that disappeared as soon as I saw the flower-bearer's face.

I felt the breath leave my lungs and gravity upend itself as I was pushed to the floor.

The door slammed shut.

It was Vince.

CHAPTER 63

CARTER

I had the entire four-hour drive to convince myself I was right, that if Emily got up in front of an audience and sang, something would shut off for Vince. She'd become public property and unlovable.

Neither was true, of course. She'd never be public property because she was mine, and she'd never be unlovable for the same reason. But maybe she'd be free of closed-circuit cameras, bodyguards, and fear.

I pulled into the Bellagio parking lot in the early morning hours. Carlos had briefed the team on the performers' lodgings and the work-arounds regarding Emily's arrangements.

—Tiny dancer? Are you up?—

I texted her from the hotel lobby and waited for an answer. The hotel was famous for its colored glass flowers, garden, and marble. It suggested tranquility without offering it. The flashing lights and buzzing, beeping, bouncing casino were ten feet away. It smelled of cigarettes and old coins as I walked through it, following the path to the other side of the hotel.

No answer from her. I texted Carlos. He never slept.

—*Are you up?*—

—*Of course I'm up*—

He called me a second later.

"What's happening?" he asked.

"It's—"

He must have heard the dinging of the slot machines when he cut me off.

"Are you here? In Vegas? Can you work? We're short one."

"Sure. Fine. Where's Emily? Do you have anyone on her?"

"The Bellagio. Fabian just got back."

"What room?"

I was answered with a long silence.

"Carlos?"

"You know I can't tell you her room unless you're working."

I hung up, frustrated. I could wait. I was a patient man. But I came to suggest a plan that would need time to implement.

You came here to see her.

I did. The plan was an excuse. I believed in it, but the best part of it would be her, and us, and making up for all the stupid things we'd said.

As if calling her to mind called her to the world, a brass bellman's cart went by.

Her pink leather bag hung from the hook, swinging with the motion as the bellman who was pushing it spoke to another, who was holding a clipboard. I followed them, trying to get a good look at the monogram.

They stopped at the elevator, speaking another language. I pretended to look at my phone, but I was really trying to get a good view of the monogram.

It was hers.

I could just follow it to her room. No problem if she was one of the first stops. If she wasn't, I'd be following them from floor to floor, and I'd look suspicious.

One bellman got out and held people from entering. Bellman Two held the doors open and turned to me.

"I'm sorry, sir. This is being used for service overnight."

"But—"

"Another elevator just arrived."

Truth. The first bellman was guiding people to the next open elevator.

But I couldn't lose sight of that bag.

It wasn't about seeing her now or later.

It wasn't about the unanswered text.

It wasn't about Fabian ending his shift.

It was my intuition. The Iron Eye catching the pink bag in a sea of bright colors.

I had to go up that elevator.

CHAPTER 64

EMILY

This wasn't my fault. None of it. If I was dead by morning, it wouldn't be because I'd opened the door or because I moved in with him in the first place or stopped singing to please him. This wasn't me; it was him.

He'd caught me by surprise. He'd knocked the wind out of me and slapped a precut piece of duct tape over my mouth before dragging me to the bathroom. I punched him. I kicked like a gymnast. I grabbed a big ceramic urn to hit him with, but he kicked it away. He was bigger. He was prepared. He was crazy. His goatee had grown out over his cheeks, and he'd lost weight. For a second I saw the handsome guy I'd loved, but he disappeared as soon as he opened his mouth.

"This is done, Em." He threw me into the bathroom. I banged against the glass shower door, but it didn't break. "I tried to do this like a nice guy. But you don't want a nice guy."

Twisting and wrestling, he got me onto the floor. My stomach writhed on the slippery marble, but he kept me still with a knee to the lower back. It hurt like hell, but the pain made me all the stronger.

He flipped me over. I scurried backward until my back was to the tub.

I couldn't say fuck you. I couldn't even flip him off because my hands were behind me. I was afraid. Very afraid. But adrenaline and a lack of options made me defiant as well.

He took me by the side of the face and got close to me. I could smell his cologne. His sweat. His own fear.

"I was a nice guy before I met you. I was fun. I had a lot of good times. Then you . . . you made it all go bad. Now it's like my friends don't even know me."

Behind the tape, I told him it wasn't my fault. And he could have his life back any time if he let me go.

Maybe he heard my muffled syllables. His hands got gentle, no longer holding my head in place.

"I keep telling them you're worth it. You had all those cameras. I always saw them, and I knew you had them for me. It was like I was there with you. You know? Like I was still in your life."

I blinked away tears. He moved his hands away and put them on my thighs. Even through my jeans, my skin recoiled.

"And you smashed them up. Like you wanted to smash me, and when you get back, you think you're gonna just sweep them away?"

He squeezed my thighs.

"Just make me disappear and move that guy in?"

He squeezed until it hurt, moving his face close.

"I don't think so."

I reared my head back and thrust it forward, bringing my forehead onto his nose as hard as I could. Bones crunched.

His scream was deafening. He got off me, hands over a nose that was shooting blood.

I got away with hands behind my back, bare feet gripping marble, then carpet. The door was a million miles away. Fucking suite. Motel 6 next time.

There were roses all over the floor. I stepped on one hard and got a thorn in the heel. I screamed behind the tape. I knew he was coming. He had to be.

The door. Right here. But the handle was for hands in front, and mine were behind, and I'd never reach the lock in this position.

"Fuck!" He was a few steps away, bleeding everywhere, coming for me. I was ready for a fight. I might kill him, and I didn't have use of my hands, but I was ready.

From the heavens, like the sound of an angel, the doorbell rang.

Then a knock.

Then the doorbell again, but I didn't even have time to hear that second ring. Vince dove for me, and I threw myself against the door, making it rattle.

"Emily?" The voice came from the other side, and just like the flip side of a gold coin, despair turned to hope.

It was Carter.

The door rattled from his side.

Why wasn't he coming in?

Vince tried to grab me and missed. Another rattle from the other side of the door.

"Emily!"

"Do not disturb!" Vince cried, though he sounded like he had a bad cold.

As I backed away, Vince advanced on me, half-crouched, one hand over his nose, the other hand swiping for me, and I thought for a second . . . what if it wasn't Carter? What if it was cleaning or room service? What if they heard a sick guy tell them to go away? They'd go away.

I lunged for the door and threw myself against it just as it swung open. I landed at Carter's feet, surrounded by security guys.

I blinked up at him. He was bent forward with his hands behind his back as if the security guys had tried to wrestle him down. A bellman held my missing pink bag, and on the floor by Carter's feet was a little envelope

with my room number and welcome message inside. He must have recognized the pink luggage and followed it to me. Thank God for that.

Carter's dark hair fell over his eyes, and when the security guys let
him go, he dropped to his knees over me. In the room, far away, there
were scuffles and curses. I was lost in relief, lost in safety, spinning away
from the intensity of what had just happened.

"Are you . . . ?" Carter was so out of breath he could barely speak.
His eyes ran over me, from face to bare feet and back to face.

I nodded. I was okay. I was all right. Everything was going to be
fine. I was safe.

CHAPTER 65

EMILY

Darlene had that faraway look she got when her brain was firing in the rhythms of the show. She was pacing the length of the platform she was supposed to perform on.

Having spent half the night at the police station making a statement, I'd been late for the sound check and run-through, but I'd never felt better.

"No, no, no." Darlene waved her hands at everything. "I can't see it. I need to see it." She jumped off the platform to the seats. "Can we play it so I can freaking *see* it?"

I pointed to the girl behind the soundboard. "Can we get it on the monitors?"

She held up five fingers and mouthed the word *minutes*.

"Oh for the love of . . ." Who had five minutes? Lines of dancers waited, ready to try again.

Carter stood with Fabian and Carlos. Thor checked things off a list. He was halfway between the stage and the back exit, but when he looked my way, I felt him right next to me.

"Sing it, all right?" Darlene shouted. "Please? Can we just do it?" She never shouted as if she were ready to bust a vein. I'd kept her up late with movies and girl talk and woken her early to be in the station with me.

"Make Him Yours" was a slow jam and the only song with a standing microphone. This was our first and only chance to get it right, mostly because I'd been late, which wasn't my fault, but it wouldn't kill me to grease the wheels a little.

I pointed at Darlene, who had her arms crossed.

"I'll only sing for you."

I took a deep breath and began. I sang in front of people, without amplification, while my dancers did their routine behind me. I didn't even realize what I was doing, except my job. Except what I was capable of.

The sound girl obviously didn't need five minutes, because five seconds after I started, my voice came over the system, loud and clear. Darlene rolled her hands to say "Keep going," so I did. She scrambled up the platform, stood next to me, and her voice joined mine. I'd forgotten how much fun it was to sing.

"Go, girls!" Simon cried behind us. Everyone was looking, even Carter from half an auditorium away. Our eyes met. What had happened in the hours since he'd shown up at my suite with security?

We'd stated our case. He explained why he'd stolen the tag, run up the stairs, slipped into the next elevator on the second floor, and run to my room.

Was that all? It felt like more. It felt as if I'd shaken off a hundred pounds of chains. When I looked at him unbound, I didn't see problems. I didn't see a conflicted man with baggage, and I didn't see through the eyes of fear. I saw what he was and what he wasn't. He was a man. Not a protector. Not a target for my past. Not a repeat of all the mistakes I'd made. He was more than all that. He was just a man. A glorious, gorgeous, strong, loving man, and he was smiling at me, and I was singing for him.

He held up his fist. It was the exact size of his heart.

I made a fist and put it against my chest.

Darlene and I used to harmonize all the time, and that day we sang her chorus as if I'd never stopped singing. I wasn't as practiced as Darlene, but the sound of us together, the way we made something bigger than the sum of us, sounded perfect. I was carried away on it, the way I always used to be.

Make him yours.

Make him yours.

Make him yours.

"See?" I said into the mic. Darlene slow-clapped. My cheeks shot through with the pink of surprise and sudden awkwardness. Simon slow-clapped. All the dancers did. When I couldn't look at them another moment, my eyes fell on Carter, who was front and center, clapping for a verse and a chorus.

"Lunch!" a voice cried over the huge space. Equipment dropped, stations were abandoned, voices drifted away. Darlene hugged me.

"You sound amazing."

"Thank you."

She pulled back, holding me by the biceps.

"I'm so glad you're all right."

"Me too."

Darlene got pulled away to make a decision or have a salad. I'd never know, because Carter was at the ends of the platform, taking all my attention.

I stood over him. He had his security badge around his neck, and his gun bulged under his jacket. He'd been given clearance to work the show with a slap on the wrist.

"It was worth coming to Vegas just to hear you sing," he said, reaching over the edge and laying his hand on my ankle.

"Saving my life last night notwithstanding?"

"One was necessary. One is just pleasure."

His finger trailed over the top of my foot. He was too far away. I couldn't smell him; I couldn't touch him. His voice was at a normal conversational distance when it should have been so close his breath warmed my skin.

I knelt on the edge of the stage, and his hand went from my ankle to my knee.

"I sound like a frog." I tucked a sliver of loose hair behind my ear and slid my hand over his. "But it was fun."

People yelled all around us. The sound system popped, and men dangled from the light racks above us. I was so happy to see Carter, none of it distracted me. I could smell lunch. Chicken and garlic and, to my surprise, brownies. I was hungry but couldn't move. Not while he touched me. Not while he looked at me as if I were the only woman in the world.

"We were so distracted," I said. "You never told me why you came all the way here."

"Because I wanted to apologize. And I wanted to win you over. And tell you that the closer you got to me, the harder I pushed you away. I kept repeating these reasons why I couldn't be in a relationship, and they were great reasons until we met. When you came along, it all changed. None of the reasons held water anymore, and that? It scared me. I fought for those reasons as if my life depended on it. But, tiny dancer, I'm sorry. My life doesn't depend on protecting what I have unless I have you."

Our clasped hands rested on my knee. His thumb ran along my finger.

"And I had an idea," he added.

"What kind of idea?"

"The kind you don't need now. Get down here."

I took his face in my hands, but my face couldn't reach his from up so high. Leaning on his shoulders, I pushed forward. He held me at the waist and lifted me, holding me up and dropping me in the circle of his arms.

Our lips found each other. He was warm and strong, and I was free to love him.

CHAPTER 66

CARTER

"It's the stupidest idea I've ever heard in my life." Emily sat across from me in a corner of the Bellagio VIP lounge, the stiletto on her crossed leg dangling from her toe. Her dress flowed over her thighs, covering everything I wanted to taste. The color had surprised me when I saw it. She called it "spite white." Her blonde hair was up in a twist, and I was going to put bite marks on her shoulders by morning. "It never would have worked."

Emily's legs had tensed into pure tight muscle, and when she crossed them I got the sense she could wrap them around a second time.

Those legs around me . . .

"Now it doesn't have to. Now you should just do it because you should."

"Go onstage with a voice I haven't trained in God knows how long?"

When she put her hands on her hips and thrust those bitable shoulders at me, the neck of her dress puckered until I saw a lavender bra.

"You sounded amazing this afternoon. And you'll sound amazing tomorrow night."

"Darlene would have never agreed to it."

The lounge had the best of everything. Colored glass flowers and gold furniture. Wool rug. The waitstaff didn't waste a second refilling wineglasses. I sat up on the leather chair and put my glass on the stainless table.

"She already did." I took her by the back of the neck and pulled her close. "Why do you think she put you in front of a mic today?"

"Oh my God."

"What?"

"You sneaky bastard." She whispered it with a sexy inflection on each first syllable. She was warming to the idea. "Why would you do that?"

"Because when I had the plan, it was about Vince. And when they caught Vince, I was disappointed you wouldn't sing." I pushed her knee until she uncrossed her legs. "You deserve to be heard, and the world deserves your talent." My hand went up her skirt to the lace tops of her stockings. "And it might be fun. And it would turn me on."

"Carter, I have a room. We . . ."

I touched skin over the stockings, kept her face to mine as my fingers found lace between her legs. "What are you wearing under here?"

"I had the bag . . . uh . . . in the car . . ."

I ran my fingernail over the texture of her panties. She was wet already.

"Open your legs. Just a little more."

I pressed my knee against hers, opening her up so I could get past the strip of fabric. Her eyelids flicked closed; her lips parted so her tongue could flick over them.

"Let's go upstairs."

"Sure." But I didn't stand. Behind us, the business of the lounge went on as I got one finger under and stroked her pussy. My own breaths went ragged. "After I get inside you." I slid a finger in. She looked as if she was going to burst.

"Can we go now?"

"Two fingers."

"I can't . . ."

I pressed her leg open a little wider.

"You can." Middle and index fingers. If she thought she was about to come, I wasn't far behind. My cock throbbed at the base. I drove my fingers deep inside her and bent them, looking for the bundle of nerves at . . .

She hitched a little.

Found it. She grabbed my sleeve as if hanging on for dear life.

"What floor are you on?"

I didn't stop the motions of my fingers or even slow down. We were so close I heard the workings of her throat. She had to breathe and swallow before she could tell me.

"Twenty-five."

"So far. Do you want to come now?"

She opened her big brown eyes. They knotted between the brows. "If you keep doing that, I will."

"What if I do this?"

I rubbed her clit with my thumb. She hissed through her teeth.

Her thigh muscles went rigid; her body fought itself to move and not move at the same time. I kissed her to anchor her face, but she didn't have enough control to kiss me back.

When she was done, I pulled my fingers out of her. She gulped air.

"You all right?"

She fixed her hair and looked around the room. I put my hand to my mouth. My fingers smelled like her pussy. I didn't think I was going to make it up the elevator.

CHAPTER 67

EMILY

When he put his fingers near his lips, the orgasm I'd had seconds before shrank to nothing, and I twitched for another. He was looking at me so intensely I had to look away, and of course I chose to look down, where his erection was stretching the seam inside his pants leg.

"Can we go?" I asked.

He stood and held out his hand. I took it, expecting to go up to my room. Instead, he guided me out to the casino, away from the elevators.

"Where are we going?"

He showed me his temporary security access badge.

"I don't get it."

"I do."

Left at the carpet. Past the cashier. Against the wall and down a short hall was a door. Putting his card under the light, it beeped and clicked.

He opened the door for me.

"Let me show you where to go if there's a problem."

We walked into another hallway. After the dim lights and excited bells of the casino, the world behind the door was flat, bright, and quiet. He showed his card to a guard behind a grate, was buzzed through another door, had a short conversation about exit strategies, turned another corner, pulled me through a door, and shut it behind him.

The room went black except for a white light coming from a box on a shelf at his elbow. Inside it, an iPad, a laptop, headphones, and a porno DVD were all wrapped in plastic and labeled. The light came from a cell phone with its flashlight left on.

"The lost and found?" He was a dark shape, lit at the edges from the phone, and he descended on me, taking my mouth with his, my body with his arms. Pushing me against a metal table that tipped, then stopped when it hit the wall. He lifted my leg around his waist. Soft met hard, grinding through too much clothing. The fabric between us should have caught fire. Should have rubbed away in the friction. Thin, weak, yet impenetrable, we had to move away to get closer.

He unbuckled, unbuttoned. I reached into the dark to get his throbbing, thick cock in both my hands. Around the back, under my skirt, he yanked on my underwear and tore the lace to shreds.

"Sorry about that," he growled.

"I'm not."

He pushed me hard against the table, and I angled to meet him. When he thrust inside me, I grunted like an animal, and again with the second thrust until he was buried inside me. I was flooded. My blood, my skin, my mind, flooded with pleasure and the need for more of it. Beating ourselves against each other impossibly fast, brutally hard, I wanted him to crawl inside me, stretch out, vault through the air with him, higher and higher.

Grabbing the leather strap of his holster and a fistful of shirt, I came with him at the top of the arc, feeling that moment when you're as high as you're going to go but you haven't started falling yet. The moment between up and down, between movement and potential, where power and pleasure joined.

CHAPTER 68

EMILY

After a long workout or a series of demanding performances, my body was sure to ache when I woke up. That was how I knew my muscles were breaking down and rebuilding. Because the pain made me stronger, it had an edge of joy. Everything functioned. I was all right. Rewards for hard work were being granted.

I woke in the Bellagio twisted in sheets, hugging a pillow that smelled like the fifth of July, with an aching tenderness between my legs. It hurt to move. It hurt to breathe. I smiled with every shot of pain.

"Good morning," Carter whispered. I opened my eyes. He was freshly showered, tie draped over his shoulders, pants zipped, not buttoned, with the ends of his belt dangling from the front loops.

"Morning."

"I was going to try for a fourth." He adjusted his cuffs. "But I thought you might need a break."

I got up on my elbow.

"Carter?"

He sat on the edge of the bed. "Yes?"

"About last night?"

"What about last night?" He slid the sheet off my naked body.

"It was incredible."

The tilt of the bed shifted as Carter draped himself over me and nuzzled my neck. He was getting hard again.

"More to come." He kissed my cheek. "You ready for tonight?"

"Actually, yeah. I'm kind of excited. And nervous."

"Phin calls that nervocited."

"I like it."

"I want all of you, my tiny dancer." His lips pressed against the place where my neck met my shoulders. "I cannot wait to have you."

CHAPTER 69

CARTER

The sun was just setting behind the MGM, and the crowd was getting restless. It was a small venue compared with the rest of the tour, but a few thousand people on the Las Vegas Strip were hard to miss. Half the women wore *Sexy Bitch* shirts. The men had matching shirts that said *I'm with a Sexy Bitch*.

I stuck by Emily while she prepped the dancers, then did ID cross-checks for Carlos and eyeballed the line forming outside the auditorium.

—*Dad?*—

I smiled when I saw the text. Part of me had been afraid he was going to stay mad and never call me "Dad" again. I would have accepted his decision, but I'd hoped otherwise.

—*Yes?*—

—*I like your tie*—

Instinctively, I patted down my blue tie. It was nondescript. Not worth liking or even mentioning.

—Which tie?—

A segment of the crowd had started chanting, "Sex-y Bitch! Sex-y Bitch!"

—The one you're wearing. It's a nice blue—

Phin was in Los Angeles, four hours away. Had he hacked into my phone? The security cameras at the MGM? The Nikon around the neck of a tourist?

—What the

"Dad!"

His voice came from the real world, almost lost in the noise of the crowd. I whipped around until I saw arms waving out of time with the chanting.

My first thought, seeing him in the line, pressed up against the sawhorses, was that he was not old enough to be hearing the phrase *sexy bitch*, much less chanting it. My mother was right behind him, and she should damn well know better.

My second thought spilled out loud enough to be heard across the plaza.

"What the hell are you doing here?"

"Nice to see you too," Mom said when I got to the line. She laid her hand on the shoulder of the girl standing next to her. "Carter, Phin's dad, this is Summer."

Summer was Phin's age, with a spray of pimples on her chin and lavender eye shadow. She smiled, elbowed Phin, then shook my hand. A man my age stood behind her. He thrust out his hand.

"Mr. Kincaid. I'm John. Summer's father."

"Carter." We shook.

"Your son has quite the head on him."

I shot Phin a glance. Was he still my son to the outside world? The kid shrugged as if life was life for the time being.

"What did he do?" I asked with suspicion.

"Fixed my wife's track pad. I thought we were going to have to toss the whole laptop. But no. I don't even know what he did."

"Me neither. Phin? Can we talk?"

"Can I get back in the line when we're done?"

Trick question. Son of a bitch, this kid made me appreciate his mother's intelligence more and more every day. If I said he could get back in the line, I was as good as saying he could stay where he didn't belong. If I said no, I was going to embarrass him in front of Summer. This kid was just getting smarter and smarter.

"Just come." I pointed to the pavement on my side of the sawhorse. He ducked under it, and I pulled him out of earshot.

"Before you get mad . . ."

"Too late."

"She had tickets. What was I supposed to do?"

"Call and ask."

"You would have said no."

He was damn right about that.

"You have no business being here. You're not ready."

"But I knew you'd be here. I wasn't trying to get away with it."

"I can't watch you and watch the client at the same time."

"Grandma's here. And John."

"For the love of generations of tradition, call him Mr. . . . whatever. Show some respect."

"Fine, fine."

Behind him, the line started moving.

"Is this the girl with the mouthy friends?" I asked.

"Yes, but it was all stupid and messed up. It wasn't what I thought. And when the thing about Mom happened . . ." He shrugged, swung his arms, craned his neck as if emotions and words were too big to get through his mouth. "She called me, and she was so nice. She invited me to get my mind off it."

He told me he'd stay home. That was a big part of his argument when he told me to come to Vegas. But hearing how this girl had stepped up for him like a true friend, and seeing him acting like a normal kid after crying in my arms for hours softened my initial reaction. I was still going to give him a hard time, because he should have asked first, but once I was done giving him hell, he was going to the Sexy Bitch preshow.

"Please, Dad," Phin continued. "Please let me stay. We'll be home by morning to feed the cat, I promise. I'll be good. I'll take out the garbage without complaining."

"You're supposed to do that anyway."

"Come on, Dad!"

He'd said "Dad" again. It had never given me more satisfaction than it did right after he knew I was his uncle.

"'Come on' is not a reason to be at an adult concert."

"You can't send me home. Summer's dad drove."

"Grandma can take my car, and I can do whatever I need to do."

The wind whipped from behind him, flopping up a moussed panel of hair as if he had a trapdoor on the top of his head. I caught a whiff of him on the breeze.

"Are you wearing my cologne?" My laugh was pure delight, but he must have assumed it was derision.

"Whatever. Fine. Whatever. I'll just, whatever, go home with Gram, and on Monday everyone can laugh at me. Great. That's just great. No one's going to talk to me anymore." He spun on the back of his sneaker with one hand in his front pocket. The other snapped and twitched as he walked back to the line.

"Phinnaeus!"

He stopped halfway between me and the line but didn't turn.

"I did not dismiss you."

His shoulders rose, then fell. He stormed back to me, hanging his head in a cartoon of disappointment.

"There's no more complaining about taking out the garbage." He didn't reply, and I couldn't see his face from above. "You are not to chant the B-word. I don't care if it's empowering to some people. It's not to you."

His head popped up, eyes wide, mouth open in a crazed smile.

"I'll be backstage looking out," I continued. "I don't want to see you drinking soda, eating candy or anything with sugar. It makes you hyper, and I know you want to be on your best behavior in front of Summer. Am I right?"

"Yes!" He threw his arms around me.

"Another thing. If the people around you are acting crazy, that's not an excuse for you to act the fool."

"Thank you, thank you."

I patted his head, mentally listing off a lifetime's worth of guidelines I'd never gotten around to telling him. It seemed too late. He either knew how to act or he didn't.

"Do you have money?"

He squeezed me harder. "I have the twenty you gave me for my birthday."

I took out my wallet, and he unwrapped himself, bouncing nervously. "You're going to need more than that." I pulled out three twenties. Teenagers were expensive. "Get Summer a thank-you gift or a soda or something. Offer her dad gas money on the way home, which is code for 'Don't spend it all at the concert.' And don't forget to thank your grandmother."

He hugged me again. "Thank you. I love you."

"I love you too." I kissed his head and gave him a last squeeze. "Don't get all mushy on me. Get out of here."

He held up his fist. "Not even big enough right now, but it's the size I got."

I bumped. "I love you too."

He ran back to the line with a rubbery grace, his gangly limbs growing to fit his newly expanded world.

CHAPTER 70

CARTER

I admit, I found out where Phin was sitting and asked the security lady at the closed circuits to keep an eye on him. She winked and agreed to. After that, I had to let it go. He was fine. He'd better be. Darlene was getting onstage in a silver bodysuit and wig, and I didn't have the headspace for him. Backstage handlers were in a flurry of activity and anticipation.

"She really is something," Emily said from behind me. I put my arm around her for a second, then let her go. I was on the clock.

"Yep."

"They always said we both had talent, but she was the star."

"It's a big sky."

She rolled her eyes at me as if I didn't already have a teenager at home, then ran to get her dancers in place for their first big number. She was the picture of competence, and to me, she was a star.

I took a call for a drunk and disorderly, caught a crasher, redirected giggling girls looking for the bathroom, and called for cola cleanup.

The auditorium went quiet between songs. Darlene's voice didn't sing but spoke the first few lines of "More Than a Sister" over the cheers and hoots of her fans. I couldn't catch every word.

. . . sometimes you have a friend . . . lost and you don't know what to do . . . lean on . . . good times and bad . . . more than a sister.

The crowd went wild at the title, and the song began with a *thump*, Darlene's operatic opening, another *thump*, and a different note from a different singer.

Emily hopped onto the stage with the dancers and a handheld mic. After another *thump*, Darlene and Emily sang together, and Emily took the first verse.

She was good.

Really good.

Maybe rough.

Maybe not silver from head to toe.

Maybe I didn't know shit, but she was the most stunning woman to take the stage. Any stage. Ever. I didn't know about show business, but I knew someone I loved when I saw her. And that was her. Shining her light, matching Darlene for the chorus, letting her take the next verse with a dance. I couldn't take my eyes off her.

I didn't realize how hard I was smiling until my face hurt.

Finally, finally, after my sister and Emily and protecting Phin from his own history, I let myself taste victory.

CHAPTER 71

EMILY

It was completely possible that I hadn't breathed since the end of the song. Or the whole time I managed my dancers. Or until the laughter and flowers had stopped and Simon picked me up in the dressing room to present the World's Next Top Diva to everyone.

Drunk on endorphins and freedom, I hugged everyone I'd worked with on the show. I hugged the venue staff. I hugged people who didn't even want to be hugged.

"I knew you could do it!" Darlene jumped on me, wrapping her legs around my waist. We'd sung together forty minutes before, but she acted as if we'd both just stepped off the stage.

"You were perfect," I said. "But I want to work on the—"

"Girl! No! You just let yourself feel good for a minute. Do you feel good?"

"I feel good."

"Can you breathe that in? That good feeling? Like this. Go . . ." She sucked air through her nose and waved her hand in the air. "Do it."

I did it.

"Feel good?"

"Feels good." She hugged me again, a good, long one this time until I caught the scent of fireworks and heard a man's hands clap in slow applause. I opened my eyes to see Carter.

Darlene broke the hug. "Take her—she's yours."

Darlene fell out of my vision, because all I could see was Carter with his crooked smile and straight shoulders.

"You were good," he said above the excited voices and laughs of the cast and crew. The show had been a success, and it was time to celebrate.

"Good?"

His smile stretched to both sides of his magnificent mouth, and in a swift motion I wasn't ready for, he swept me into his arms and picked me up until we were nose to nose.

"You didn't sound anything like a frog."

"What did I sound like?"

"Like you belonged up there."

His kiss was firm and strong, sealing his words with action.

"You know where else I belong?" I asked.

"With me."

I touched his nose. Correct.

He kissed me again. Someone popped a bottle of champagne, and the spray got on us, dripping between our faces. I tasted it and laughed, but he wouldn't stop kissing me.

Nothing was guaranteed.

Life wasn't sure, protected, or secure.

But he made love feel as if it wasn't a risk.

Love was the good part. The joy. The reason.

Love was the one thing worth protecting.

EPILOGUE

EMILY

I had sounded like a frog on the Sexy Bitch Vegas preshow stage. I watched it a hundred times, and though hearing myself was less painful every time, I was awful.

But I went up there for every single show, and I got better every time. Darlene's gift to me was never the gift of access or opportunity. Her gift was the space to practice, rehearse, repeat. By the time we set up our last show at the Staples Center, I was ready to make my leap without her.

Carter's first priority was Phin's well-being, so he didn't travel constantly with us. He worked with the security crew when he could, especially in the summer. Berlin. Paris. Melbourne. Sydney. Sometimes he came with Phin, who insinuated himself with the stage techs with such disarming charm he became part mascot, part apprentice.

The Staples Center show was about to break records. Tickets had sold out in seven seconds. Scalpers were getting obscene amounts of money for the worst seats. The calls and offers I'd been putting off would have to be dealt with soon. I was going to have to make choices about my career I'd always dreamed of making. Choices between contracts. Between agents. Between money and creative control.

"You look well rested." Kandi, the makeup artist, brushed powder on my forehead. I'd sweat it off before the first verse, but I let her put it on anyway.

"I am." I smiled. The lights on either side of the mirror made my teeth sparkle.

"Getting laid every night," Darlene interjected from next to me. She'd just sat down to get herself done. Late. Always moving. Always pushing.

I'd gotten into Los Angeles two days before and spent both nights with Carter, eating dinner with his family and spending the evenings on the porch holding hands and talking about everything in the world.

He'd moved Phin's bedroom to the other side of the house for good, solid reasons. It was hard to keep silent when he made me come so hard.

"This tour's been great," I said. "But I can't wait until I'm really getting laid every night."

"Mmm hmm," Darlene agreed. "A girl has needs. Hear that."

"You're done," Kandi said. I got up just as Carter's buzz came from my pocket.

Phin appeared behind me. He had clothespins all over his shirt, a ring of zip ties around his belt loop, and a headset he compulsively touched as if he needed to make sure it was still there.

"That's a lot of equipment," I said.

"Have you seen Dad?"

"Not yet."

"I want to go up on the racks."

"I think—"

The boy held up his hand and touched his earpiece as if something of earth-shattering importance was coming over it. He ran away as if he were late to solve the world's problems.

I checked Carter's text.

—*Have you seen Phin?*—

318

I texted him back as I walked down the hall. The industrial carpet absorbed the sound of rushing feet in either direction. Security. Tech. Performers.

—Looking for you. He wanted to go up on the racks—

—Hell no—

Liam stopped me. "Is she in makeup yet?"
"Just sat down."
"Cheers."
He hurried past me.

—Where are you—

Gene Testarossa, the agent with two watches, caught me on the way to the greenroom.

—On way to stage to check marks. You?—

"Did you look at the deal memo I sent?" he asked. "It's time sensitive."
"I did. I want—"
"They want you. You're a hot commodity, lady. Let's make something happen." His watch flashed, and he glanced at it, giving me an excuse to look at my phone.

—I have something for you. I'm in Security Four—

"Let's talk on Monday."
"Lunch at Spago. No one says no at Spago. It's got GO right in the name."

He pointed both index fingers at me.

"All right. Hey, do you know the way to Security Four?"

"No idea." His watch flashed again. "Gotta go!"

—I have no idea where I am—

I turned another corner and wound up in a sea of fountain soda canisters and stacks of food racks. I plowed forward because I knew the security area wasn't where I'd been.

—I'm heading for the stage in five—

I magically exited into second unit costuming, where the dancers and onstage musicians had their gear.

Simon enfolded me in a hug.

"Last day!" He did a shimmy. He'd dyed his hair pale blue.

"Which way to the stage?"

He pointed. "Out that door, right, then left at where Thor's standing."

—On way—

Simon grabbed my elbow. "I'll take you, and we can talk."

"What are we talking about?"

The dancers waved, smiled, or ignored me. We were a well-oiled machine, and they needed no guidance from me anymore.

"We are talking about our future."

He hit the bar across the double doors, and we went into a hall-way that was wider than my house. Equipment and people swirled in constant motion.

"We have a future?"

"How does that make you feel?"

Phin was on a ladder. A really high ladder.

"Unsafe."

"What?"

"Phin!" I called out. He turned. "Did your dad say that was okay?"

I got a thumbs-up.

"Your future," Simon said, pulling me close and forward at the same time. "I want it to be my future."

"How so?"

"I'm just going to say it."

"Good idea."

He stopped short and got in front of me.

"I love dancing, but I can be something more. Like you."

"Being a working dancer is a big achievement."

"But being a choreographer is bigger."

"Ah." He must have wanted to move into my position with Darlene. "I can—"

"And you, girl, you are about to need a choreographer."

"Me?"

"You. And me." He pointed at me, then him, and crossed his fingers.

"Oh, Simon, I don't think I'm going to be that big. Just small clubs and stuff."

He made a right, then a left, shaking his head slowly. "You got no idea."

"I do. I'm just not Darlene. That's fine."

My phone buzzed.

—*I'm here, TD*—

TD meant *tiny dancer*, and I smiled.

"When you find out you're wrong, you'd better call me first."

I could see the empty seats under the impossibly high ceiling. A few more steps, and Carter came into view with his suit and ear wire.

"I will. I promise."

Simon kissed my cheek. "Now let me go beautify."

"Go."

Carter saw me and held his hand out for me. He was stillness in the chaos. A buoy on a tumultuous sea. I took his hand and let him anchor me.

"Hey. I'm not trying to snitch, but I saw Phin on a ladder."

"It's fine." He brushed his lips over mine. Such a tease. "You look stunning. As always."

"I can't wait for a week to go by without this gunk on my face."

"Turn around." He gently pushed my shoulders so my back was to him and I faced the seats. It was a sight I was used to now, but not with him behind me, shifting around.

"Okay, what?" I asked. I thought he was going to talk dirty in my ear or run his hands under my dress. Both would have been welcome, but neither would have taken that long.

His lips brushed the base of my neck, running shivers up to my ear.

"I've been a very patient man. You've slept all over the world."

We'd talked every night, and when we were in the same city, we shared a bed. It hadn't been enough, not by a long shot, and whenever we parted ways, the pain of separation was almost physical. I missed him every moment, not for the safety but for the pleasure of his love. I felt as though I'd had plenty of good moments, but the great ones belonged to him.

"I'm back now." I touched his hand as it rested on my shoulder.

"You are. And I want you to sleep in my bed every night. I want your body next to mine every morning. I want your voice to be the last thing I hear at night and the first thing I hear when I wake up. I want you with me."

Before I could agree, he reached above me. I caught a flash of metal and red.

"I want you to move in with me."

He placed a red ribbon around my neck. I touched the weight on the end. It was a key. Shiny and new. For me. I couldn't stop looking at the way the dull brass caught the lights, as if it was so much more important than its color suggested.

"Carter. I . . . Wow."

"You'll have plenty of room. I'll clean out the garage, and you can use it as a studio. Mom's moving out, since Phin's mostly grown up now. And he loves you. He really does."

Did he? That boy gave me almost as much happiness as his father. He made me laugh every time I saw him.

"I'm his biggest fan." I turned to face Carter and put my arms around his shoulders. "And yours." I looked at the key and let it drop. "So, yeah. Let's do this."

"I love you, tiny dancer."

"I love you, Carter."

We kissed with all the warmth of two people who knew how to live and how to love.

AUTHOR REVIEWS

Montlake Publishing

Five "we got this" stars. This company really did its research. I especially like Charlotte Herscher as the developmental editor; Christopher Werner as the acquisitions editor; and their superior taste in designers, in particular Shasti O'Leary Soudant, who owned the best WTF moment when I saw her beautiful cover.

Beta Readers

Five stars aren't enough for Kyla Linde (dancing) and Jean Siska (legal accuracy). They are flawless. The author, however, probably let an error slip through. Review to come!

Family

A billion "inspiration" stars to the author's husband and two beautiful children. Before you ask, we don't have pets because I'm allergic, but if we did, it would be a yappy little dog.

The Team

Two stars for Social Butterfly PR for pure originality and constant support. Docked three because it's boring how organized and knowledgeable they are all the time, every time. Especially Jenn. I'm totally over her perfection at her job.

Partners

One star each for all my girls, up to a bazillion, especially the talkers of shop, the Slackers, and the rest of you guys who share and support every damn day. Five for Amy Tannenbaum for doing a terrific edit and always explaining stuff to me that I should already know but don't.

The Indie Community

DNF

It looks like I'll never get to the bottom of this well of good spirit and generosity. When I talk to artist friends about how the indie writing community supports one another through drama and poor sales, how mentoring and data sharing are normal, they can't even believe it. They think I'm exaggerating. Meanwhile, I don't know how anyone functions without friends.

Five "Best for Last" Stars

Readers, fans, bloggers.

All the stars in the sky.

ABOUT THE AUTHOR

© 2014 Erin Clenendin

CD Reiss is a *USA Today* and Amazon bestselling author. Born in New York City, she moved to Hollywood, California, to get her master's degree in screenwriting from USC. In case you want to know, that went nowhere, but it did embed TV story structure well enough in her head for her to take a big risk on a TV-inspired erotic series called Songs of Submission. It's about a kinky billionaire hung up on his ex-wife; an ingénue singer with a wisecracking mouth; and art, music, and sin in the city of Los Angeles.

Critics have dubbed the books "poetic," "literary," and "hauntingly atmospheric," which is flattering enough for her to put it in a bio, but embarrassing enough for her not to tell her husband, or he might think she's some sort of braggart who's too good to give the toilets a once-over every couple of weeks.

If you meet her in person, you should call her Christine.

Made in United States
North Haven, CT
10 January 2022

14415408R00200